Wahiba Sands

Freedom's Home Series

Larry McGill

Atlanta, Georgia

Larry McGill
Atlanta, Georgia
www.larrymcgill.com

Publisher's Note: This is a work of fiction. Names, characters, places, and incidents are a product of the author's imagination. Locales and public names are sometimes used for atmospheric purposes. Any resemblance to actual people, living or dead, or to businesses, companies, events, institutions, or locales is completely coincidental.

Book Layout ©2017 BookDesignTemplates.com

Wahiba Sands/ Larry McGill. -- 1st ed.
PAPERBACK: ISBN 978-1-7339877-0-7
EBOOK: ISBN 978-1-7339877-1-4

To my family, friends, and co-workers
who have always inspired me

For you, Dad
Richard McGill
"The Colonel"

The greatest accomplishment is not in never falling, but in rising again after you fall.

—Vince Lombardi

Acknowledgments

The characters in this book are purely fictional, but the encouragement and inspiration come from a lifetime of stories, places, and in some cases, personalities of people I have met, or who have touched my life. I want to recognize those who have encouraged me to take this path and certainly continue to do so.

To my loving family and my adoring spouse Joanie, this is for you pushing me to chase this dream I had of writing.

To my Dad, a true American hero, who has always been there for me. To my sisters, who gave me encouragement and faith, I thank you. To my children Tanya and Richard, who help me keep my sense of humor, along with my two stepsons, Josh and Jake. Never a dull moment, and certainly, I used some of the humor that you have afforded me. To my aunts, who gave me a sense of humor and have always kept a smile on my face. Secondly, to my friends and coworkers, who I am so blessed to have. I have traveled the world with Brian and Mark, and they have been ever so supportive. I thank you. Ken and Anna, thanks for teaching me about faith. You are true friends. And to my Sigma Chi brothers, true friends who have been the basis for the humorous side of some of my characters.

Last, to Diana Grabau and Amy Blackburn, my editor and assistant, who were my partners in crime on this first swing at the plate. You have both been patient, tolerant, and thank goodness, talented. I could not have written this without you. I hope there are more to come.

I researched a hundred different quotes in an attempt to be witty or perceived in some scholarly way, but in the end, as I know I have missed somebody in my acknowledgements, I will just say thank you, to all my friends, colleagues and associates who gave me a great deal of material and inspiration for this story.

LarryMcGill

Wahiba Sands

Map of UAE, Oman, and Yemen

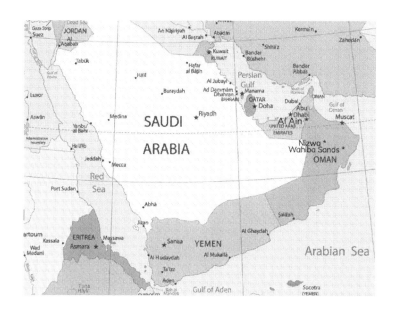

Contents

CHAPTER ONE

The Meet

September 1995

Stretched out full-length on the couch at the Sig house nursing a bit of a hangover, Michael O'Shea picked up his phone, but the call had already disconnected. His mother. He'd only been away at his first semester of college for a week. Was she already checking up on him? His exhaustion had more to do with the first day of fall conditioning for the University of Texas Longhorns football team than it did with the late-night card game with drinks.

Don Carpenter walked in with a bottle of Jack under his arm and said, "Hey pards, get your butt up! The Chi Os are havin' a mixer tonight, and they're the hottest parties on campus!"

"I don't know, this couch feels pretty good. I feel like I've been hit by a truck," Mike said.

"Aw, you wuss, you don't wanna miss this thing." Don threw the bottle of Jack Daniels at Mike, who caught it one-handed and pulled the corked lid out with a *thwunk*. He took a pull, closed it, then threw it back at Don.

"All right, all right already, I'm coming. I need a shower. Stop by the jock dorm and pick me up. What time does this shindig start?"

"Now," Don said, "so get goin', and I'll see you in a few."

He'd have to call Mom back later. Mike's body protested the movement and he groaned with pain. After showering, he put on golf shorts and a Sigma Chi T-shirt. Don pulled up in his '72 pickup, with a drill pipe bumper, two fenders in different colors, and no window in the back. Mike couldn't help but laugh. The torn seat covers and hole in the floorboard added character to its appearance. He reached through the window to open the door, as the outside handle was broken.

"I see we're takin' the babe magnet tonight!" Mike grinned and slid in on the cracked vinyl. "But what I don't get is, why do you drive this hunk of junk to a party that has one girl to three guys? Do you not want to find a nice gal and drive her around in your brand-new Bimmer? She dang sure isn't gonna want to go out with you in this tank!"

Don smirked. "Ya know, Mike, I want a gal that likes me for me, and I figure if'n she sees me drivin' this boat and still wants to be with me, she's my type of gal. Besides, the stereo in it is worth more than the truck." He cranked up the gritty blues-rock of Lynyrd Skynyrd.

As the truck jerked forward, Mike shook his head. "That's quite the strategy. I hope it works for you." They took off, cutting up and laughing all the way. Mike reached back through the window with no glass and pulled two Rodeo Cold Buds from a cooler with no ice, then they turned onto the dirt road toward the Party Barn.

They wheeled around and parked in front of the old barn in the lineup of pickups, tailgate facing the party. Don's music blasted from the truck and heads turned to watch them leap out. Mike, laughing at one of Don's antics, waved at a couple of his buddies on the team and Don whooped and hollered at everybody within earshot. They headed straight for the keg and pumped two beers into red plastic cups, mingling as the local band tuned up for the evening.

A cool breeze wafted through every so often, bringing intermittent relief to the hot Texas night. This Friday party was the typical first Greek mixer of the year, and the girls were decked out in their best shorts, skirts, tank tops, and cowboy boots. Mike and the other guys scanned the offerings. They hooked their thumbs in the front pockets of their Levi's and tried to be cool. For a bunch of eighteen- to twenty-year-old freshmen and sophomores from small Texas towns, this was the big time. University of Texas sorority girls and all the beer you could drink, with great country-rock music—this was as good as it gets. Mike and Don joined in the revelry and the party continued on, the music and fun driving every thought of classes and sports out of their minds for the near future. Don, in his element, was surrounded by a bunch of big-haired girls with low tops and short shorts. He kept them in stitches, entertaining them with one joke after the other, his tall, lanky frame topped by a mop of hair the color of sand and a wide smile. Having heard all Don's jokes four or five times before, Mike sat back on a bale of hay and watched his friend's antics with a grin.

As he tapped his foot to a little Willie and let the evening breeze waft over him, a flash of red caught his eye. His gaze fastened on her, mesmerized by the way she filled out her short, one-piece outfit. With her light-streaked soft curls and fun-loving expression, she looked like she belonged in a movie trailer, not at some college mixer in a barn. She entered with an easy confidence, and all heads turned. The air was sucked from every male chest. Hair pulled back, it cascaded down her back like a waterfall. She stopped a moment to raise the wine cooler to her upturned lips, and when she finished drinking, her amused smile remained.

Mike's eyes followed as her long slender legs carried her over to talk to a few friends. One of the guys on his floor in the dorm rested against the side of a pickup, and he reached out for her. Steve, he thought, a wide receiver. Trying to get her attention, Steve said, "Hey babe, if you were a parking ticket, you'd have 'fine' written all over you." The "fine" was stretched out suggestively. *Wow, real charming,* Mike thought, his body tensing.

The girl inclined her head, being nice, but obviously wanting to move away. Steve set his drink on the fender, and as she turned and began to move, he grabbed her and swung her around. Her drink fell from her hand, droplets spraying up like a fountain, and she pulled her arm back and tried to break free of his big-handed grip on her delicate wrist.

With a cat-like reaction, Mike was between him and the girl in a matter of seconds. Steve released her as Mike faced him down.

Mike said, "Okay, pards, that's enough." He turned and fastened on her mesmerizing green eyes. Though caught in that timeless moment of eye contact, he wasn't lost enough that he couldn't see the fist coming at the side of his head. He ducked and hit Steve in the gut, following that with a slamming hard right to the side of his head. His blow knocked Steve backward into a group of local thugs who pushed him back toward Mike. At that point Mike's right cross landed such a blow that it smashed into Steve's nose, now certainly broken, as blood gushed out. The guy wobbled and fell to the ground, spitting blood.

Steve's friends rose and started toward Mike to avenge their buddy. One of them muttered, "Big mistake, cowboy."

As they came at him, Don, a tall but compact ex-golden gloves state finalist on the UT boxing team, stepped in and the two of them took on the five in what might be described as an old western-style saloon fight. As more Sigs showed up to see what was going down, some joined the fight and it was all over in a matter of minutes. Mike, lip bleeding, turned around and searched for the girl, but she was gone.

"Who was she?" Mike asked Don, having grabbed him by the collar.

With a bit of a drunken slur Don said, "Well, hell son, I don't know."

"Dammit, Don, you know everybody! By the way, thanks, cuz, but I need you to find out who she is!"

Don said, "All I know is she's a Chi Omega, but I'll try." He scratched his head and scanned the dispersing crowd. "Now, come on, buddy, there are lots of good lookin' fish still here."

But Mike wasn't interested. Like a song, he only had eyes for a light-haired beauty whose name he didn't yet know. He couldn't get her off his mind, searching for her in the crowd until the party began to wind down at 2:00 a.m. All had a large time, especially Don, who had

cornered a little brunette from Kilgore, Texas. Short and
cute, with short brown hair, she was built like a gymnast
and was, in fact, on the UT gymnastics team. Don was
smitten.

"Come on, buddy," Mike said as Don's girl
scampered off. "Good thing she's leaving before she sees
you get into your rusty bucket." He climbed into the old
truck, mashing his hat down on his close-cropped
straight blond hair that had lost any semblance of order
in the fight. He pulled his phone out of his pocket. A
sharp crack jagged across the screen on top of a series of
messages from his mother wanting him to call. There
were only three. Surely it could wait until morning.
Couldn't it? Maybe something had happened. He tried to
gauge his level of intoxication and whether he'd be able
to talk coherently without worrying Mom. He thought he
could do it. He gingerly touched her number in his
Favorites, trying not to cut his fingertip on the broken
glass.

"Hey, Mom," he said when her soft voice answered.
He apologized for calling so late and told her he'd been
out at a party and was headed home. She'd know he'd
been drinking, but he doubted it would be any surprise to
her. Her voice sounded tense, congested.

"I wouldn't be hovering over you, son, except that
this is important. Your father has been injured, and I
thought you should know about it."

"What do you mean? Injured? How? How badly?"

"I don't have all the facts, even now," she said. "But
he has been away, and apparently the mission put his
safety in jeopardy. He has been beaten 'within an inch of
his life' was how it was said. I don't know any specifics.
I'm waiting by the phone."

"Where is he?" Mike asked. Don had climbed into the truck and started her up, the rumble shaking both Mike's drinking hand and his phone hand. Mike had filled his plastic cup with remaining beer from the keg before heading to the truck. He looked apologetically at Don when it splashed out onto the floor mat. Don shrugged and stayed silent, realizing the call was serious.

"You know they don't say," his mother continued. "'Somewhere in the Middle East,' is all they ever tell me."

"That doesn't sound very good. Do you want me to come home? I could jump in the Wrangler and be there in three hours."

"No, you stay there and sleep it off. There's nothing you can do here but hold my hand, and you know I don't need you to do that." *That was Mom, always putting on a strong front.*

"Let me know as soon as you hear anything, Mom. I'll leave my phone on its loudest ring."

"Thank you. It strengthens me just to share it with you. I don't want to tell the girls until I know more. Don't worry, your father is a strong man."

Several days passed while Mike and Don nursed hangovers. He'd heard from his mother again, and she assured him that although his father was badly beaten, he'd be okay. He was bound and determined to attend Mike's opening game against TCU in a few weeks. His mom told him they'd catch up then and they'd tell him everything they could. While Mike tried to work out the soreness from the daily beatings on the field, the girl occupied his thoughts nonstop. By Tuesday morning, he feared she had become an obsession. Coming back from a Trig class, he bent over to unlock his bike, and when he looked through the back wheel, a beautiful set of smooth, curvy female legs tensed as their owner pulled her own bike from the rack. As he rose, a soft, feminine voice said, "So, you're my knight in shining armor?"

It was her.

With a smirk on his face, he said, "Well, I guess so, but most of the time in storybooks when you save the damsel, she at least sticks around to say thanks."

"Oh, sorry about that. My ride was leaving, and you looked like you had things well in hand."

"I dropped my beer, nursed a fat lip for a couple of days, and dang near started a street brawl, so the least you could do for a wounded knight is buy him a beer." He'd never had to use lines before to try and get a date.

She laughed and started to walk away, saying, "I don't know you well enough, Sir Knight."

"That is what I am trying to remedy, My Lady." He gave a slight bow. She wasn't warming to the idea, so he said, "Come on, one beer. By the way, what's your name?"

Her hair whirled around, and she was almost at a jog when she hollered back, "Stacy. Stacy Lyons. I'm late for Civics, but I work down at the pub. If you stop by tomorrow, I'll buy you that beer, Sir Knight."

In a flash, she was gone. Again. Mike, not accustomed to this elusive, slippery feeling, felt the loss, like a catfish that slips from one's hands back into the murky pond water. Until now, any girl he'd ever approached had looked at him with the same desire he had toward Stacy. The proverbial shoe was now on the other foot. He had been the catch, the one who could do the selecting, but now—like a kid in a candy store—he was not being allowed to have any. This unfamiliar lovesick feeling was driving him crazy. He could hear

Don now. *What in the hell is wrong with you, son?* Mike was too old for puppy love. He'd never had a problem getting a date, until now.

The more he thought about Stacy, the madder he got. He was *not* going to chase her. That evening he sat at the kitchen table trying to do homework. After thirty minutes of reading the same page over and over, he slammed the cover shut. His self-assurance shot to hell, he stood up, walked into his room, looked at the floor-length mirror and said, "Mike O'Shea, what is wrong with you? You are not going down there to chase that girl!" The image in the mirror moved as he flexed his muscles. Did she notice his physique? His hard, bunched muscles? He lifted his shirt to see whether he needed to work on the definition of his abs. He'd made it a goal three years ago, when starting high school football, that he'd work out to his max at every opportunity. So far, it had paid off. But why not with Stacy? Was he too cocky?

The next day after football practice he told himself the same thing again, that he would not go chase the girl. When that didn't work, he mumbled it out loud. "I ain't going!"

After starting an English paper and getting nowhere, he slammed his MacBook shut and got in his Jeep, gunning it a bit as he drove to Don's dorm. He honked several times until Don walked outside wearing his gym shorts and a "Keep Austin Weird" tank top, and, as always, his faded, stained Longhorn hat. He walked over to Mike's passenger window and said, "What gives, cuz?"

"Get in. We're going to get a cold one."

Don grinned and jumped in the front seat next to Mike. He looked over at his bud and said, "Great. Where we goin'?"

Looking straight ahead and almost snarling, Mike said, "We're goin' to the pub."

"I know that place. Coldest beer in the city and usually some pretty ladies attached to a mug. I haven't been there in a while."

Furious with himself for his lack of control, Mike couldn't stay away. He just couldn't. They walked into the dimly lit college pub. She had her back to them behind the bar, her long, blond-streaked hair bouncing every time she moved. She finished drawing a Bud from the wall tap and carried it to her customer at the side bar.

Don's eyes widened as he laid eyes on the object of Mike's discontent. "Now I get it. You found her! Ya know, pards, her name is Stacy."

Mike glowered at Don. "How'd you know that?"

Don grinned. "I asked Amy about her."

"Who's Amy?" asked Mike.

"She's that gal I met at the party last Friday. We went out Saturday night and got a bite and I asked her for you. I never seen you get all google-eyed over a girl before."

Even madder now for letting himself be in such a position, he grabbed Don's arm and tried to swing him around. "Come on, let's get out of here and find another place."

Don pulled away and looked at him like he was crazy.

At that moment he heard her sweet voice say, "I didn't think my knight in shining armor was going to show up." His head swiveled, and her emerald eyes locked on his. She smiled. A thrill shot through his body and he smiled back. The stirring inside softened him down into a malleable lump of clay.

Don jerked away and said, "Hi-ya, Stace, I'm Don, and this here—what was it you called him—knight? Well, he's my pal Mike. But don't mind him, he ain't real good with the ladies, but I'm working with him! Ha!"

All three laughed and the ice was broken. Don always seemed to be able to lighten the mood and get some laughs going. Mike was genuinely grateful.

They sat at the bar as Stacy waited on customers. Every chance she could break away, she stood across from Mike and Don and listened to another of Don's jokes, laughing and smiling, jokes he'd told a million times. As the night wore on and Stacy's shift neared an end, Mike drummed up his courage and said, "Hey, would you like to get a bite to eat?"

"No, I can't. I have to study for an accounting test tomorrow." The focus of Mike's desire had sucked the air right out of his sails.

He said, "Oh," then threw a twenty on the table and turned to leave. He'd never been turned down when asking for a date. Another painful first.

As he motioned to Don to leave, he ventured a look back and heard her say with a smile in her smooth voice, "But I don't have anything tomorrow night."

Don came back quickly. "Great, where we goin'?" Mike looked over at him with that tough West Texas look, and Don, aware but not taking the hint, said, "Why don't Amy and I meet you two over at Busters for some dinner?" He turned to look at Mike and said with a grin, "My treat."

"All right," Mike said through gritted teeth, "on one condition." Don looked puzzled. Mike smirked. "As long as you don't bring that damned ole truck!"

Don laughed and said, "Deal!"

Mike turned to Stacy. "That all right with you?"

She laughed and smiled and said, "How long you two been doing this comedy act?"

With a smirk, Don said, "I'm trying to pry this boy out of his shell!"

Stacy said, "Sounds good. I love Amy to death. We'll have a great time. See you at six-thirty at the Chi-O house." She turned and left through the back door.

Mike turned to Don, hit the brim of his hat, and laughed. "Well, I guess dinner is on you tomorrow." They swung into the jeep, cranked up the music, and sang along to Garth Brooks all the way back to the dorms.

Several weeks later, after managing to get Stacy out on a handful of dates, Mike asked her to go to Ft. Worth with him for UT's opening game against TCU. Mike, starting as a freshman, was excited to have her come. Besides that, his whole family would be there, and he wanted them to meet her. Mike had dated plenty of girls before now—high school proms, dances, movies—but he'd never been serious about any of them. Besides, his silly sisters didn't think any of them were good enough for their brother. This would, he realized, be the first *real* girlfriend he'd ever brought home. He shook his head a little. Could he call her his girlfriend? He'd only known her a few weeks, and between a full load of classes, labs, and football practice, he had only seen her a few times, and always with Don and Amy.

At first, he was afraid she would say no. He told her that she would have to ride up with Don and Amy, as he had to go on the team bus. He would, however, be allowed to ride home with them the next day. He told her he'd reserve a room for the girls, and he and Don would bunk together. Laughing, she said, "Sure, sounds like fun, and I get to watch my knight kick some TCU Horn Frog butt!"

Mike was excited, but now he had to break the news to her. "Do you mind if the four of us meet up with my family for dinner afterward? It's the only time I'll get to see them."

She tilted her head and giggled. "So, after weeks of semi-dating, you want me to meet the family?" Mike turned red and started to say something when she interrupted him. "Just kidding, Sir Lancelot, sounds like fun." She jabbed at his chest and laughed.

Mike laughed also. Wow, we are semi-dating! Well, that's a start. He smiled.

***

Stacy leaned forward, forearms resting on her jeans. Her eyes found Mike standing on the sidelines. He bounced on his feet, back and forth. Then he scooted down the sidelines and trotted back. He was nervous. As a starting freshman, his entire family had come to see him in his first Longhorn game. Stacy and their friends were sitting in the student section of the stands. Don, Amy, and other friends were cheering, the burst of color from their burnt orange jerseys with Mike's number on them lending an early promise of autumn, bonfires, and pumpkins to the warm, breezy, early fall day.

Mike's family occupied seats with other reserved season ticket holders, and with seventy thousand screaming fans, they would not meet up until dinner that night. Kickoff was at twelve o'clock, and UT was slightly favored, as Texas had not fared too well against the Horn Frogs the previous two years. But this was a new team, a new coach, and a five-star recruiting class. Stacy, optimistic that her boyfriend could help the team on to victory, joined in with the others as kickoff commenced.

The newspapers and ESPN had all reported that Texas could be the dark horse. They pointed out that the team had a great recruiting class and a new coach that had gone after team speed. Maybe this could be the beginning of a string of championship runs, she thought. Things had shaped up well so far.

"Look, Stacy, your big strong linebacker is quick," Amy shouted over the cheers as Mike sped up the field and brought down the ball carrier.

One of the local papers Stacy read had said Mike O'Shea possessed outside speed and quickness not seen since D.D. Lewis, one of UT and the Dallas Cowboys' all-time greatest. She sat in a dreamlike trance as Mike rushed all over the field. It seemed they were calling his name over the loudspeaker every defensive play. On one blitz he hit the Horn Frog quarterback so hard the ball came loose. He grabbed it and went forty yards for a Longhorn score. This being only their first game, the plays seemed to Stacy the stuff legends were made of. She could dream for him, couldn't she? When the game was over the Longhorns had won, with a score of 29–14. Stacy's face glowed when she saw Mike burst from the locker room carrying the game ball. This guy, the strong, quiet type, had depth to him, and she planned to discover how deep it went.

CHAPTER TWO

The Injury
September 1995

Stacy stared in amazement as she watched Mike on the screen in the bar. She had no idea this guy she'd been semi-dating was such a stud. Her sorority sisters had warned her about dating football players, because they tended to be a "love 'em and leave 'em" bunch. She knew he played, and he'd mentioned it on occasion, but as she sat looking up at Mike's skirmish smile, she was mesmerized. She looked down at the orange jersey with the number 38 on it that Mike had given her. She couldn't help but be proud to wear it. When they left the stadium, she'd heard fans talking about Mike and how this was UT's year. She smiled and shook her head, a smile lifting the corner of her mouth.

Don, of course, was lit up like a firecracker. You would think he'd raised Mike himself. "How 'bout my boy!" he yelled at the top of his lungs, and fans all around punched the air with high fives.

Stacy, Don, and Amy were waiting at a local sports bar where they had agreed to meet up with Mike. The bar sat across the street from where they'd catch up with Mike's family. Stacy identified a few TCU fans in the bar, but most had gone, leaving the die-hard sports-bar types along with UT fans wanting to stay and celebrate while waiting for the rush of traffic to clear.

They sat in the corner, ordered drinks, and laughed and talked. All three paused to watch as ESPN showed Mike's touchdown play. Stacy, still in shock, could only marvel at the crowd of UT fans, all cheering and having a great time.

Stacy had always been the one boys chased. As her high school's tennis star with a high academic record, she'd been homecoming queen her senior year but had never dated anyone seriously. She had never met anyone who felt like her equal—either in intellect, drive, or passion for life. But Mike was different—he was quiet, smart, and as her girlfriends put it, "the catch of the campus." Mike gave no pretense of being aware of his good looks or stellar abilities, except that he seemed overly confident around girls. Something within her wanted to knock him down a notch or two in that department. She didn't want to be easy. Other than being overly confident around women, he came across as humble, funny, and caring, with good manners.

As she sat watching him on TV, she said to herself, Stacy, this is a good guy. You don't have to lower your standards for him. In fact, girl, you better quit playing so hard to get and get on your game. When she came out of her daze, the entire sports bar erupted as word spread like wildfire that number 38, Mike O'Shea, had just walked in. She'd never seen anything like it. Mike tried to make his way over to the table, but hands grabbed him to stop and sign autographs and have his picture taken. He shook the hands thrust out at him like a politician running for office, not a wet-behind-the-ears college kid.

***

Mike sat down next to his friends, pumped up and excited, feeling pride to have them as part of his inner circle. With dark hair still damp and face flushed, Mike looked over at Stacy and said, "Can I have a sip of that beer, young lady?"

He laughed and toasted with his friends. They all knew this was a big day for UT and for all of them. As the adrenaline wore off, Mike grew quieter and he tried not to grimace when the pain from getting beat up in the game set in. Division I football was not for the meek or weak. He held Stacy's hand quietly as Don and Amy carried on about the game and the fact that their pal was all over the TV. What seemed like hordes of people stopped by their table asking for Mike's autograph. He kindly obliged each one, posing for a few pictures with a few people's preteen kids while things calmed down in the bar. They hung out for an hour before they crossed the street to Morton's Steak House to have dinner with Mike's family.

As they walked, Don leaned over and said, "You okay with us coming and all?" Mike looked at him as if to say, *Are you crazy? Of course!* The two friends walked behind the girls. "Look Mike, this is the first time Stacy is going to meet your folks, and we don't want to intrude."

Mike stepped back. He hadn't really thought about it. Don was right, he had never introduced a girl to his family, and when he talked to his mom, he told her that

Don and two other friends were coming, not that he was bringing a girl he was crazy about. "You're part of the family, Don. Don't go weird on me. This is hard enough already."

They walked in, and off to the right was a bar with ESPN on and another with the local news, all showing highlights of the game here too. When Mike strode through the doorway, word spread again, and everyone clapped and cheered. It was obvious that most of the folks in the restaurant were from Austin. Mike asked for his dad's table and they were shown to a private room in the back. And then the party began. Mom and his sisters, Sharon and Kim, all hugged and kissed Mike and greeted Don, who had spent many good times with the family. Stacy, Don, and Amy took in the family dynamics from the wall, and before he got around to introducing the girls, he noticed his father hadn't gotten up. A hush came over the room. Mike had seen his father and he was anything but calm now.

His tall, brawny father, the man Mike had idolized since his adoption at the age of eleven, seemed to be stuck in his chair. His face was various shades of black, blue, and yellow, still swollen after three weeks. He had a patch over one eye and a cast on an arm. A pair of crutches leaned against the wall behind him and he looked weak and exhausted.

"What in the hell happened, Dad?" Mike said. "Why didn't any of you tell me how badly you were hurt? I thought you were done with the dangerous shit." He turned to Stacy and his sisters and apologized. "Sorry for the language, but I'm a little shook up here."

His father lifted his good arm, and even that appeared to be an effort. He waved Mike over to the empty chair beside him. "Sit down, son," he said quietly. Mike, still in shock, hesitated. He wanted to punch something, anything. He wanted to kick someone's butt, but there was nothing. Nothing on which he could take out his anger and frustration. So he mastered his rage and sat, his normally cool, friendly blue eyes now dark and steely, like tungsten. Nothing more was said, as no one knew how to continue.

After what seemed like an eternity, Ann, Mike's mom, smiled and said, "Now, who do we have here?"

Mike introduced Stacy and Amy to the family, but of course, the sisters were checking Stacy out. They all broke into smaller chattering groups.

Ann leaned over to Stacy and said, "Don't be too taken aback. You must realize, you're the first girl Mike has ever brought to a family gathering. His sisters are very protective of him. I'm sorry about that."

Stacy smiled and said, "I get it. I think if I were to bring Mike home to meet my folks, it would be worse." They laughed.

Don started in with his antics. Mike's sisters chatted with Amy, finding a lot to talk about. After a few minutes, Amy sat back and rolled her eyes at Don, who was telling a joke even Amy had heard before, but his delivery was worth another laugh. Stacy sat between Mike and Ann. Mike's father, the general, sat still and quiet with a slight smile on his face, listening and watching. Tales were told, and the room buzzed with chatter and laughter. Mike and his father recounted a few plays from the game and gave toasts to the family and guests. The general was clearly very proud of his son, and Mike bided his time until he could talk to his dad privately. In between Don's stories, the girls grilled

Stacy, and though they were polite about it, they obviously enjoyed the new development.

"So, Stacy, what's your major? Or are you still deciding?" Kim asked. Kim and Sharon were seniors this year. Part of Mike missed being at home with them. Everything he knew about girls he'd learned from his younger twin sisters.

"Just general courses this year. I don't think it matters what major I choose if I want to get into law school, but I'll probably pick something like economics or political science."

Sharon raised her eyebrows. "Cool," she said. "Sounds hard, though."

"I think it's fascinating to learn about how the world governments work and how business entities make decisions about what really matters to them and their people," Stacy said.

They all ordered, and conversation continued. Everyone relaxed and let their guards down. Generally, they had great times together when they went out for family dinners. They'd managed to pull it off about once a month over the years, and all enjoyed spending the precious time together. Time and money well spent, Mom and Dad always said. Mike agreed.

Mike and his father pushed their chairs back a ways from the table while everyone else continued to banter and laugh.

Mike and his father both spoke at once. "Let me go first," the general said. "I know you're upset to see me this way, but I assure you, except for a broken arm and torn ligaments, my injuries are all soft-tissue damage that will heal. You understand, I'm sure, that nothing is gained by sitting back and doing nothing and letting evil proliferate."

"But Dad, you've had your years of field work. I thought you were finished with the dangerous stuff."

"I had to make a decision to act recently due to a friendship I'd made ten years ago. My trip wasn't supposed to hold any risk, but in this business one can't always predict where the danger will manifest. This time it came out of nowhere, and I had to fight my way out of a situation. The three that attacked me got the upper hand, but I did some damage before they left me for dead. They ran off when some of our guys showed up."

"I know there's more to the story," Mike said. "Do you know how frustrating it is to your family when you can't tell us any details?"

"Yes, I do, son, but some things *must* be accepted when the stakes are high for our country and its people. My family is also serving their country when they sacrifice a normal family life for the danger of this one. I know you didn't choose this life for yourselves, but I have hoped and prayed that all of you would willingly join me in a life of honorable service to the country."

"Well, let me just tell you, it's damn hard sometimes," Mike said. "We all love you and can't stand to see you hurt." Mike's voice shook and he let his gaze drop, embarrassed at his emotional words.

"Thank you, son." John gave Mike a warm smile and a pat on the arm, and Mike stood and hugged his dad carefully, so as to not cause more pain. Mike knew there would be no more said about this. He'd have to accept it and focus instead on the good things they had. In some ways, the threat of danger made the everyday moments of life that much sweeter. None of them took anything for granted, especially him. Bad memories of the orphanage threatened to invade his thoughts, but he pushed them down and smiled at his father.

When he sat back down, he could feel the almost audible sigh of relief and peace that came over his family. They knew this accounting between the two strong men they loved had to happen.

After dinner, Mike's parents and sisters headed back to the airport Marriott, as they had an early flight the next morning. The four said their goodnights and best wishes, and Mike stood by while his mother pulled Stacy aside.

"Looking forward to seeing you again and doing some girly things next time," Ann said. "We could treat ourselves to a mani-pedi and then go shopping." Her invitation was a clear indication that Stacy had been deemed an acceptable girlfriend for their son.

Stacy smiled gratefully. "I'd love that."

***

Mike, Stacy, and their friends checked into the hotel. The girls freshened up in the room next door, while Don brought in a cooler and a bottle of Jack. After he and Don cleaned up, they invited Amy and Stacy over for a nightcap. Mike was beat. He tried to stay awake, but he had a huge bruise on his thigh where a 305-pound lineman hit him with a clip. Full of steak and wine and with his head on the pillow, he dozed off, then he startled and looked around the room. No one was there.

A soft knock sounded at the door, and as he got up he said, "So you've locked yourself out, Don." He opened the door and Stacy stood in front of him in her thigh-length royal blue silk robe, soft, tanned legs showing beneath the hem, beautiful and sexy.

Only inches apart, she looked into Mike's eyes and said, "Do you mind? Amy and Don want to be alone."

With a sudden burst of adrenaline and desire, he kicked the door shut behind her, took her into his arms, and they fell onto the bed. Their passion consumed them, unlike anything either of them had experienced before. First tender, then with a rush of heat, his body bonded with hers perfectly. This was sweaty-hot explosive lovemaking, the stuff dreams are made of. Their passion lasted most of the night, with breaks of exhaustion from both. Sensual and climactic, their heavy breathing finally subsided, and they held each other tightly. Mike never wanted to let go. This was the real deal. He knew it and could tell she knew it too. They were everything each other wanted.

Mike drifted off to sleep. Sometime later, he jerked awake, his sweat having soaked the sheets and caused a teeth-rattling chill from the cold room air. One arm was wound in the sheet, and both felt heavy and weak, as if they'd been trapped underneath him. He groaned. Bright morning light filtered through the drapes, and that helped him to recall the nightmare that had awakened him.

He'd been buried in sand up to his waist. Heavy boots kicked him repeatedly while men with hate-filled Arab voices laughed and danced around him. Dark, glossy brown eyes, like the plastic ones on a stuffed animal, glared through what appeared to be a Halloween mask. They lasered Mike as he struggled to free himself in spite of the impossibility of it. Loathing his helplessness, he roared at them, "Just wait! You'll get what's coming to you!" He tried to shake it off and he scooted back under the covers in a dry spot against Stacy. She pulled his arm tight around her and the spread over them both, and he fell back to sleep.

CHAPTER THREE

The Warrior
Oman

Ali Al Sharif woke on his mat as he did many mornings, his foot shaking rapidly back and forth. Though the events that had changed his life forever happened ten years ago, it seemed like yesterday. He'd been an adult for almost that long, having been thrust into the role too soon. He still couldn't get the screams out of his head. He rose off the mat, stepped outside the tent, and spit on the ground. His sandals scuffed the desert sand as he paced. His torment had reached the pinnacle of physical and mental sickness. He moaned, his eyes glassing over in an almost rage-like distortion in the bright morning light. Soon, he promised himself. Soon he would be avenged.

The unkempt youth who approached was nothing but skin and bones. "My sheik, can I bring you some morning refreshment?" he said.

"We'll break camp midmorning," Ali said. "For now, feed yourselves what you have and bring me some coffee, *minfadlich*." The boy nodded. He couldn't be more than fifteen. Ali knew what it was to be fifteen. At that age his life had irrevocably changed course.

"My master, are we going to the city?" another of the youth said, bringing him his requested cup of the spicy brew.

"*Sah,*" he said, nodding. "Clean your weapons." The boy hustled off to spread the word, as Ali knew he would. He'd have to make an announcement to his small troupe soon. But first, he needed to drink his coffee and outline his plans. They'd have just enough time to encamp at the wadi nearest Sheik Saud's farm if they left early midday.

Ali cursed the events that had led to this. If he didn't get some revenge soon, he feared the rage inside might eat him alive. When he'd been the age of this young boy, his family's migratory warring Bedouin tribe had roamed the Yemeni desert as nomads and thieves, stealing from anyone they could. When the Sunni tribe attacked his tribe's camel caravan, his father and the other men were sitting around chewing gat, a hallucinogenic stimulant that pushed the entire clan into an emotional frenzy. Though chewing gat was a daily occurrence for many in the region, serious chewers experienced heightened feelings of invincibility. The drug worked a lot like speed. While the men chewed, their saliva streamed down the sides of their ratted beards in red streaks. By the time the attack came, the men had been chewing for several hours. The raid had not been thought out clearly by the Sunni group, and was more a spontaneous emotional attack, to rob and destroy. Even so, Ali's tribe members underestimated the strength of the Sunni caravan and the firepower within their group.

Ali's father, brother, and two uncles were shot and killed immediately by a Russian AK-47. Fifteen-year-old Ali, who had been sitting by himself some distance from the men, saw the grenade land ten meters from him. His delayed response to the grenade's danger caused him to be too close when it exploded. They would have killed him too, but as he lay unconscious, covered in sand and blood, they thought he was dead already.

When he came to, he could hear his mother and sisters screaming and sobbing. The Sunnis showed no mercy as they beat, raped, and pillaged, taking everything of value his family had. It didn't matter that the attackers had come from only one tribe and not the whole nation; the only emotions Ali could generate after the attack were hate and its companion, rage.

The right side of his face suffered the worst injury. Burned to the bone, it took months to heal, and he endured excruciating pain. Medical supplies and practices in the area were medieval at best. The third-degree burns scarred him for life. He vowed he would never forgive any member of the Sunni nation, nor forget how they decimated his family.

From that moment, even at the young age of fifteen and as the new head of his family, Ali Al Sharif swore to Allah revenge—death to all Sunnis and their Western allies. As most Bedouin tribes would do, he took his family and retreated quickly to the backwater-laden mountain wadis. After the attack, it took almost a year to deal with his injuries. His face would not heal, no matter what they tried to do. Because of the severity of the wound and his anger, he would let no one attend to the injury but his mother, Sarasa. They had no access to plastic surgeons who would operate on a Bedouin boy with little or no money. Ali's hatred grew every time he looked in the mirror, and after a while, he refused to look at a mirror at all. He knew things were hard for his mother, but she and his sisters had healed in a few weeks. Melina's rape and subsequent pregnancy at the age of thirteen caused almost insurmountable problems, and there was no one to solve them but him. Locals were afraid for Sarasa, as she was considered dirty or tainted by the men who had many wives. With no husband, she was looking at a life of constant struggle, a problem that was now heaped on young Ali's shoulders. Bitterness engulfed him as he considered how grim the future looked for all of them.

Ali didn't blame his mother, but he was distant from her, and especially so with his sisters. He, like other men, couldn't stand to look at them in their disgrace. Their lives had taken on a bland routine of hoarding goats, milking, selling at the local market, and scratching out a lifestyle of poverty. His mother had to sell everything they had just to keep them fed, and when her first grandchild was born, there were no celebrations— only disdain, and another mouth to feed. The tribe avoided them. His mother became more of a burden when she fell into a depression with little hope for betterment. She learned to expect nothing from life and struggled daily to endure it.

As the family moved from one location to another, they sold their milk. It fell on Ali to barter and negotiate when they needed to sell, as women were not allowed to do so. If they ran into a family with small children or infants, they could usually sell all they had each day, but some weeks, it was slow. As Ali grew, so did his appetite. Sarasa found it hard to keep up with him—not only to care for his needs, but also to have any influence over his hatred. His decline began, with a mother he loathed, a sister tainted with a rape baby, very little food, and no money, all because of the Sunnis.

His wound healed, and he grew to be a tall, muscular Shiite Muslim. He learned to hunt and to go to the villages and steal. One of his cousins taught him hand-to-hand combat. The cousin had learned the skills from the Yemeni Secret Police. In agreement with Ali's cause, the cousin taught him how to shoot and use a knife with complete stealth.

Although gat chewing was a common and accepted pastime, Ali resolved never to touch the drug. It jarred his senses and clouded his thinking. He swore he'd never make the mistake his tribal elders made, sure that their mental state had affected their ability to assess the threat to the caravan and react quickly.

With all his terrorizing and criminal activity, he was careful to not let his mother know about or see him commit heinous crimes. A slim devotion toward Sarasa seemed to be the only shred of humanity he had left— supporting his family was the remaining fragment of honor he held in memory of his father, but he felt this to be more a duty than anything done out of love. Love was something he didn't understand.

At the age of nineteen he moved his family from a nomadic life to a white villa overlooking the Arabian Sea not far from Salalah, Oman. The countries of Yemen and Oman border the Arabian Peninsula to the south of Saudi Arabia, and the two countries are roughly the same size and shape, bent or curved rectangles lying on their long sides along the Arabian Sea. Salalah is the nearest major city to Yemen, about eighty kilometers from the border. Here, away from the tribe, his mother showed improvement, and Ali's assistance was no longer needed, except financially. Piracy became a part of his operations in this location. He raided ships and killed rich tourists, smuggling goods in and out of the beaches of both Oman and Yemen. His frequent trips to Nizwa to buy medicine for his wounds had brought him into proximity with those who introduced him to the black-market weapons trade. He could relate to this clandestine activity, and it pleased him that the trades would be highly untraceable. His first trades were small, as cash was required up front. As he parlayed multiple deals into more money, the size of his deals escalated. Eventually, he was able to buy automatic weapons, grenade rockets, and finally, heavy artillery, and he found willing buyers in the African republics that were constantly at war.

He started out small. He'd wait up until late at night and then sneak out and go raiding. Far to the east, in the old city of Sana'a, Yemen's largest city and the center of its governorate, he'd rob and steal everything he could get his hands on. His uncle was a policeman in the city. He functioned as Ali's inside man, giving him leads on who to attack and when. He taught Ali how to fight— first, hand to hand, then with weapons, knives, pistols, and a deadly garrote for strangulation. He'd catch fat and happy Sunni merchants leaving the city and would kill, thinking nothing of it. After all, they'd sent his father to Allah. He would continue his quest for wealth, having learned early on that money could buy almost anything, and although he could have used the money and lived large, he existed in a simple tent. Indulging himself was impossible. The relentless hatred drove him, and it was all he cared about.

As he learned the skills of criminals, he developed an expertise and adroitness few could attain. He never hesitated or regretted anything taken from the Sunnis or their masters, the white-faced infidels. His wealth grew, and his fearlessness became legendary. In only a short time, he and his uncle had to rent a storage building on the outskirts of the town of Sana'a to hold their plunder. They'd take the goods all the way across the two countries to Nizwa or Muscat, on the eastern border of Oman, nearly 2500 kilometers, and sell them for gold. While there, his uncle taught him about women. Ali had an insatiable appetite for women, and because of his disfigurement, he knew they would not accept his advances, so he forced himself on them roughly. This became a way of life. He bought expat whores from Russia and Poland and kept them in both cities, laughing and mocking them as he took them. After this abuse, he'd use these whores to gain influence with other tribal leaders. This slave trade had earned him another lucrative path to fortune.

***

Ali approached the small group of young fighters he'd recruited. There must be near fifty of them. He had provided them with incentives and a role model to follow, and he'd given them a cause to believe in and fight for and fed them small portions of praise and reward for serving him well. Ali alone knew of his own deception and the depths to which he'd go to accomplish his plans. He gave them instructions before saying, "We head out in one hour. We will show the Western scum and their Arab allies who is great, Inshallah!"

"Inshallah!" the young men shouted back.

CHAPTER FOUR

The General

Oman, Three Weeks Earlier

If General John O'Shea prided himself on anything at all, it would be the sense of honor instilled in him by his own father. As he sat waiting to deplane at Oman International Airport in Muscat, he allowed the painful thoughts to wash over him. His father had lived his life with as much integrity and grit as anyone John had ever known. John himself had reaped the benefits of his father's strength and commitment. His father's rapid decline in health had taken him completely by surprise, and he had been too young and immature to realize that death could occur to the man he held in such high regard. His chest tightened with sharp regret. He'd failed to heed his mother's request to come see the man who had sacrificed so much for his family. He'd needed to be there, but he'd been chasing his own goals, and far too soon, his father had succumbed to an overwhelming staph infection and died.

Now the only way to honor his father would be to instill those qualities in his own children. No doubt this regret toward his father factored into his actions when he'd adopted Mike. Dad would have loved to see his grandson. The boy had gone from an abused, wounded child who'd experienced horrors a grown man would find unbearable to a strong young man who knew his own worth. Now Mike was off to college with a bright future. His father would have been so proud. John nodded his head in honor of this thought and shifted his focus to the task at hand. He always enjoyed his time in this beautiful country and looked forward to seeing his old friend, Sheik Saud.

General O'Shea stepped off the plane to a sweltering heat that took his breath away. If he'd worn rubber-soled shoes, they would be melting already, which explained why the Arabs wore only leather sandals. The VIP arrival team was there, along with a US Embassy guardsman. Standing to the side was his old friend, Master Sergeant O'Dooley, affectionately called "Gunny" as both an honor and an endearment.

The guardsman was decked out in his finest blues. After exchanging salutes, the guardsman stuck out his hand and said, "Welcome to Oman, General. It is an honor to meet you. The ambassador was held up and extends his apologies, so I'm afraid you're stuck with me. I'm Lieutenant LJ Sullivan, sir."

The general smiled. "No problem, Lieutenant. I prefer a marine anytime over a politician, but let's keep that between you and me and not piss the ambassador off, if that's okay with you."

LJ winked and nodded his head, then smiled back. "Roger that, sir." He picked up the general's bag and asked him to follow.

The general turned to O'Dooley, held out his outstretched arms, and they embraced, accompanied by a few backslaps. "O'Dooley, you ole dirt eatin', hell-raisin' grunt, I thought they would have mustered you out by now."

"By God, General, they've tried, but after that little incident you helped me out of a few years ago, they sent me over here to stay out of trouble. Damn glad to see you, sir!"

"Well, it's obvious that the two of you already know each other, so please follow me." Lt. Sullivan held out his arm to move them out of the heat. They were ushered into the smoky VIP lounge while they were awaiting passport approval. They sat at a raised table and ordered drinks.

O'Dooley shook his head and cracked a smile at the memory. "I have nightmares to this day about that Turkish hellhole we were in. I'll never forget how you dragged my butt for three blocks out of that riot and saved my bacon. I am beholden to you, sir."

"Ah hell, son, you would have done the same. How's the leg, anyway?"

"Good as new, sir, and ready to return the favor."

"I hope you don't ever have to, Gunny. That was quite the cluster, wasn't it?"

"Sure was, General, but we made up for it."

"Yeah, we did at that, Gunny. Those Syrians high-tailed it back across the border, singing all the way."

The general and a small detachment of marines had been in the throes of war exercises with a Turkish Special Forces task force when a Syrian group crossed the border and invaded a small Turkish town, killing, raping, and stealing everything they could get their hands

on. Because of their close proximity to the raid, the
general, O'Dooley, and the detachment rushed in to quell
the disturbance and calm the Turks down after the
incident. Unfortunately, O'Dooley had been injured in
the melee, having taken a bullet in the leg that splintered
his femur.

As the men caught up in the lounge, Sheik Saud's
first cousin, Salah, walked in. The general had broken
bread with Salah on several occasions. The man
approached, then smiled and said, "*Salam alay kum*,"
and embraced the general. "My general, it is so happy to
see you!"

The term "my" preceding a name was one of affection
and respect. The first time John had heard this form of
personal address he'd been taken aback but had grown to
appreciate it.

"*Wah lay kum salam*, my old friend," the general said,
a tone of affection in his words as he returned the
embrace.

Salah smiled. "My uncle is waiting for you at our
farm in Wadi Hifa! He sends his blessing and is happy
you are here to be with us."

The general turned and thanked the VIP staff with a
little "*baksheesh*," which he remembered was a tip for
services. They all bowed and left happy. The general
then turned to LJ and said, "Lieutenant, are you coming
with us?"

Lieutenant Sullivan said, "No, sir. I just wanted to
make sure you got here safely. I am headed over to pick
up the ambassador, and we will catch up with you at
dinner." He saluted again and walked away.

"*Fadal*, come with me, my general," Salah said
warmly as they walked up to the decked-out Range
Rover. Its windows were tinted so dark he could not see

in. The general's keen eye picked out two other Range Rovers, one in front and one in back, with four security guards in each. The general didn't miss the .45s bulging through their long flowing galabias.

When they got in the car, the general leaned over and said, "Okay, Salah, what's with all the bruisers escorting us?"

Salah's typically smiling face and jovial disposition changed immediately. "My general, there is much trouble with some of the Yemeni peoples who have come across the mountains. They are threatening some of our leaders. This is why Sheik Saud has asked to see you. He trusts you and also has some valuable information he needs to share with you." As the general nodded, he listened intently to Salah. "I must say, my general, we are all happy you are here."

His eyes focused on General O'Shea, and almost pleading, he said, "These are very bad peoples, and we need your help and information. My general, we think it is *him* that is here. 'The Warrior,' from Yemen. It is him that is killing some of our peoples and robbing our families. He always has a plan that is fitted for the attack, different every time. We need your satellite access to locate him and take him out. Our satellites are not strong, and he hides during the day in the passes and moves around. Our images are not clear or quick enough to track them, and this is what my sheik wants to discuss with you. He dares not do it on the phone, as these Yemeni peoples have ears and eyes everywhere."

The general listened intently as deep concern washed over Salah's face. The man said, "The sheik will tell you what is requested when we get to our farm."

Salah, silent now, watched gravely out the darkened window. After some time, he again spoke. "He needs your help, my general. It is most important, or he would not ask. It is not for himself he asks, but for our great leader and father, Sultan Qaboos. My sheik fears for him."

"Not to worry, my old friend. Let me speak to your sheik and we will see what can be done." The general gave a soft pat to Salah's outstretched hand. He believed the country contained many fine Arab people, whose only desire was for peace and effective governing. Sheik Saud had been a close friend of John's for some time now.

They rode in silence for the next forty-five minutes as the general thought through what Salah had said. What resources did he have at his disposal here in country that could assist his old friend? He'd have to check with the naval base in Bahrain.

As they drove through a narrow pass that opened up to a large valley, a sultan's palace came into view. The general, as in the past, was amazed at its beauty. Lush hillsides were covered with enormous date palms. A small stream running through the property emptied into a manmade water reservoir, then a small waterfall emptied into another creek used for watering cattle, camels, goats, and horses. The contrast of the green fields against the desert was an oasis to behold.

Breaking the silence and changing the gloomy air that had engulfed the SUV, Salah said, "Look there, General—there is Hercules." He pointed at a huge, shiny, jet-black horse with a star on its forehead. "Sheik Saud is grooming him to run in your Kentucky Derby."

The general smiled and said, "He's a beaut, but can he run?"

"Like the wind, my general. We have enough time to teach him how to get out of the blocks, and then he will be magnificent in the races!"

They rounded the fence-lined mountain curve and came face to face with the full breadth of the palace. The ten-foot-high walls gleamed with fresh white paint, with everything in its place. Rows of exotic plants and flowers lined the street that led to the main house, with a circular driveway that surrounded a huge fountain. Marble horses reared up, spitting water, like fire-breathing dragons. The fountain was a beautiful work of art. Sheik Saud had hired a team from Italy to come and carve it, Salah said. Like something out of Florence, the sculpture was a masterpiece. The skill of the Italian artists was obvious, even to John.

The Range Rover curved around the drive and pulled up to the massive steps that led to the massive doors. The palace looked like pictures he remembered from his childhood copy of *Arabian Nights*, a book that had captured his imagination as a boy of twelve years. He admired the palace's raised sphere, pointed ceilings, curved walls, and marble floors. As they entered the main hall into the house, he once again enjoyed looking at the classic works of art and murals from the rich history of Oman. They entered a grand room, whose upholstered straight-backed chairs had undoubtedly been hand-stitched and gilded with gold. These chairs hugged the circular walls while rich Persian carpets covered the marble floors. Tall and narrow repetitive windows ran the entire width of the room, overlooking plush gardens with ornate Roman statues that stood like sentinels throughout the manicured lawn.

Sheik Saud sat in the middle of this room in a large carved chair, his stately posture and serious facial expression conveying the importance of his position. He rose as the general and Salah entered. The men smiled and embraced, their endearing words spoken softly, the men's care and unwavering respect for one another apparent. When greeting old friends, it is customary in the culture to speak and display affection for a prolonged period as a show of respect and caring. This can seem awkward to those who are not familiar with the custom, but for those who are, it is something to behold and to cherish. John's American compatriots could take a lesson from this kind of devotion.

Dressed like those in power typically are for an important function, Sheik Saud wore his gold-threaded Omani head cap and his robes, with golden streamers that hung down to his waist. The black robe had gold stitching around the edge. This type of outfit represented power, strength, and importance. The sheik's attire had been donned for John and represented no ordinary meeting. This was serious, or he would not have been summoned to Oman.

Salah had said that in Arabia people had begun calling the terrorist "The Warrior," or the "Warrior Sheik"—John had never come face to face with him but had heard a little bit about his background and reputation. The word on the street was that this warrior was a dangerous man whose reputation seemed to grow by the day. Smart and shrewd, he was not someone to take lightly.

Sheik Saud clapped his hands and asked the servants to bring coffee. A festive atmosphere gripped the room in spite of the serious upcoming meeting. They moved to the grand dining hall where rugs covered much of the floor.

"*Minfadlich*," the sheik said to his old friend. "Sit, sit please, my general."

They curled their legs and sat on the Persian carpets and the servants returned, bearing hourglass-shaped copper and brass Omani coffee pots with long spouts, filled with the steaming brew, strong with the smell of cardamom. Dates accompanied the drink to lend some sweetness. Sheik Saud talked of the horse Hercules, his farm, the upcoming World Cup, and how Oman would fare in the games in Qatar.

Sheik Saud asked politely in a soft voice, "How is our beautiful Anna Beth and the girls? And your son Mike? How old is he now, twenty-one?"

The general smiled. The sheik had been so taken with Ann's full name when he first heard it that he called her "Anna Beth" at every opportunity. John said, "Thank you, my sheik. Ann says hello and to give her best to Fatima and all the children of our great sheik. I have brought presents for all, as well as Fatima's favorite pecan pie. The girls are fine, and they've sent gifts for your daughters. Ann sent chocolates, and Kim and Sharon sent the newest Arabic fashion magazines." He smiled and bowed his head before continuing. "Mike is still only nineteen, my sheik. He has a ways to go, but he is turning into an honorable young man. Studying at the university this year."

"When we visited you in Texas, the boy struggled with his anger at school. Have you made progress with this?"

"Mike will always have a strong instinct to protect others. I recognize this as good. But he needed to learn control and use it effectively for the betterment of others. The abuse he suffered in orphanages caused his repressed anger. With further training, he will have it under control. At least that is what I hope."

The sheik nodded respectfully and stood, indicating John should follow. They entered the dining room. John would have to wait while the usual customs took place—dinner, entertainment, and niceties—before the business at hand. This business might be addressed tonight, tomorrow, or the day after, depending on how Sheik Saud wanted to handle the situation. The Omanis felt no need to walk in and get right down to business, as Americans do. This was Arabia, and patience, along with being a good guest, was the accepted protocol. So John relaxed, deciding to take it all in and enjoy. He was tired but made sure not to show any sign of this.

The officers ate with the sheik, while the rest of the team dined in a different room. Bob Johnson, the ambassador, arrived along with his entourage, which included Lt. Sullivan and Major Chris Edwards, all escorted by a detachment of marines. The male prominence was apparent at the stations at which everyone sat, the seating order entirely scripted and dictated. The ladies also dined separately, as this was still very much a man's world.

The food arrived, and it was a feast. Lamb and fish were served, all on large round trays similar to Spanish paella dishes. Brown rice with dates and spices filled out the meal. The food was magnificent, as always. For dessert, Turkish coffee, syrup-drenched dates, and baklava from Lebanon were served. After dinner, everyone moved to another room for the entertainment. John watched as others entered and were seated. The ladies came in right before the entertainment, and then

Fatima arrived, dressed in black and completely covered. The two second wives followed. One might describe them as "lesser." They were present to display Sheik Saud's station as an important leader. Fatima was the first wife, the dominant one. She was in charge of all domestic affairs. She caught John's eye as she entered and dipped her head, a slight smile lifting the corner of her mouth in greeting as she led the women to be seated behind the men. She was quite a woman, John thought. Intelligent and strong, an equal to the sheik, yet deferring to her husband, as custom dictated.

The ceremonial atmosphere reflected typical Arabic hospitality, and great effort and extravagance had gone into honoring this friendship and meeting. Whirling dervishes provided colorful entertainment, followed by an acrobatic team flown in from Asia. These entertainers astonished their audience in how they could move, bend, jump, and fly. They would rival any of the top entertainments in Vegas, even with all its Cirque du Soleil from all over the world that provided a break from the gambling tables.

John leaned toward the sheik and said softly, "*Shokrun,*" showing his appreciation.

The sheik had visited John at his ranch four years previously, wanting to learn how to set up a proper stable in Western fashion. The Arabs longed to be appreciated for their traditions and expertise with horses, but their care of and facilities for the animals needed to be modernized. Though their horses were treated with great respect and value, the sheik wanted to see how the animals were cared for in the Western world before upgrading his own methods and operations. It appeared to John that the sheik had made some progress, evidenced by the new stables. With high ceilings, many windows, and the indoor arena, the facilities were airy and beautiful, displaying the elegance of Arabic architectural elements.

John had tried to explain to Ann that a sheik of Saud's importance commonly had up to four wives. It was somewhat expected and accustomed for him to have at least three. Ann had a fit over it. But even she had to admit that Sheik Saud and Fatima were very much in love. Typically, having more than one wife displayed wealth and order in the eyes of the Arab world. Fatima's children with Sheik Saud would be the dominant, or "first as it is known"—the other children sired by Sheik Saud and his other wives were lesser in the order, but Sheik Saud loved them all and treated each basically the same.

With three wives and a dozen children, a great balancing act must take place by all parties involved. John had observed in only a few visits that Sheik Saud was a soft-spoken man who demanded great respect and did not involve himself in the domestic squabbling and issues that took place in his household. This was Fatima's job, he'd said, and John watched her carry out her duties with grace and class. Therefore, the sheik's household was loving and orderly, with few domestic issues. He had always been a great and fair man. Other household staff showed him immense respect and genuinely praised the sheik for his skill with such a balancing act. He traveled internationally with only Fatima, as he knew the customs of the Western world were to have only one wife. Thus, he and his first and most beloved wife got to know the O'Shea family.

The entertainment continued as John reminisced, now with pipers who arrived with flutes, along with the traditional Bedouin Omani drums. Many rose to their feet and the music and dance began.

The Saud family had a grand time at John's ranch. They all shared many laughs and became close. Once a person enters into the trust of respected Arabs, it is both a great honor and a great privilege to be considered a friend. Their culture requires a tremendous loyalty, not only given in good times, but also an expectation in dangerous times. The men had a history of significant favors between them that cemented their loyalty to one another.

When the general first met them, he had saved the lives of Sheik Saud and Fatima as they were on their way to a diplomatic gathering with other prominent leaders. Neither he nor the sheik had ever forgotten it, but the incident was never mentioned by either man, according to custom.

The entertainment finally wore down. No business had been discussed the entire evening. All guests were required to stay the night and were provided with palatial suites. The emphasis this evening had been on the celebration of two old friends, as this was a sign of respect and honor, which always takes precedence over business. It was agreed that the ambassador, the two officers, and John would meet with Sheik Saud at nine o'clock the following morning. Pleasantries were exchanged, and the guests were escorted to their rooms. The general was grateful for the short evening, as he was still jet-lagged and in dire need of sleep.

CHAPTER FIVE

Sheik Saud
Oman

The alarm went off at 7:30 a.m. John rose, showered, had a cup of coffee, and read the international news placed on his tray. He opened his curtains and stepped out to his balcony to watch the horse training taking place, amazed at the care and patient attention to detail evidenced by the precision of gait the trainer was demanding. He could have watched for hours, but it was time to head to the meeting.

When the general walked in, Sheik Saud and the ambassador were already in conversation. This was to be expected, as there was always much business to discuss. The atmosphere was much different than the festivities of the previous evening. The general walked up slowly, and both Ambassador Johnson and Sheik Saud rose and greeted him.

The ambassador said, "You're just in time, General. We were discussing the Warrior and his whereabouts." His voice rose with emotion as he continued. "General, this man is nasty and very dangerous. He seems to have a hatred of all Westerners and those who are allied with them, making Sheik Saud and Sultan Qaboos his enemies."

"I'm well aware of this, Mr. Johnson," John said. The man had a tendency to derive a distinct personal importance from his position, and he wanted to make sure others recognized it. This wasn't the first time John had seen it. *Diplomacy, John,* he told himself, refusing his impulse to answer any more sharply.

Sheik Saud said softly, "This, my general, is why I have asked you to come."

He looked older today, and neither his voice nor his look held any happiness. "We need to stop this Yemeni and either jail him or kill him. He is behind many deaths, and it is rumored he is raising an army to overthrow His Majesty Sultan Qaboos, all glory to his name."

Ambassador Johnson addressed John and said, "General, you have access to many methods of search, as well as satellites with the latest technology, which I don't have access to, and certainly the Omanis don't."

The ambassador had a habit of gesturing expansively in his fervor, unlike their hosts. The general hoped the arm movements weren't offending the sheik. The Arabs had laws about gestures, which Bob should know. He'd be lucky if his gesturing didn't get him into trouble of some kind.

Bob continued. "This warlord moves at night and takes refuge in the caves during the day."

John knew that the Omani military, small in number, were limited with how much area they could cover and still protect the ministers.

Sheik Saud spoke again. "This, my general, is where we were hoping you could help us. We know you and your government have intelligence and the ability to see deep into all lands worldwide." Almost pleading, he said, "We need you and your giant bird-in-the-sky to help us find this scourge so we can kill it, for all to be safe. We are worried that his followers have infiltrated the Royal Palace and will have a run at Sultan Qaboos, all honor to his name. This, my general, we must not let happen. Can you help us?"

The general had been thinking about this since Sheik Saud's cousin Salah had given him a heads-up. What could he and his government do to help? He'd have to pull a few strings with the Navy stationed in Bahrain. He had a close, long-time ally running the Fifth Fleet there. They had satellite imagery of the entire region, and certainly it would be no big issue to find this guy. He would have to call in some favors.

What John had learned over the years was that the key to these types of meetings, or what should be flat-out said, was diplomacy at its finest. The general had to have the appearance of being able to solve all their problems yet ensure that Sheik Saud and the ambassador got all the credit. Ambassador Bob Johnson was first rate, in spite of his personality quirks, and they needed to make sure he was seen as a problem solver to the sheikdom. So John did what all military geniuses would do.

He listened and then said, "Now that I understand your problem, I'll gather my resources and find a way to help." John knew exactly what needed to be done, but he didn't want to show his hand yet.

All agreed they would meet two days later in Muscat and the general would give a briefing on what action could be taken. The general looked at his old friend and said, "Don't worry, my sheik, we will figure out a way to defeat this threat." This was John's way of communicating that he had a plan and could help. All were agreeable, and John and Bob left together.

As they walked down the hall, the ambassador glanced over at John. "General, thank you for your help with this situation. We can travel back together after lunch. This is a little more sensitive than Sheik Saud mentioned, I'm afraid. Did you see the small militia protecting his palace as we entered? They are armed with heavy artillery."

"Yes, I noticed, Bob. I suspected not everything was being brought to the forefront."

Bob said, "Listen, I know Sheik Saud well enough to know that he will not allow anything to enter his grounds. He has more firepower than what I even saw. His team could hold off a small division of marines, if necessary. I also know that it's Sultan Qaboos's safety that has you both most concerned."

John shook his head, his brisk pace betraying his anger. "How in the hell did this get so far out of hand, Bob?"

Bob lifted his hands and shrugged. "My impression is that they hoped to take care of this Bedo warrior themselves, but they underestimated both his recklessness and the sheer number of his young followers. You know as well as I do that it is a matter of pride, especially for these Arab countries, to handle their own problems. They underestimated the threat. Someone was trying to protect his own neck by keeping a low profile. Someone wanted the glory of taking him out singlehandedly. Hell, there could be a lot of reasons."

"And now—"

"Now, he is attacking Sunni caravans wherever he can find them, and he and his followers are terrorizing others and hiding out in the caves."

"And that's how he's come to be known as the Warrior. The Warrior Sheik. Unbelievable." John rubbed his eyes.

They stepped off the elevator. Both rooms were on the same floor, both with seaside views. They shook hands, and John thought he might catch a short nap before lunch. Though his mind swirled with tension, the surroundings were made for relaxation. When this nasty business was over, he'd bring Ann and they'd party and relax. She would love it.

Two hours later, Bob and John walked toward the SUVs. Lt. Sullivan and Major Edwards waited with the doors open, along with two other SUVs, one armored car, and two machine gun-mounted jeeps manned by marines. The general looked over to the ambassador and lifted his eyebrows. Bob shrugged and said, "You can never be too safe."

As they reached the armored car, the general watched the marines load his bag and check their equipment for the three-hour drive back to Muscat. As the team took its leave, Sheik Saud stood at the top of the stairs in his dignified stance. He lifted a hand and bowed.

CHAPTER SIX

Ali Al Sharif

Oman, August 1995

Ali Al Sharif paced among the tents and looked over the valley to the sheik's palace. The huge structure with its lush grounds and lavish landscaping turned his stomach. He wiped the sweat that dripped constantly down the side of his face, irritating his wounds that never seemed to heal completely. He had worked out a plan—an ambush—and he had high hopes that Allah would bring them victory, if only to strike fear into the rulers. Yes, it would bring their wrath on him, but he knew they would not be able to stop him without help. His contact in Saud's house had informed him of the American general's visit. His elation at this opportunity had him eager to move in, but he must wait.

They traveled as light as they could, but fifty young men required pack animals and carts to carry weapons, food, and water. He'd send his young men to the attack site in small groups so as to avert notice. He may not have the most well-outfitted, sophisticated army, but with Allah behind him and the fire inside, he would have the victory.

By his early twenties, Ali had developed a reputation as a cold, merciless person, one not to be taken lightly. On one occasion, he had an order for multiple weapons, and he risked all his cash on one bold move. This would be the score that would boost him to the next level and allow him to really enrich his pocketbook. He met with a supplier he had done a couple of deals with, but Ali did not trust the man. The meeting took place among the tents outside Nizwa, Oman's former capital city. Ali paid three hundred thousand dollars in cash to cover the order. He and the supplier agreed to meet the next day in the same place, where he would receive the goods. Ali showed at the scheduled time, but the supplier was nowhere in sight. Ali had been robbed. His rage flared.

He tracked down the local that had provided him with the name of the arms trader. He found the man in a tent that evening enjoying coffee with friends. Ali entered the tent and asked where the arms dealer was. The Arab replied, "*My lash. Fadal, fadal.* No worries. Go away." Ali pulled out his Glock .45 and shot everyone in the tent except the go-between. Ali then grabbed him by his hair, dragged him outside, and tied him down to stakes pounded into the sand.

The man would not talk. Ali and his man took their time, removing his fingers one by one. By this time the man could not have talked even if he were willing. Then, with a rust-covered ax, Ali chopped, and the man's left foot flew into the air. Not wanting him to bleed out yet, Ali's men seared the bleeding stump with a red-hot metal poker from a nearby charcoal fire. As the man screamed, Ali smiled. When he could get a word in, he demanded,

"Where is he? Where is my money?" The man would not answer, whether from shock or loyalty was unclear.

The tortured Arab fell in and out of consciousness while his blood soaked steadily into the sand. When Ali took hold of the ax and raised it to remove the remaining foot, the tortured man choked out in a whisper, "They are at Mahmood's coffee shop near the fort."

Ali knew he was not lying, as he could see the fear in the man's eyes. He turned to his trusted followers and said, "We go."

As he turned to leave, he shot the tortured man in the left eye, smiled his grotesque smile, and left. They found the gunrunners who had stiffed them coming out of the coffee shop. Ali and his men waited, then followed, wanting to be led to where the crooks were staying. They watched from afar as the gunrunners entered an old warehouse. The overbearing heat during the day postponed most transactions until well into the night. Ali would wait as long as it took.

At 3:00 a.m., Ali and his band struck. They entered the old dwelling next to the warehouse and found the arms dealer and his men asleep with Russian whores in their rooms. Ali and his men roamed from one room to the next in the old dwelling, causing total carnage. As the screams rose and fell, a sliver of satisfaction coursed through his veins. Ali and another follower dragged the dealer who had swindled him outside by his mop of curly hair, then tied him to a post. Ali found his money in the man's camel saddle laying against a wall near the door that opened into the warehouse. It was there that Ali Al Sharif made his fortune. The bag contained four million dollars. Arms and artillery, along with tanks, missile launchers, cannons, and crates of Russian AK-

47s filled the warehouse. He decided then and there to take it all. Certainly, the man he had tied to the post was just a middleman, but Ali saw this acquisition as pure gold. The African in the Congo would pay top dollar for these weapons—at least five million, based on the sheer amount of cache Ali had found.

He walked back out to the warehouse. The man who had stolen from him paced back and forth, distraught about the threat to his men. Ali said, "What is your name?"

"My name is Basim. In the name of Allah, I beg you, show mercy. We will give you anything you want. Anything."

"I will have it anyway," Ali said, smirking. "Your actions have shown me your plan was to rob me. Otherwise you would not be comfortably sleeping. What have I done to you, my brother, that you would steal from me? Have I not always treated you fairly and with respect?"

The man fell on his knees and babbled out rapid excuses. "O great warrior, have mercy! We did go to meet you. We must have the time wrong. We did not and would not steal from you!"

Ali ordered the thieves to be lashed to the weight-bearing poles holding up the ceiling. They watched the frightening madman in terror, as all knew what was about to happen. Ali drew his sword from an ornate sheath and slashed the heads off the two Arabs tied next to Basim, the leader, in two lightning-quick strokes. Basim screamed and begged. Ali smiled again, then grabbed this last man by his hair, looked him directly in the eyes, and bared his teeth. With a blood-curdling yell, he slashed the blade across his neck and the man's head tumbled off. He raised the bloody prize for all his followers to see. Then he yelled the mantra that always accompanied and justified such acts. "Allah Akbar! Take everything!"

And with this act of murderous vengeance, Ali's reputation grew. He would hide in the canyons and crevices of the wadis and they would not find him. He took on the name 'Warrior Sheik,' and this title quickly became his brand throughout the two countries. He would make sure his name inspired fear and trembling in everyone who heard it.

Contemplating again his own resources, he knew he had the means to carry on for a long time. He'd been wrong about how much he'd get from the sale of the weapons. He hadn't made five million dollars from his source in the African Congo, but rather eight million. This success enabled him to move on to bigger and more profitable deals. His reputation grew and quickly became legendary, and by sharing his wealth, he amassed loyal followers in the young Arab men who wanted money, women, and all that goes with it. As he worked closely with the young men, a remnant of boyish longing rose in him and the realization of what he could have been stabbed through him. He found he could relate to the young men, and by showing a smattering of kindness to them, he could get them to emulate and praise him, following without reservation. Too easy, he thought, as he wielded his power over them.

His wealth continued to grow, and his scars appeared like medals of honor to the young Arabs who followed his teachings. He used his wealth to bribe the lost souls of young Bedouins who wanted out of the old way of life. He built an army and hand-trained them, and all had a fanatical loyalty to follow him to the death. He gave them hope, money, and purpose—the means to forsake the old ways to have a better life. They had fast cars and new Land Cruisers, gold watches and Russian women. This kind of recruitment came easy to him, because he knew instinctively what they needed, or what they were lacking, because the same need was inside of him. He gave them vision and the sense of belonging to a great cause. He had the anger and fury necessary to carry out his revenge, and he fed it to them. These young Arabs idolized Ali and what he stood for, and as he taught them, he brainwashed them with hate. They would sacrifice anything for him. He was the core on which all their beliefs were centered. He was their prophet, their mentor, and their warring sheik, whom they would follow to hell and back—and if necessary, would die for.

Now, ten years after the attack, he had accumulated everything he needed—maturity, firm resolve, resources, and the ability to hide his activities and whereabouts. More than ready to carry out his revenge, he now had an opportunity to strike. His men had planted their IED during the night and they were ready.

He cursed the Americans and the Omanis for their partnership, their alliance against him and his goals. He planned and waited patiently, with a clear head and a burning, festering, tormenting hatred to avenge his family.

CHAPTER SEVEN

The Message
Oman

The meeting with the sheik had gone well, John thought. Their friendship was still strong, and John didn't take that lightly. He looked forward to telling Ann about it, as she had so enjoyed entertaining the Saud family.

The air in the desert was still and hot. Sweat trickled down John's back as the team headed toward Muscat. All eyes scanned the surrounding terrain as they traveled. A few select areas could be troublesome, as most of the ride home wound through barren desert. Forty minutes into their trip they had only one of these areas left. As they drew closer, the hair on the back of the general's neck stood up. He'd become sensitized to this eerie feeling over the years. As he watched their convoy snake along ahead, an explosion in the jeep in front of him tore through the air, sending billows of gray-white smoke skyward. Chunks of wreckage fell around and on top of them, and they swerved to avoid the worst of it. The three marines in that jeep, John knew, were now dead from the IED. All heads swiveled to the ridge, close to a kilometer away. Time began to crawl, and the other vehicles slowed to a stop as gunfire erupted from their remaining jeep toward the ridge where they'd detected movement. Major Chris Edwards could be heard on the radio with headquarters in Muscat, asking—yelling—for support.

Their car and the two SUVs were blocked from moving forward by the burning wreckage. One of their SUVs was isolated from the rest of the convoy, out in front of the burning jeep. Everyone jumped out and dashed to the ditch for cover. John struggled to look through his scope while small arms began firing on them. The rush was on. Several small groups of terrorists ran down the ridge toward them, one group carrying an RPG. The first wave, on foot, was repelled as everyone in the American convoy returned fire. When the smoke cleared, they could see that the Yemeni attack team had been decimated, and as the Americans took stock of their situation, the young marines looked to the general for leadership. Their CO had been taken out in the first jeep. This was the first time for most of them, and certainly the ambassador, to be in this kind of ambush.

The general quickly evaluated the terrain and yelled, "Sergeant, get to the water in the vehicles! Grab what ammunition you can and haul your butt back here!"

"Roger that, sir!" He and two other marines made a run for the vehicles. They grabbed all they could carry and started back to the ditch. As John and others watched, a small, camouflaged group jumped up from the sand and fired their RPG. As the grenade sailed through the air, John yelled, "Incoming!"

As the sergeant and the marines jumped into the ditch, the other jeep exploded, then all was silent, with the exception of the crackling and popping from the burning jeeps. Heated air from the fire washed over them.

The general had been in many such tight spots. He focused ahead to consider their next steps. The terrorists would attack at nightfall. Even though the major had already contacted the rest of the marines in Muscat, the time of day worked in the enemy's favor. He checked his watch. Three-thirty. To gather, arm, and get to them would take a team about two and a half hours, making their arrival close to dark. Shadows would begin to fall well before dark as the sun disappeared behind the mountain wadis that lined both sides of the road. If they could hold out until then, they had a much better chance of surviving.

Digging in, they took what cover they could and prepared for the expected onslaught. The heat was stifling. They had minimal water and no shade. They also did not know the strength of their adversaries. Had they been attacked by a small force or a whole division? How well armed? Was this the Warrior's doing? What could John do to save his small unit?

Time wore on while they sweated, and finally the sun began to edge behind the mountains. The Yemenis would attack any time now, and John was right. Intermittent small arms cover fire began, giving the impression of an old-time raid by Apaches. The enemy came at the group from three directions, yelling and firing as they attacked.

Ali watched through his binoculars from the hilltop. He did not care that he was sacrificing his men. Most were only boys, not men, and they ran straight into the gunfire of the Americans. The carnage spread out like a killing field before him, bloody and gruesome. With no regard for his followers, Ali sent them to their deaths. Occasionally, one got close to the foxholes the Americans had dug into, but it soon became evident that the Yemenis had no artillery larger than an RPG or they would have used it.

The general turned his head to the side. Dirt, sweat, and in some cases, blood covered the faces of the young men in the ditch, and a steely composure had crept into their eyes. Their months of training had taken over, and John could see that over the last couple of hours these boys had become men—war-hardened marines who believed there was no "quit." This had to be the Warrior's work. The general looked at his watch. Worst case, they had to hang on another hour, but then help would arrive.

Twenty minutes later, fifteen more young recruits charged the Americans from behind, distracting them. Again, the carnage took place, with most of the young Yemenis killed or wounded while the Warrior Sheik scoffed at the dying. His two-season fighters, four of them, again attacked the rear, catching one marine squarely in the chest with a .45.

General O'Shea wiped the sweat off yet again, his eyes burning from the irritation. He spit the grit from his mouth. When he heard movement behind him, he whirled around. Two of the Warrior's men had come over the dune behind them. One of the bloody Bedouins came straight on and managed to get close enough to take a shot. His bullet tore straight through John's right inner thigh. The attacker jumped on him with a knife. He grazed the general's forehead and hit him in his right eye with the butt end of the knife. The Yemeni began beating

on the side of the general's head where blood trailed
down from the cut in his forehead. As John turned his
head to avoid being hit anymore in the face, the Arab
twisted above him to get a better angle, and his full
weight came down purposely on the general's left arm
and snapped it. General O'Shea lay on the ground now,
the attacker kicking him repeatedly. John tried to grab
the foot with his right arm, and just as he had a hold on
it, he heard a .45 go off. He cracked his bleary eye open
enough to see that Gunny had put the round in the back
of the attacking Arab's head. Gunny then turned and shot
the other terrorist in the head as well.

The general cracked his swelling eye open and looked
at his savior. "Well hell, Gunny, I guess it's your turn to
return the favor. Now drag my butt out of this hole and
watch the arm. I think it's broken." Gunny lifted him out
and grabbed the field first aid kit. The bullet had entered
John's upper inner thigh. Blood pumped steadily out of
the wound. He tied a tourniquet above the hole, nearly at
the groin, then injected the general with morphine. The
bullet had gone clean through, it appeared.

"Gunny, where's the ambassador? Have you seen
him?" He could feel the energy draining from him and
his voice sounded weaker to his own ears.

"He's cowering in the ditch, sir," O'Dooley said.

"Make sure he stays safe, would you? It would be an
even bigger disaster if Bob were to go down. We need
him."

As this was taking place, lights became visible down
the road. The cavalry approached. Cheers erupted from
the young marines. How many of his little unit were left?
Several ACPs and a string of armed jeeps rushed in,
accompanied by clouds of dust. They positioned

themselves between the damaged convoy and the enemy. Machine guns blasted away at the mountaintops as darkness fell, and the Yemenis scattered and ran. The terrorists had killed a handful of marines for sure and injured others.

They all paused as a voice sounded from the top of the ridge. "Allah Akbar!" The eerie, drawn-out sound echoed down the slope and through the valley, sending a chill through all who heard it. The voice held a distinct note of triumph, the general thought, before his eyes closed completely and he faded into unconsciousness.

The marines had shown up just in time. The wounded general had a nasty black eye, a badly broken arm, a hole in his leg, and multiple contusions, but he was alive. Gunny's attention to his injuries had been first-rate and had no doubt saved his life. He was loaded into a military Red Cross vehicle. With morphine on board, he didn't remember the ride home. When the general came to in a hospital bed, Gunny O'Dooley occupied the chair next to him. The general looked over and said, "Guess you saved my bacon this time, Gunny."

"Roger that, sir!"

The general looked O'Dooley in the eye and said, "How many, Gunny?"

"We have five KIAs, sir, and three wounded, including you." Gunny sat, holding his hat in hand and lowering his head.

"How many bad guys, Gunny?"

"Twenty-eight confirmed, and five wounded. Their wounds are being addressed and we have them safely confined."

With the sternest voice he could muster, the general said, "Gunny, I want them alive. We need to question them. Don't let the locals kill them! You hear me, Gunny?"

"Roger that, sir!"

"I mean it, Gunny. We need more intel on the Yemeni sheik."

Those were the last words the general said before his eyes rolled back in his head and he passed out.

Gunny O'Dooley left the general in capable hands and departed to look in on their prisoners. There'd be hell to pay if none of them were alive for the general to question.

CHAPTER EIGHT

Beginnings
1988 Ten Years Earlier

John O'Shea entered the pub right at happy hour. Siné Irish Pub, near the Pentagon, had been the favorite watering hole of he and his close friend Major General Jack Shouple. He'd flown in from Texas after his friend's insistence that they meet. He and the major general had a long, global history across many different ops over the course of their military service. In fact, both of them had a hand in conceiving and hatching John's recent idea to form an organization they casually called "PAL."

Jack Shouple's closest officers called him "Jack" rather than "Major General" at his insistence, as it made him feel closer to his men on a personal level. It was the major general's mission to sell their brainchild to the few governmental civilians who were involved with the military branches, and he had taken this responsibility with grave seriousness.

John O'Shea had arrived first after his flight from Austin and was perched on a barstool enjoying the smells of hops and malt, fried fish, and pie crust. The wait staff hurried past his seat with plates of fish and chips and shepherd's pie. He'd been there only ten minutes when his old friend Jack walked in. John had already ordered two boilermakers, and they waited on the bar. Jack, whose thick, graying hair and broad smile sat atop a regularly maintained, trim body, looked down at the two drinks and grinned at his long-time friend. "My God, John, you ole mule-skinner, how long has it been?"

John stood and they embraced with bear hugs, slapping each other on the back a few times.

"You look great, John," the major general continued. I see you haven't forgotten our tradition."

They had been together in the Sinai after the Six Day War and helped secure the Mitla and Kiddi passes after the Israelis had caught the Egyptian army and overrun them all the way back to the Suez Canal.

Jack raised his glass and said, "Here's to getting it right!"

John smiled. "Back at you, and here's to Kenneth Lee." Kenneth was a fallen comrade on that op. They downed their boilermakers and turned the mugs upside down at the same time, chuckling and removing the shot glasses from their mouths.

"Okay, Jack, what do you want from me, and why am I here?"

Jack grinned. "That's what I love about you, John, direct and always to the point. You're being summoned by the Secretary of Defense to hear about your new job, but I thought you would rather hear it from me."

John O'Shea set his water glass down with a clack on the bar. This was unusual, as he rarely met with political figures in his role. Usually it was the major general or his immediate boss, General Ed Perkins.

The waitress stopped by and said, "You gentlemen want another drink?"

John shook his head, smiling at the cute young waitress. "Come back in about ten minutes and we'll be ready." He turned back to his old buddy. "Spill it. Now."

"Okay, you know that special forces task force? The one where we'd have our hands untied, where we can make up our own rules like the enemy does? The one we always talked about."

"Yeah, what about it?"

"Well, John my boy, I got 'er done!"

"What the hell are you talkin' about?"

"You know, our little 'drinkin' thinkin' we used to do, sittin' at the Sinai bar."

"Yes, that new branch of the military we both knew would be necessary if we are to keep our homeland safe," John said. "Remember, I think you were the one that nicknamed it PAL—Protecting American Lives."

"Kinda corny, but the boys in DC bought it—hook, line, and sinker—and I got it funded when we confiscated that Saudi's money being laundered in Turkey." He grinned like the Cheshire cat. Jack clearly had more to say. It was the major general who had sold their brainchild to the civilians who were involved with the military branches.

"I convinced them that five hundred million would fund the project for a couple of years, giving you time to prove out our little scheme." Jack delivered this revelation with a satisfied grin.

John just stared. The major general had gone and sold their brainchild to the civilians involved with the military branches. "What do you mean, giving *me* time?" I got four more years and I am done. Besides, you seem to forget that I already have a job."

Jack grinned and said, "Yep, you're right. Just not the one you've been doin' lately. I got you fired, John. I told them you were too old to be running around in field ops with Navy SEALs."

"You did what?"

"That's right, you are no longer employed by the navy, General." Jack said, still smiling. He reached over and slapped John on the back. You and I are going to get to work together again! That's right, your ass is officially mine again."

General John O'Shea hesitated, taking a few moments to digest the new development. Now that it came right down to it, was he ready to move out of field ops? On the other hand, this was his brainchild, and it needed to happen. If he could be the one to get this operation off the ground, he was all in. He admired the audacity of his old friend to take it through channels and make it a reality, even to the point of altering John's own position.

"So how do you like them apples, General?" Jack said, a slight uncertainty in his voice now.

"You have got to be shittin' me, Jack. What have you done?" John would make him sweat, at least briefly.

"I'll tell you what I have done, old friend. I just gave you your dream job. You get to run your own little clandestine army, navy, and marine branches of the US military. I know PAL sounds a little far-fetched, but they bought it like kids in a candy store!"

John smiled. He had to hand it to the major general. The man had quite the knack for getting things done. He could persuade even the orneriest burro into moving ahead.

"They loved it because there were no politics involved, and we already have the money upfront. No need for a vote in the House or Senate, and if we do good, all them 'political seagulls' will be fightin' over who gets the credit! We got it, John, and there's no better man to run this than you. You get to pick your own team from all branches, with no hesitation from the Joint Chiefs. I'll tell you this, it wasn't an easy sell, and those boys headin' the other branches are not very happy, so don't expect a lot of cooperation from them." Jack smirked. "They were hopin' to get their grubby little paws on that money. I convinced those politicians that we needed to approach certain terrorist activists differently than in the traditional military way, and I pointed out that the CIA did not have the military training or background to handle full-out ops."

John O'Shea sat back, eyes leveled on his old friend, measuring up the new development before reacting.

"I told them we had to stop waitin' to be hit and go after the sons of bitches that are comin' at us, and it would take military folks to do this, not some spy guys."

Finally, John spoke. "I never expected this wild idea we cooked up would actually fly, Jack."

"Apparently they agreed to it when I told them you were just the one to head this. By the way, your boss, Ed Perkins, is not a big fan of mine right now. He thinks the world of you, but he is pissed off at me. I guess he figured as long as you were handling things, he wouldn't have to fool with the division you were heading up. Anyway, he certainly had no kind words to say about me after I went ahead and got the deal done, so I am not expecting a Christmas card from him."

John's mouth quirked up on one corner. "So Big Ed is a little pissed at me right now." His smirk widened and he said, "Well, he is a hell of a guy. He's a great general and a good soldier, so he will do the right thing. Besides, if this is gonna work, we will need him later on."

"Roger that!" Jack said with a big grin and a look of relief at John's apparent cooperation.

Their food arrived and they both dug in. "What's new in your family, John? How are the girls?"

"I guess you haven't heard, but we have a new member of the family."

"Oh? I didn't realize Ann was pregnant. When did this happen? It hasn't been that long since I talked to you last."

"Just last year. We adopted a boy from the orphanage. He's something else. Had a rough go of it in foster care. He's got a fire inside of him from years of abuse, but he's coming along. He's twelve now. Name's Mike."

"Well, congratulations. I look forward to meeting him someday. I'm sure he'll do great in your family. How are the girls taking it?"

"They love him to death. They try to mother him, but he's a year older and bigger than the two of them put together. He's very protective of them, so it's a complementary arrangement."

As they finished their steak and martinis and a couple bottles of wine, it finally hit John what this new arrangement might entail. In a kind of panic, he said, "Jack, where is this headquartered? Do I have a facility? Am I going to have to move my family? I need to talk to Ann about this. I promised her and the kids this was our last move!"

"Relax, General," Jack said. "I have already taken care of all of this, except the 'talking to Ann' part." His smug satisfaction at what he had accomplished was irrepressible. "You remember the old Navy base closed by Clinton during the base shutdowns? Well there is one small facility fifteen minutes from your house in Austin. We used it in the mid-1990s to house political prisoners and an overstocked warehouse. There might even be some stuff you could use there—unofficially, of course."

Thus, the new agency was formed. The only caveat was that General John O'Shea had to give up his field command to lead the new division. Although his heart and soul were with his men in the field, he knew the vital importance of this new agency. He needed to step into this position. After all, he'd been the one to conceive of it in the first place. It would be Jack's job to oversee the newly formed PAL organization, and John welcomed that change. When they joined forces, J and J, as the two had been nicknamed by the oversight committee, were a formidable pair.

The two enjoyed a nice meal, catching up on all the news since they'd last seen each other. John ordered each a Cognac, and then it hit him again. "Jack, I have one final field op I have to do before I start. Sheik Saud has contacted me. Says he needs me, and you know damn well he doesn't trust any of our other generals after the Gulf War promises weren't kept. Besides, it's time I meet him in person. I have to go."

"Okay, okay!" Jack agreed, holding his hands up like he was going to be robbed. How long and when do you go?"

"Next week, and two weeks, tops," the general said, smiling.

"Now, damn it, John, don't go and get yourself killed, or I am gonna be really pissed at you!"

CHAPTER NINE

The Ranch
Hill Country, Texas 1999

John O'Shea stood alone on the escarpment looking out over the Hill Country he loved, under the wide Texas sky. He'd ridden out here to the western edge of his five-hundred-acre ranch in the light of early dawn. Red-tailed hawks circled in the sky before him, much like his thinking, which he badly needed to square away on several fronts. Careers were at the forefront, both his and his son's. Now that Mike and Stacy had graduated, they were coming home for the long Memorial Day weekend, and he and Mike would talk.

After his serious injuries in Oman four years ago, he'd made the difficult decision to return to field work with the PAL teams. He'd breathed a sigh of relief when the decision had been made. Though he was nearly fifty years old, he'd kept himself conditioned over the seven years he'd been a paper pusher. At the age of forty-eight, the desk and the burden of out-of-control politics was neither what he felt he was born to do nor his idea of

where he should have been with a second star on his
shoulder after a stellar career of doing away with bad
guys. He'd moved to the desk job in order to start and
run this branch of America's quasi-CIA and Homeland
Security Special Forces team. Like most government
agencies, PAL had come under attack, with budget cuts
being the politics of the day. He knew that if he hadn't
made the move back to the field when he did, he'd be out
of the action for good, and his division would be
doomed. He believed he still had a lot to offer his
country, his foremost objective being to see what he
could do to increase PAL's success rate on the ground.
Going back to the field had been and continued to be a
hard sell to the organization, but especially to his wife
and family. He knew Mike had been profoundly affected
by his injury four years ago, and he wondered if that
would negate his attempts to lead his son into the
organization.

John and Ann had both wanted a boy to round out
their family with the twins, Kim and Sharon, so they'd
gone to visit the orphanage. Most parents want to adopt a
newborn, but when the general first saw Mike in the
Home for Second Chance Boys—watched him stand,
walk with a swagger, and shake his hand with his head
held high—he knew. He and Ann knew the boy had been
passed over many times for adoption, and yet he still
impressed them with his strong spirit. Mike's look of
deep sadness was now long gone.

John felt great satisfaction over what they had been
able to do for Mike. Instead of a life of crime, drugs, and
prison, the young, scared boy was introduced to
manners, respect, and loyalty, and he had embraced it all,
eager to please and outwardly grateful. He was smart—
not just street smart. He could think on his feet now. His

son was a perfect match for the PAL organization. He and Mike were close, and although the general had not confided in his son about his real work, for obvious reasons, he was convinced Mike was suited for a life protecting the American public from threats.

He'd glimpsed the boy's dark side and believed it was only semi-controlled, but most of that dark side could be brought under control with training. When the whistle blew, adrenaline took hold as though a switch had been flipped. He had experienced this himself many times, that place where everything turns to slow motion. John could see this happen much more strongly in Mike. The brain speeds up and bodily reflexes quicken. When Mike talked about it, he'd say it felt like he was "in the zone." After watching Mike through Tae Kwon Do, boxing, and four years of college football, he could see the young man had the toughness to succeed in jobs others would shrink from—jobs that demanded toughness be pushed to its limit.

Mike had questioned him many times about his military career, and John had told him all he could. Mike knew that, early on as a Navy pilot, John had been shot down in the rice paddies of Vietnam. He then transferred into the marines and served in Special Operations Capable forces, but Mike knew nothing concrete about the covert organization, PAL, that John had been a part of for the last ten years, and since he'd returned to the field, the work had taken him away from home a lot. As his career had progressed and he'd received his second star, he felt like that was a sign that his work would someday come to an end and the reins would be turned over to the next generation. He had fought for this program. As the different agencies struggled for turf and who would do what to keep America safe, this elite group from all branches of the armed forces proved to be a success well beyond what was first envisioned, and now its position was cemented as a vital force in the country's counterespionage, in spite of funding and politics.

The O'Shea family employed a young Native American couple, Joe and Hanna, for whom they'd built a home on five acres at the back of the property. They were all fond of the couple, who took good care of the ranch when the family was absent. They tended the horses and cattle, kept up fence, and plowed, planted, and harvested hay. The ranch did little better than break even, but they hadn't bought it for the investment—they'd bought it because all the O'Sheas enjoyed the outdoors. When the family came, Hanna always had everything in order in the sprawling ranch home. The family had spent most holidays here.

Whenever John needed to have a discussion with one of his children or impart "life's little lessons" as they had come to be known, he loaded them up in his F–150 and they went out to the ranch due west of town, located at the beginning of Hill Country. It was called "Broken Arrow," BA brand, after a Native American tribe that had once lived there but had long since gone. The O'Sheas bought the place some years back when the market crashed, and John and Mike had spent a lot of weekends and holidays chasing white-tailed deer, hogs, and turkeys. They planted sunflowers for dove season and raised pheasants, which were now bountiful on the property. One of the major forks of the Trinity River ran right through the acreage, and the three ponds overflowed with sizable largemouth bass. The region appealed because of its topography and its vineyards and caverns, being the dividing line between the American Southwest and the Southeast. The ranch was the family sanctuary. They all agreed they felt most at home there as they bonded, laughed, played card games, and engaged in the usual tricks and pranks. This place provided something the hard-working family needed—a temporary haven, a taste of the ease of life. Along with the kick-back atmosphere, the family conducted most of their inner-circle business at the ranch. He hoped Mike would relax enough to talk about his future.

***

Mike shifted smoothly through the gears of his Jeep Wrangler as he and Stacy headed to the family home in Austin. He loved his Jeep and hadn't had enough time to get it out on the road over the last few years. This trip home and out to the ranch would be a place he could relax after the four grueling years of UT football and studies.

Four wonderful years had flown by and Stacy and Mike had been inseparable, but over the past few months both had felt the pressure of graduation and what would happen between them when it was all over. They had both tried to broach the subject of their rapidly approaching decision, but neither wanted to face the brutal truth of inevitable separation, so for the most part they'd avoided the painful issue. But time continued to march closer to school's end, and both knew they had to face it head-on during this three-hour drive into Hill Country. The getaway had sounded like heaven. But first he'd have to cut the tension that entered the vehicle when he'd picked Stacy up. He reached over and took her hand, but Stacy pulled back.

"Mike, we have to talk about our future."

Mike grimaced and his jaw flexed.

"You know I love you," Stacy said. "You also know that I have worked my butt off to get into Harvard Law. I've dreamed of this since I was a girl. What are we going to do about us?" she said, pleading for him to come up with an answer.

He didn't have one.

"Stacy, you have to do what you have to do. You've already been accepted and made your decision, so what else is there to say?"

"That's not an answer, Mike!" A tear started down Stacy's cheek.

Mike stared at the road ahead. He, too, was hurting.

"I don't know, Stace! I know you have to go, but I'm still wrestling with what I want to do. I don't see myself going into law and putting myself through three more years of school." Mike gripped the wheel harder, frustrated. "I'm thinking of doing what Dad does or something similar—FBI, Navy SEAL, Homeland Security—something like that. I'm going to talk to him this weekend."

Stacy shuddered. "We'll just have to see what happens. I have to tell you, I don't want you to go that direction. Not after what happened to your dad."

Almost pleading, Mike said, "Stacy, we can manage this. Three years is not forever. We will make time during breaks and holidays, and we can talk every night."

The stress was still building, and Mike could do nothing to fix it. "Damn it!" he said, slamming his fist on the steering wheel. "We're in a hard spot right now and there's nothing we can do to avoid it. I know you're thinking about Dad, but just because he was injured doesn't mean I would be. He's much older. You and I both know I'm custom built for something like that. Although I can't even say for sure what he's doing. He's never talked specifically about it." Stacy looked at him sideways. "Because he can't. But maybe now is the time and I can get him to talk about it this weekend."

After a few minutes of silence, Mike raised his arm and put it across her shoulders. Though she was struggling with her emotions, she did scoot under his arm. She reached her hand up and felt for his.

For the next twenty miles neither said anything. Facing the reality that many college sweethearts face, Mike realized that if either gave in, resentment would be sure to follow, and both were smart enough to recognize this. It seemed a no-win situation, at least for the near future.

"I admit I'm afraid you'll decide to follow in your father's footsteps. After what happened four years ago, that terrifies me, Mike. Why don't you apply to Harvard and follow me there? Get a graduate degree in international relations and get your PhD if you don't want law. I know you're interested in that. Then we can be in similar fields, and we'll be together."

The lack of sound, not even radio, was intense, and neither knew what to say next. Mike finally said, "If it is meant to be, we'll make it happen. Please know that I love you." This was not easy for him to say.

Well aware of his own introverted nature, Mike preferred to be a listener, and believed he was damn good at that. His confidence had grown over the last four years, and now, in top physical shape, he felt prepared for whatever life decided to throw at him. Maybe his years as an orphan hadn't been for naught. The hardships had made him strong, but he had to admit the stress of the decisions had been weighing on him. He couldn't stomach another four years of college. Or even two. The thought of sitting at a desk studying any longer made him cringe.

Mike's father wanted him to go out to the ranch early the next morning and have the girls catch up later for a barbecue. Stacy would go with Kim and Sharon to the Hidden Spa for several hours, and his father was pushing for this time to talk. Mike was a little taken aback, as it was not hunting season, and for the life of him he couldn't think of anything he'd done recently that would trigger a trip to the barn. When he asked, the general told him he wanted a little time with his son now that school was over. Mike knew better. Historically, whenever his father said "Let's head to the ranch," it usually meant one of three things. Either you were in trouble, he wanted to go hunting or fishing, or he had something on his mind about which he required your undivided attention with minimal distractions.

CHAPTER TEN

Family Times

Hill Country, Texas

Five a.m. rolled around, and Mike drove to the ranch to meet his father. They poured a thermos full of hot coffee in the kitchen and headed out. Not much was said at this early hour, but Mike sensed something weighed heavy on his father's mind. He knew better than to press it. He would wait, and his dad would eventually get around to talking about whatever was stuck in his craw.

Joe met them at the barn. He was trying to get the first cut of hay in. He wanted to try to get three cuts out of the field this year and the first cut put up in the barn this weekend. His helper at the ranch had gone to Mexico for a family wedding, and Joe needed extra hands. So father and son spent most of the morning walking behind the trailer, throwing bales of hay and then stacking square bales the old-fashioned way in the tin-roofed barn. Both men were covered in sweat, pieces of straw stuck to their flannel shirts. They needed a cold one. Joe left to fetch Hanna, then headed to town to pick up the best steaks in the state of Texas. The small town right outside the ranch had one of the few butcher shops that still cut meat the old-fashioned way. Big, thick, and cooked on a charcoal fire, the steaks were a real treat—the entire family's favorite meal, along with the conversation and Hanna's pecan pie.

They packed up the saddle bags, the fishing rods, and a six-pack of Bud, and each climbed on his favorite horse. John rode the big black stallion, and Mike mounted his favorite paint. Both knew exactly where they were going, down to the big mesquite tree that provided shade at the river's honey hole, which was filled with fish. Mike was curious, and maybe a little anxious, about what his father wanted to speak to him about. He waited, though patience was not one of his strong suits.

A cool breeze hit them, and with a Bud in hand and lines in the water, John the father, not the starched General O'Shea, started in with small talk—about school, UT football, whether bird season was going to be abundant this year, and Mike's two sisters' latest shenanigans. They sat and laughed in the mild breeze, then John grew quiet. Mike sat in silence, listening to the river and the wind whispering in the evergreen leaves of the Texas live oaks.

"So, Mike, now that you've graduated, I'm sure you've been thinking hard about your future. Do you have any thoughts about what direction to take?"

His dad knew Stacy was headed to law school. Mike hadn't mentioned anything about following her. He took his time to answer, staring at his bobber wobbling in the watery ripples.

Finally, he said, "I've given this a lot of thought. I've watched and listened to you for some years now. Your career seems to have made you content. You've always said that service to one's country is necessary for all others to have freedom. I think—I'm not sure yet—but I'm looking to the military, CIA, or FBI. I know I won't get rich, but money isn't everything, and service to one's country is honorable." His father listened and watched him intently, but he looked proud, Mike thought. He probably felt relief that all his talks about service had paid off.

Mike continued. "You know, truthfully, I'm scared, Dad. I'm not sure I have overcome my childhood yet. I know you've seen and been concerned about my inner demons. I know they're there. Sometimes I just want to lash out at injustice, and a cold inner rage takes over, especially when adults are harming children. It's really hard to keep it under control. What will happen when it's tested in a hot situation? Will I do more harm than good? Will that rage come out and hurt others? I'm not a hundred percent certain I can always control it."

"Son, you've been through therapy and you have come a long way. I have seen you mature and learn to exert control over your rage. Going through further military training will cement those lessons. You'll never be rid of it, that's guaranteed. It works that way for all of us with childhood wounds. But that is not a bad thing. There's a Biblical lesson my mother taught me long ago that I've never forgotten. It goes something like, 'You intended to harm me, but God intended it for good to accomplish the saving of many lives.' If we don't feel passion for something, we won't do what it takes to fight the evil. The fact that you have that passion and, with the opportunity to use it for good, you will be highly effective." His bobber plunged below the surface and he yanked up on it, but his soggy worm flipped out of the water with nothing attached. He took a long drink of his beer and recast.

"Your mother and I have talked long and hard about whether we want to see you enter a branch of service that would endanger your life. She, as most mothers do, looks upon such a thing with her nurturing heart and is not sure she'll be able to handle another of her men in harm's way. My beating on the mission four years ago and my return to the field did nothing to ease her fears, as you know. But she is stronger than she realizes."

Mike nodded. They'd all thanked the Lord above for sparing him from disability or death. They talked for nearly an hour while the fish bit, catching one after another and throwing them back, laughing and ribbing each other as only a father and son can do. They opened a second can of beer to start the weekend off right and then it grew quiet again, except for the chirping of the golden-cheeked warbler.

"Dad, Stacy and I are at a crossroads. You can probably guess by now how much I love her."

"It's written all over both of your faces, son. But I can appreciate that you have a crisis going on in your relationship over your future. Your mother and I have been down that road ourselves."

Mike recast his fishing line and sat back. "Stacy's headed to Harvard Law in a couple of months and wants me to come. But that's not what I feel is right for me, as much as I'm going to miss her. I think I need to follow my own path until we're in a position to make our relationship permanent."

"That sounds like a good way of looking at it," his father said. "Sometimes our emotions can get the best of us in love and affect our life's decisions. We can find the inner strength we need to push through and pursue our goals even when it means postponing what is most dear to our hearts. We have to take a level-headed, unemotional look and evaluate what makes the most sense for our lives overall. Your mother and I had to sacrifice what we wanted in the moment in order to achieve the life goals we both needed and wanted to accomplish. We forced ourselves to look at the big picture, and it helped us to endure the times apart. If your relationship is strong, there is something to be said for absence making the heart grow fonder."

"You seem to have a very strong marriage. It's an inspiration to all of us."

"Yes. I think enduring the tough things made us strong. That has benefitted us in more ways than one."

Mike's father seemed reluctant to fully speak his mind, but he told him he'd like to walk him through his offices and let his men speak to Mike. He asked Mike not to jump both feet first into anything until they had a chance to discuss his decision after that. So they set a date for the following week for Mike to stop by his office and grab some lunch. Fair enough, Mike thought. He was highly curious by now about the work his father kept tightly concealed.

They kept a few fish, threw some back into the water, and headed to the house where they were sure the girls were up to something.

***

"How are my girls?" John's booming voice echoed in the lofty kitchen. Ann had returned just moments before, and the three girls, Kim, Sharon, and Stacy, were showing off their nails. Ann moved to give him a hug.

He wrapped his arm around her and squeezed. After twenty-five years of marriage, he was still smitten with her. As in most military families, the absences strained the family unit, but Ann had held it together, and she brought balance to the complete warrior, the largest part of his persona. Best friends, she made him laugh and they were at peace with one another. What more could a man want?

Mike approached the girls and peered over his beer can at the nails—curious, but not wanting to show too much interest.

"Look, Mike, Stacy got nude polish with this cool gold filigree design on the ring fingers." Kim's innate enthusiasm was infectious.

"Nude, huh? What's nude polish? And what's a filigree design?" The girls all looked at him in disbelief.

"He doesn't know what the color 'nude' is," Sharon said, the first to catch on. "Guys don't buy 'nude' anything."

"Hey, don't kid yourself," Mike said. "We might not buy it, per se, but we sure as hell *like* it." He winked at Stacy, then took her hand and held it up under the hanging lights. "Now those are some fancy claws."

She smiled and he kissed the back of her hand before releasing it. "Thank you. And how was the fishing?"

"Dad beat me out by one itty bitty sunfish."

"All in all, Mike's catch weighed more than mine, though," John said, graciously handing off the glory to his son. Mike's smiled gratefully.

Sharon, not to be left out, winked at Mike. "Look at my nails, bro," she said, holding out her fingers. They were painted black, with tiny white daisies in the center of each one.

"Pushing up daisies already?" he said. She pushed him, and he twisted around and quickly got her into a hold. "And how's that boyfriend of yours going to like this? Are you still going out?"

"Who?" Sharon said, eyes flashing at the thought. "You mean that scumbag, Nate? If he shows his face 'round here again, he'll be the one pushing up daisies."

"You want me to deal with him?" Mike laughed, not totally in jest.

"If he comes around, you are welcome to do whatever you see fit. I don't want nothin' to do with him." Sharon's eyes flashed and her boots clicked on the tile floor as she helped Ann with meal preparation. She moved gracefully, like her mother, her hair gathered up in a clip and her cropped top tied in a knot above her skinny jeans.

Ann sprinkled seasoning on the steaks. "This boy has the looks but not the charm. Sharon gave him a good chance. She went out with him several times over the last two months, but there was no substance to him."

John watched the interchange with interest. He could see Mike's blood boiling. From the start, Mike had instinctively taken on the duty of preserving his sisters' honor. A typical Southern dad with two strikingly beautiful daughters, John could be a little overbearing. But he adored both girls, and of course, no man would be good enough for them. It reassured him for Mike to take over the role of protector during his absences. Mike took it upon himself to "cull the boys" who came by the dozens to call on the younger girls, and not many made the cut. At times during the teen years this would put a strain on the relationship between the siblings, but the way Mike handled it made the difference. He'd use a look, or, when the girls weren't around, a direct approach—an intimidating presence that was unmistakable to the wrong kind of guy.

John and Mike grilled the steaks and they all sat and ate, opening a couple of bottles of Opus, their family's favorite red wine. When all had their fill, the girls shooed off their mother and father. "We'll get this, Mom," Kim said.

John winked at Ann and curled his finger, indicating she should come with him. He led her down the hall to the bedroom, then shut and locked the door, taking his still-beautiful wife in his arms. She had lost only a sliver of her allure. Once having donned the cover of Sports Illustrated magazine as an Olympic athlete, she still possessed a rock-solid physical presence and an intelligence that had served her well as coach, businesswoman, and ambassador.

"Did you have any success talking to Mike about PAL?" she said.

He lowered his face into her soft blond hair. "I've asked him to visit me at the office next week. I want this to be his decision, with no fatherly pressure."

"You're a good man, John," she said, arms around his waist. "That's the right way to handle this. Mike is perfect for the job. I think he'll embrace the opportunity without reservation, much as I hate the thought."

"We'll see," John said. "Our kids are all turning out to be great people. They've had their bouts of mischievousness, but overall, you've done a fantastic job, my dear."

"They've had a great role model. I can't take full credit for them."

"They have your looks," he said, tenderness underlying his words. You always wonder whether looks will go to your kids' heads, but I've seen them put each other in place when one gets arrogant or pretentious."

"I have seen it too," Ann said. "Where'd they get that from?"

"They're smart yet humble. And they've brought so much to our lives. Naming them after our long-lost relatives was a good move. Our heritage will be carried on through our children. I pray they continue to be God-fearing, yet not fanatical."

John bent over and Ann lifted her face to his to share a tender kiss.

When they went back out, the dishes were done, dried, and put away, and the four had gathered around the game table to play their favorite family game, The Settlers of Catan. Ann and John grabbed some after-dinner drinks and pulled up a couple of chairs.

And so, the game commenced. Laughter, camaraderie, and fun—this was relaxation at its best, a much-needed peaceful interlude in the stressful chess game of life.

CHAPTER ELEVEN

The Decision
1999

Mike's Wrangler looked out of place in the parking lot full of conservative vehicles, especially with the dirt still clinging to it, glaringly conspicuous against the flame red. He and Don had tried out the new off-road park for a few days, sleeping in the bunkhouses and hitting up all the new trails. Leave it to the unmaintained car wash to leave his flame-red Jeep all smudged and spotted. Good thing no one else was around. This place looked so nondescript that Mike wasn't sure he was in the right place until he saw his father's white Lexus sedan, conspicuous amongst the predominantly black vehicles.

Mike had never fully understood his dad's role in the military. When Mike asked, his dad would say he did "whatever they need me to do." The way he said it prevented Mike from questioning his dad's occupation. Like others who were family or knew the general, Mike referred to him as an officer who ran a division of the marines, which included special ops and other special forces in various departments. Mike often asked his dad about his day, but again, it was the way the general answered that kept Mike from persisting. Over time, Mike just let it go, though he knew that becoming a general, especially a two-star general, was big. Such a position came with sacrifice, long deployments away from home, and odd hours. Certainly no eight-to-five job, like other kids' dads.

Mike pulled up to the manned gate, said his name, and showed his ID. He was waved right through after the marine told him which building to go to. As he drove through the facility, it looked like many of the government buildings were used for official business and not meant for public tours. The façade of the buildings appeared cold, plain, matter of fact.

Mike walked into what seemed like a sterile environment, with only a smattering of pictures on the wall, mostly of past naval battles and, of course, the current president, vice president, and secretary of state. Mike paused at the desk after he entered and was required to sign a confidentiality agreement before proceeding. Mike's escort was a naval captain who had come to meet him at the lobby entrance. Bill Glasses had so many medals and ribbons pinned to his dress blues that he looked like he might fall over, or at least ought to be standing with a lean. Captain Bill wasn't much for small talk, certainly not one to be found working at a theme park. He was all business, answering "Yes, sir" and "No, sir" as his patented answers. As Mike walked down the hall, he had an eerie feeling he was being watched. He had never been in the building before, much less his father's office. Nor had the general ever been a participant in "Bring your Dad to School for Show and

Tell." His mom handled the domestic appearances. They moved down the hall through what made him think of prison doors—one had to have both a badge and a retinal scan before any of them would open. Mike would bet that everyone in this building was accounted for.

As they came to the end of the hall, a monitor on which they appeared, live, was in full view. The door buzzed and partially opened, and Mike followed Captain Glasses into a waiting room. Behind the desk sat Sandy, his dad's long-tenured assistant. Mike had met her before when his parents invited her to spend Christmas Day at their house. His parents often invited others who had no one to be with for the holidays. Now in her early forties, Sandy was a brunette who surely worked out frequently, as she was still nice on the eyes. Through conversation with Captain Bill, Mike learned that she was very good at her day job and had once been a field operative.

Sandy got up and walked around the desk and hugged Mike. Bill gave her an indecipherable look. A little coldly, Sandy told Bill he could return to his post. Bill got up and left without saying a word.

When he was gone, Mike said to Sandy, "What gives with the captain?"

"It's a long story," she said. "When he and I were younger, we had a fling. It is just as well forgotten." It appeared to Mike that Bill hadn't wanted it to end. Tough thing to have to work in close proximity. She motioned for Mike to follow her into his dad's office.

Mike was immediately struck by the photographs on the walls—pictures of young John O'Shea, his family in different vacation areas, war photos, and field shots of old comrades. Mike walked across the large, well-designed room to his father and shook his hand, then took a seat on an oversized leather chair opposite his father's desk. His chair was lower than his dad's, giving the general an intimidating presence before a word was spoken. This was probably by design, Mike thought.

After thanking and dismissing Sandy, his father told him about the organization. The agency was called PAL, which stood for Protect American Lives. A clandestine division, the public and most US Senators were not aware it existed, so there would be no flak from anyone if PAL were to simply disappear. The organization reported only to the secretary of defense and the president, with full autonomy to do whatever necessary to protect the country.

But John O'Shea knew the true value of the organization, and thank goodness, the president did too. Over the past ten years since the agency came into being, they'd stopped multiple terrorist attacks, many equivalent to the trade-tower disaster. Four hostile governments had been overthrown and five dictators wheedling genocide ousted, as well as numerous kidnapped American citizens saved by the department. More importantly, PAL kept America's enemies in check and off balance, serving as a guardian of democracy. It had become the most successful military branch of the service since guerilla warfare and terrorist activities replaced the great wars, largely due to John O'Shea's leadership. It was often hard to find out who the real enemy was—who was behind it and what their next move would be, but their success had impressed the powers that be.

Since PAL's inception, John had been in a prime position to do what he deemed necessary to protect the United States. Gary Casswell, his contact who worked in the middle of the Sultanate of Oman, met secretly with factions and leaders of the Mutawah, the fanatical religious police of the Middle East who were camped outside Nizwa. As a local CIA agent with a cover, Gary functioned as an oilfield wildcatter looking for the next big strike in the oil-rich sheikdom.

Mike listened in awe to the vital workings of the covert organization as well as the position and work of his own father. Now everything made sense. John O'Shea stood, motioning for Mike to follow him. The general walked him into PAL's soundproof and IT-protected war room. All of his top staff were there. The folks sitting around the room were all seasoned veterans who had shared, participated in, and led many of the successful missions that PAL had been tasked with over the years. All of them were senior officers, highly decorated, and most importantly, handpicked by the general, their loyalty beyond reproach. All remained willing to step in front of a bullet for anyone in the room, and many had done so.

Structured like any corporate board room, the exceptional difference was that the decisions made in this room could cost lives, overthrow governments, or even start conflicts worldwide. And as with most corporate boards, this one included two types of personalities. The conservatives, who are slow to act, and the fighters, who will quickly jump into action. The general was the balancing force for the team. His word was the final decision on go-or-no-go policy; on deployment; and on the spend that needed to take place. With all John's years of service, his skill and experience was such that his decisions were seldom questioned. He had the final say, and he merited unwavering loyalty.

The team topic for today recognized that as the leaders of this esteemed organization had aged, so had the field officers. They had no succession plan in place, no trainee or intern program, and all knew that shoring up the division was imperative for continued success. The meeting started with an empty page and discussion took place on what optimum field operatives should look like. As the white board filled with criteria, it became obvious to Mike that what was being described looked exactly like him.

When this meeting ended, the general took Mike through a door that appeared to be part of the wall paneling in the back of the room. They stepped through. A glass wall ran the length of a long hall. Through the glass, giant screens displayed world globes, with complex diagrams that looked like the Mafia's family trees from different regions of the world. Satellite images projected a variety of scenes, showing everything from troop movements to desert camp embankments and overhead surveillance. Telephoto shots were shown, focusing on one or more individuals on the screens adjacent to it. The name of the special agent in charge of each region and the latest update that had been sent were displayed. Each were color-coded in regard to the danger, or potential danger, the respective cases revealed. Mike stood still, stunned at the sheer size and scope of what was being monitored. Now that he was in the loop, he understood. There must have been eighty to a hundred different missions projected onto what looked like small think tanks. The rooms were split into U-shaped conference rooms with about a dozen people in each. All were focused on their respective screens. The enormity of what was taking place in front of him was hard to grasp.

After the general's thorough tour and explanation of PAL facilities, he led Mike back to his office and offered him a cup of coffee. Mike accepted gratefully. He needed a few moments to digest all he had seen. He'd known from the moment he walked in what his decision would be. Well aware that this decision would push him to develop and use every shred of his inner capacity, his gut told him this was right for him. His sense of honor and dignity, along with his fighting spirit, rose up within him, and he nodded his head. He would follow this path, and one day he and Stacy would be together. He hoped she would be able to be proud of him.

The general sat patiently behind his massive desk, waiting. He sipped his coffee from the sturdy brown mug Kim had made for him in high school art class. Everyone in the family had one of Kim's mugs, and all agreed she had some serious artistic talent. Mike lifted his eyes and smiled, the mug a symbol of family cohesiveness, as he and everyone used her mugs exclusively for their morning joe.

"I've made a decision, Dad," Mike said. "I'd like to begin the steps necessary to become a part of the team."

"Thank you, Mike," his father said. He didn't smile, but the look of serious pride in his eyes warmed Mike. He knew it wouldn't have mattered if he'd decided this wasn't for him, but he also knew that he'd just given his father a much-desired gift.

This momentous decision seemed to be a fitting cap to an adoption success story. Mike's soul swelled with gratitude for the family who had brought him in and loved him like their own from the first day. He could never repay any of them, or his country, enough.

The two men strode down the hall, backs straight and strong, traversing what seemed like two city blocks. They passed walls of brightly colored screens displaying information on every mission, then entered a briefing room with ten of the highest-ranking officials in the US sitting around the table. Mike knew most of them, but a few he didn't recognize. All stood as they entered, and the general told them to be seated. All eyes shifted back and forth between Mike and John O'Shea. The general introduced his son. They all clapped, congratulating him on his decision and wishing him well with his training. And so it began.

CHAPTER TWELVE

The Early Years
Texas, 1985

Mike had learned not to cry in front of anyone, but it was dark, and his fingers throbbed, and his right eye was swollen when the tear oozed out and ran down his cheek. Dim light came from under the closet door. He squinted his eyes to look for something he could use to beat on it or pry it open. This time, Lenny had slugged him in the face, grabbed him by the hair, and dragged him across the linoleum floor before tossing him in the closet. He'd slammed the door, catching Mike's fingers and smashing them, skinning them and probably breaking the bones, too. Because Lenny couldn't close the door completely, he opened it just enough that Mike could remove his bloody fingertips before he slammed it again.

Maybe today was his birthday. He didn't know. He thought he was eight, but he wasn't sure. Other kids brought treats to school, but he would never get to do that. This was the second time this week he'd been put in the closet. The last time, Lenny kept him there for two days. Once, someone threw a piece of bread and a juice box into the darkened space, but that was all. He had no place to go to the bathroom, no water, and only a dim light at the bottom of the door crack. How long would it be this time? It was Sunday, so maybe Lenny would let him out to go to school the next day. Both Mike and the government rip-off artist Lenny knew that Mike was required to go to school. If he missed much, they would come to the home and check on him, and maybe take him away. Lenny wasn't about to let good money leave his pocket. His rug rats provided him the majority of his income. Eight was the maximum allowed by the state, or he would have had more of the little bastards in his three-bedroom, two-bath track home. He and his "squaw" took the master bedroom with a bath attached, leaving the three orphaned girls one of the other rooms and the five boys squeezed into the back bedroom. Each room contained only one queen-sized bed. The three skinny, fragile girls fit in their bed, but because of their size, only two of the boys had room on theirs, leaving the other three to sleep on the floor.

Lenny grumbled constantly about everything he provided them. After all, he said repeatedly, he gave them sleeping bags he'd picked up at an army surplus store ten years earlier and he didn't get paid a dime more for providing beds and pillows. All eight kids shared one bathroom. The toilet constantly clogged and made the whole back of the house smell like a sewer. Lenny either never noticed or didn't care, even though he was a plumber at a local factory, working the graveyard shift. At five-foot-eight and overweight by a hundred pounds, he looked like a bowling ball, with hair all over his body except his head. Though Mike and the others feared him, they called him "medicine-ball man" behind his back.

Awhile back Mike heard Lenny grumbling about his hair plugs not working. He was right. Now he looked half crazy. Mike had plenty of time in the closet to think about how much he hated this foster home and the fat, balding man who rarely bathed.

The young woman Lenny had brought back from Chili years ago was sedated on pain killers and cheap street drugs. She spent her years in a haze, watching TV, doing laundry, and occasionally cooking for the kids. She spoke little English, and no one knew her name, only that Lenny called her "the squaw." When she got whiny or talked back, he took the belt to her, too. She was a prisoner like they were. Lenny spent the money he got for the kids at the horse track every weekend, squandering their milk money on jockeys and winning just enough to keep him going back. These things percolated inside, and Mike's anger grew.

Mike lost track of time. Why was Lenny so enraged? All because he didn't get up fast enough and get Lenny a beer from the fridge? Four days ago, he was punished the same way because he wouldn't eat the spinach the squaw made.

On Monday morning, Lenny yanked open the door. Mike covered his eyes as the light blasted in. "Get out, punk. Get your butt upstairs and clean up for school. Now!"

Mike raised his arm to protect his swollen eye from the blast of light. He'd been in the dark for twelve hours, and his eyes needed to adjust. When he lowered his arm, he looked up at Lenny with hatred and without fear. Lenny smirked at Mike, grabbing his chin in his big paw. "Listen here, you little bastard, if someone asks you about that shiner, you tell 'em a baseball hit you, got that?" He swiped his nose across his sleeve. "If you don't, you'll be back in the closet again." He pushed him down on the floor toward the staircase.

With pure hatred, in the deepest adult voice an eight-year-old kid could produce, Mike clenched his small fists and said, "Lenny, someday you're going to get yours, and when I am older, I will see to it!"

Lenny jumped at him, causing Mike to stumble toward the stairs. He turned and ran up them, his fingers and hands covered in dried blood. His eye was swollen, puffy and purplish-black, and bloodshot. His shirt showed blotches of blood from the belt.

"You hear me, Mike? I mean it, dammit, if they come tonight, you'll have hell to pay!" Mike kept going. He'd felt the belt before. As he raced up the stairs he passed Chad, who looked at him with wide eyes. Mike would have run away, but even at this young age, he felt a loyalty to his friend and classmate Chad. Chad was seven, and Mike knew that if he left, Chad would be abused—not only by Lenny and the squaw, but by the other kids at school. The boy was weak and a little slow but was a kind kid. In low-income schools, the weak often suffered. With Mike there, at least none of the other kids picked on Chad, and he could try and keep Lenny away from him.

This existence was what Mike thought life was about. This was his third foster home in six years. He could not remember his birth parents. All he could remember was work, the belt, beatings, hunger, and being shuttled from place to place. Before Lenny's hellhole, he'd been on a farm where the kids were slave labor, but at least they were fed well. The farmer knew that if he fed them, they could work harder. He'd still be there working before and after school if the farmer hadn't been drunk and fallen under a combine that ran over and killed him.

He arrived at school that morning with Chad, two other boys, and one of the girls. As they got off the bus, four kids from a local gang of thirteen- and fourteen-year-old boys started to pick on the two other boys, and then one of the gang members pulled a girl's skirt down toward her ankles. When Mike, who was big for his age, stepped off the bus and saw what was happening, he erupted. The rage had been brewing his entire short life and had swelled into a volatile dark side. He jumped off the last step and ran straight to the boy who had ahold of the girl's skirt and with all his might and weight behind him, he slugged the kid in the nose. The boy's hands flew to his face and he stumbled and fell to the ground screaming, blood pouring through his fingers. Mike went straight at the others, swinging his fists. He scratched and bit and did everything he could to keep from getting hit, but the three overpowered him, tore his shirt off his back, and kicked him while he was down. Mike got a few licks in, but he took the brunt of the attack. The bus driver noticed what was happening and called for the teacher on duty to take Mike to the office and two of the others to the school nurse.

Mike sat outside the principal's office with a torn shirt, a black eye, and smashed, bloody fingers. He also smelled bad, as he'd had only a quick minute to rinse off that morning before the bus came. The principal, in her mid-thirties, had seen a lot in this low-income school district, but when she saw this eight-year-old child, her breath caught in her throat. His nose ran, his fingers bled, and he had a black eye. But this was not what bothered her the most. His back was exposed through his torn shirt and he had many bright red welts on his back. She'd seen this before, and knew this boy was enduring repeated beatings. She struggled to regain her composure as tears came to her eyes. She crouched down in front of Mike and looked him in the eyes. Mike wasn't crying, but his stare held a deep sadness. Mike not only wore a lost look, but his eyes held hatred. This boy had no life—no birthday parties, no Halloween, no Christmas—only work and pain. Her arms flew open and she held him close, not caring that he was dirty, smelly, and bloody.

As she released him, she took his hand and told him to come. They proceeded to the nurse's office, and like most offices in poorer districts, they were small, understaffed, and overwhelmed with the sheer number of kids they had to treat. The nurse had just sent the other two boys to class. The principal pulled her aside, and in a clipped voice she said, "I want you to take a picture of this kid's injuries—his face, his arms, his legs, and his back."

"I don't have a camera," the nurse said.

"Find one. Find one now. I don't care if you have to go get the yearbook camera, I want pictures of this boy. Do you understand me?"

"Yes ma'am." The harried nurse rushed out the door, not bothering to even look at Mike, much less treat his wounds. The principal directed Mike up onto the examination table herself. She found clean gauze pads and gently cleaned the blood from Mike's face and hands. Mike's young mind was occupied with what Lenny would do to him once he found out. He started to shake, and the principal spoke softly.

"It's going to be okay, Mike."

The nurse returned with a Polaroid camera, and the principal took Mike's shredded shirt off while the nurse snapped pictures. Still silent, Mike knew this would be trouble. Lenny would beat him and throw him back into the closet, but he held his emotions and thoughts to himself. His life was a nightmare that would not end, and at eight years old he couldn't understand why this was happening to him. He'd seen kids on TV who had mothers and fathers and a home with a bed but had no idea why he didn't have the same.

After his fingers were bandaged, he stood and looked at the principal. "Can I go back to class now?" he said. He needed to get away from these two ladies, but it was probably too late. His fears were realized when the principal left and told the nurse to get him something to eat but keep him in her office until she got back.

The principal called the police and social services. After briefing them on what they were about to see, the three entered the nurse's office. All three were stunned and couldn't speak. Mike was sure this would be trouble. "Looks like he's been in a head-on collision with a Mack truck," one mumbled.

"I want to go home," he said, pleading with the three adults. The social worker and the police officer glanced at each other. They approached Mike and looked him over, then looked at the Polaroids. After a few minutes the nurse came in with a sandwich, chips, a piece of apple pie, and an orange juice. Mike was starving. He consumed the food like a wild jungle boy.

When it was gone, the principal said, "Mike, are you still hungry?"

Mike nodded and whispered, "A little, ma'am."

The principal sent the nurse after another meal, then asked when he ate last.

Mike was afraid, so he didn't answer.

"Was it yesterday?"

Mike nodded his head.

"Yesterday evening?"

Again, Mike said nothing.

"Mike, it's okay, you can talk to me. Was it yesterday morning?"

Mike looked up at her with a darkness in his eyes, then nodded. He was now positive this would not end well. He didn't panic, cry, or whine, he just ate his sandwich and said nothing. The three others left him with the nurse. A kid-friendly judge issued a warrant and an officer was dispatched to meet with Lenny and the squaw. They were going to make sure he didn't go back home.

Mike was being taken into protective custody, with his first stop at a local hospital to get him checked out, treated, and nourished. The principal had come back with a clean shirt from the lost and found. As Mike put it on, he could not believe how clean and soft it was. It was the nicest piece of clothing he had ever worn. He was missing one of his shoes, so the principal got him a pair of tennis shoes left from last year's basketball team. Even used, they were much better than the ones he'd had on that morning.

More nervous than ever, Mike watched his new shoes kick out and back in front of his chair. No one had ever treated him this well before. Most of the time at school he sat quietly, bothering no one, not participating in class, and not caring. He knew he could do the work, but what for? Nobody cared, so he did only enough to get by. One day he might see it differently, but for now he wasn't able to care.

***

The doorbell rang and Lenny cursed. Why weren't any of his rug rats getting up to answer it? He wore his typical stained wife-beater T-shirt, a stretched-out pair of gym shorts, and his crocs. He had lost at the track that afternoon, and his entire paycheck for the week was nearly gone. His foul mood provided the excuse to down half a fifth of Jack Daniels, with beer chasers. He threw his empty plastic cup across the room. It bounced off the wall and left a streak of beer running into the grungy carpet.

"Somebody get the damn door!" he screamed. Worthless kids. Lenny knew they were afraid of him, but that's how he liked it. They caused him less trouble that way. After a third ring of the doorbell, Lenny lumbered over and jerked it open. Two police officers looked him levelly in the eye. Two plain-clothed folks stood behind them.

"Yeah, what do you want?" Lenny snarled. He reached for the knob on the screen door, locking it.

"Are you Lenny Cormier?" asked the older of the two officers.

"Yeah. What do you want?"

"We have a warrant to search your premises. Please step aside."

"The hell, you two! What for?" Lenny wasn't about to let these bozos see that he was nervous. He puffed up his chest and crossed his arms.

One of the officers, a towering ex-marine, said, "Mr. Cormier, we have a warrant, and that is all I need to say. Step back, unlock the screen, and move away from the door." The older officer reached for the handle.

"I don't give a damn what your papers say. Now get the hell off my porch!" He slammed the door in their faces.

The older officer told the two social workers to step back behind the cars. The ex-marine pounded on the door again, and Lenny opened it with a shotgun in his hand. "I told you, you're not a'comin' into my house, and that's that!"

The older officer held up his hands as though in a stickup and said, "Mr. Cormier, I would advise you to put the gun down and cooperate with us. This is not going to go well for you." The officer did not see him as a threat, which made Lenny even madder.

Lenny snarled and raised the barrel of his shotgun, swearing like a caged animal. He stepped back and slammed the door. The officers returned to the patrol car, discussing the situation. Lenny was drunk and worried, therefore unpredictable.

Lenny stood behind the door. He'd showed them. After a few minutes he peeked out the blinds on the side window. Why weren't they leaving? He tried to think more soberly. He laid the shotgun down and paced back and forth in his small living area, beer sloshing from the bottle while he drank, his fear escalating.

He watched out the window and could hear the officer call for backup while the social workers pulled their car down the street.

Lenny worked himself into a state of hysteria. He heard sirens and began to sweat. He drank faster and swore under his stale breath when he saw two more police cars pull up. He snatched up the shotgun and moved to the front door. As he reached for the handle, the door exploded open, knocking him three feet backward, over a small table, and onto the floor.

It was over in seconds. The police kicked his antique shotgun out of his reach, cuffed him, dragged him outside, and read him his Miranda rights. As they moved through the house, the squalor and smell nauseated and sickened them. The squaw, skin and bones, her hair looking like a rat's nest, lay passed out in the bedroom, and six younger children huddled in a small room upstairs, wearing filthy clothes.

"Hell, this is a pigsty." The ex-marine spit out the words, then approached the boys, who were undernourished, dirty, and afraid. He crouched in front of them and held out his hands. They all scooted forward to be near this big strong man, sensing he was there to protect them. They had not experienced this before but were hungry for it. The marine wrapped as many as he could into his strong arms.

The children were removed from the home. They would be given a bath, new clothes, something to eat, then split up and sent to new foster homes.

The Adoption
Texas, 1987

Confused and still afraid, Mike lay quietly in the hospital bed. He hadn't slept in a bed for two years. The sheets were clean, and he had taken a shower. He had never had a shower before, but once or twice a week he'd taken a bath. He stood under the hot water as the soothing rainfall cascaded over him, cleansing more than his body. They gave him a pill, and after a short time, his pain was gone. After pulling on fresh hospital pajamas, combing his clean hair, and brushing his teeth with some toothpaste that tasted like candy, eight-year-old Mike felt something unusual—happiness. A pretty teenage girl came in carrying a tray of food, which she set on his bedside table. She raised the back of his bed.

Mike smelled the hotcakes, but as he thought about eating, he got scared again. The volunteer had worked at the hospital for over a year and had seen this fear before in the eyes of an abused child. She said softly, "Don't worry, no one is going to hurt you anymore."

For the first time in over a year, Mike let someone see a tear slide down his face. It was as if his past suddenly evaporated. The girl pulled the tray closer and lifted the plastic cover on a gourmet meal. "Thank you," he whispered. "What about Chad and the others?"

She smiled. "Don't worry, they will be fine. They are being taken care of too. Now you rest and eat breakfast. I will be back and we can talk."

Mike smiled and nodded, then went to work.

They kept him lightly sedated for a couple of days and he slept while his wounds healed. This low-income hospital for kids felt like a Ritz-Carlton hotel to Mike. One day a nice man in a black suit and white collar came by and brought Mike new clean clothes.

The man's name was Father Rich, and he was in his mid-thirties. He explained to Mike in language he could understand that he was an ex-boxer and street gang member who'd hit rock bottom fifteen years earlier and found the Lord, turned his life around, and entered seminary. The church where he'd received his new life calling ran an orphanage, which he viewed as an opportunity to help young children avoid the path he had taken. His biggest joy in life was seeing his "flock," as he referred to his kids, find good homes. Mike was a little old to be coming to his home, as many of the kids arrived as toddlers.

Father Rich sat on the side of the bed. Mike looked at him intensely with his blue-gray eyes, evaluating what kind of man the Father was, using the finely-honed instincts he'd already developed in his short life. "I'm going to take you back to my church and find you a good family to live with, Mike. I know what you've been through, and where you're going won't be anything like where you came from."

Mike frowned. "What about Chad and the rest of the kids?"

Father Rich smiled at Mike's concern. "They've all been taken care of. They'll have new parents and we make sure they go to good homes." His soothing eyes and calm, warm disposition helped Mike trust him, but he kept his guard up. After all, up to now he'd had bad luck with adults. Mike put on the new clothes and followed Father Rich to an old Dodge van that looked like a wreck.

"She may be old and a little beat up, but the engine runs like a top. Please climb on in." They started down the road to Mike's new home. On the way, Father Rich stopped in front of an A&W restaurant. When they reached the counter, Father Rich ordered two large root beer floats from the acne-faced sixteen year old working behind the counter.

Mike had never been in a restaurant. He'd seen commercials on television, though. Father Rich watched his new boarding school protégé with great interest. They sat at a booth and the boy brought over two frosty mugs filled with ice cream and root beer.

"Dig in," Father Rich said. Mike hesitated only a second.

After swallowing his first big bite of real ice cream laced with the sweet taste of root beer, Mike grinned. He couldn't get the spoon to his mouth fast enough. Father Rich said, "Slow down. Enjoy. This is all-you-can-eat Tuesday, so you can have another if you want."

"Really?" Mike grinned back. He had two more big pints of the signature dish and was about to pop.

They got back in the multi-colored van and pulled up in front of what looked like a castle. Its huge wooden front doors were intimidating, until they entered. A large cross hung on the wall in the entry with a man nailed to it.

After making his usual sign of the cross, the priest looked down at Mike and said, "That is Christ our Savior. You will get to know him well."

Mike tried not to show it, but this frightened him a little. He nodded. They walked past the wooden pews and went out the back of the church, crossed a courtyard, and entered a long building.

Single beds lined both long walls of the first room. At the end of each neatly made bed sat a trunk. Apparently, girls lived in this room. Each trunk had a number painted on it, and most were pink. Some had dolls, and many had stickers of cartoon characters decorating them.

Father Rich said, "This is the girls' side." They continued down the corridor. The next room doubled as a cafeteria and a gym, tables stretching out like the lines of a musical staff. At least fifty girls notated the benches on one side and boys occupied the benches on the other side. The noise struck Mike as deafening, but since it was all happy chatter, he drew in a sharp breath, the sweet sound lifting his chest with a relief he couldn't contain. Tears sprang to his eyes.

Father Rich watched Mike. He said, "This is where you will eat every day." All the children were dressed in uniforms and paid him little or no attention, all focusing on their lunches.

The next corridor contained offices on both sides. Mike read the signs as they passed—Nurse Snyder, Father Haworth, and Father Rich. His new mentor entered the last room and motioned for Mike to sit. In a quiet cadence, Father Rich explained the rules of the orphanage.

"We do everything here on a schedule. You'll shower every day, eat three meals, spend seven hours in class, and three hours in some sort of extracurricular activity." Mike had no idea what an extracurricular activity was. "There will be absolutely no fighting. You will dress in the uniform and make your bed every day. If you follow the rules, no harm will come to you. We want your stay here to be productive and informative. In return for good behavior, we will provide meals, an education, and will work to find you a good, permanent home. Do you understand?"

This was a lot for an eight-year-old boy to take in. Without a word, Mike nodded.

"Don't worry, you'll get the hang of it. Most kids fall right in and actually enjoy their time here. Our kids are placed into great homes, nothing like what you came from."

Mike looked at him in bewilderment. In a soft voice, Father Rich said, "Look Mike, I know how badly you and the others were treated. You don't need to be afraid now. Lenny can never harm you again. He was sent to prison." Mike smiled inwardly at this news.

The Father pulled out a Polaroid camera and snapped a picture of Mike. He placed it in a folder, then got up and said, "Follow me." They continued on down the hall, stopping to pick up uniforms and get a haircut. When they reached a locker room, Mike was instructed to shower before donning his uniform. This would be the only time he'd shower alone, as everyone did everything together—school, recess, meals, and games.

Mike was given the number 112. He had to repeat it ten times to Father Rich. This number was written on the inside of his underwear, shirts, pants, socks, and shorts.

Even his shoes had the number written on them with a permanent marker. The sign over his bed and the number on the footlocker matched as well.

"Spend some time resting and take a nap if you want," Father Rich said. "You'll start tomorrow." Mike's head spun with the whirlwind of new experiences, and he doubted he could fall asleep, not knowing what to expect next, but he drifted off, rousing only when he heard voices.

A noisy mob of young boys entered, and all began undressing, putting on shorts and sneakers. Most paid little or no attention to Mike. He sat at the end of the bed and watched with amazement as the daily routine of over fifty kids unfolded in front of him. Suddenly, he was shoved from behind and he fell to the floor. A chunky, freckle-faced kid, the biggest kid in the room apart from him, looked down on him and laughed.

"Hey, newbie, listen up." The kid puffed out his chest. "You need to know right now. I run this place and you will do as I say, or you're askin' for it!"

When Mike stood and met him eye to eye, he could tell the kid was bluffing. No one else in the room matched his size except Mike. The room quieted and Mike leaned forward. Whispering in the kid's ear, he said, "Don't ever do that again, or you'll see what happens." He stepped back and looked the boy up and down, recognizing his fear. The room remained quiet, all eyes fixed on them. Mike turned and walked away.

The next day was his first to follow the routine. The big kid continued to eye Mike with hatred. Mike didn't care. He'd fought bigger kids than this one, and the boy would be slow. After lunch, as Mike walked out of the cafeteria to the yard for recess, the kid stepped in front of him and shoved. Mike landed on the ground, but he rolled backward, jumped back to his feet, and with cat-like reflexes he hit the kid in the face and then pushed him backward to the ground. He jumped on top of him, then hit him with all his might. He swung hard, and each punch found its target—first his jaw, then he blackened his eye, and the final shot gave the bully a fat lip. As he drew back his arm to swing again, he was pulled off the boy with a jolt. His attacker remained on the ground, crying.

"Okay, slugger, that's enough." Father Steve, who Mike had not yet met, pulled him away and stood over him like a giant. "You're the new kid. Didn't Father Rich explain the rules about fighting?"

The entire school had circled the boys again. Out of nowhere a paddle appeared, riddled with evenly drilled holes, and Father Steve said, "Okay, George, you know the drill."

George, now pleading through his tears, said, "No, no, Father Steve, it was the new kid's fault."

"George you're lying. I saw the whole thing. Lying's gonna cost you an extra lick."

At this, George wailed. Mike stood in front of the Father, body stiff and fists clenched.

In a softer voice Father Steve said, "Mike? That's your name, isn't it? You'll be next." He turned to George and said, "Grab 'em, George."

George continued to wail as he turned and reached down. His bulk prevented him from reaching his ankles, so he grabbed his calves. Father Steve gave him three quick licks with the holey paddle and then said, "This last one is for lying."

He turned to Mike and said, "Mike, you're going to have to learn to walk away when someone picks on you.

As Father Rich said, we won't tolerate fighting, so grab 'em."

Mike bent over and grabbed his ankles and received three swats. His backside was going to explode, he thought, but he didn't cry, and when he stood, he turned and looked Father Steve in the eye. "I will not let anyone hit me or try to pick on me, so if this happens again, I am ready." His normally intense blue eyes had dulled to a platinum gray.

To Mike's surprise, Father Steve said, "I appreciate that, but rules are rules. Let's just hope no one comes after you again." He smiled. "You're the first one to take big George down. I don't think anyone is gonna mess with you again." He winked and walked away.

The others on the playground erupted with cheers, and Mike received many pats on his back. A few said, "Way to go, Mike!"

Mike turned and walked over to Big George and stuck out his hand. "My name's Mike."

George whipped the tears away with his sleeve, took his hand, and said, "George. George Stephenson."

"Let's don't do that again, George." Mike smiled. "I know I can take you, but my butt's so sore I don't want to mess with that Father Steve again."

"Yeah, me neither."

A few months later, Father Steve called Mike over. "We have two privileged openings available. You can either earn a little money cleaning the cafeteria, or you can take a position at the new karate school. We had a request to send someone to work there."

Mike considered this, then said, "I would like to learn karate."

"Figured you'd say that," Father Steve said. "Karate it is."

Mike was elated, though a little scared. What had he gotten himself into? Would he have to fight all the time? He'd have to take it as it came.

At the orphanage one either worked, boxed, studied, or played in the band. No idle time was allowed. As Mike's karate lessons began, he understood, even at his young age, that this would be a way to bring out his inner pain so it could be dealt with. He knew he needed it. Some days, even though he was relatively happy, the dark feelings consumed him. But Mike loved being physically challenged. He was good, and none of the other kids in the class wanted to spar with him, so Mike sparred with the older kids and the black belts. He grew taller and filled out. Now ten, he'd been at the home for two years.

After karate one day, Mike heard a girl scream when he walked back through the dorms. One of the newer kids, a young teen a few years older than Mike, had straddled her. He'd pinned her, and she was struggling. The boy held her arms down with his knees and had a fistful of her hair to keep her from thrashing her head back and forth. It looked like he was going to force a kiss on her. Mike jerked the young teen off, and the girl sprang to her feet and bolted, trying to straighten her uniform and crying. The boy turned and tried to hit Mike. Big mistake.

Mike stepped wide and the fist missed his head. He ducked and hit the kid in the midsection, causing him to lose his breath. Mike slugged again and the kid fell to the ground. At this point, Father Rich happened through the door. Mike stood over the kid, fists clenched, preparing for him to get up and come at him again. He did.

Father Rich yelled, "Enough, Mike, enough!" Just as he said this, Mike spun around and struck the kid in the side of the head with a roundhouse kick, knocking him over and laying him out. He turned to Father Rich and said, "*Now* he has had enough."

Mike's unruly blond hair stuck out at odd angles, but Father Rich could see that his eyes held a sense of surety. Of justice. He quietly said, "Okay, both of you. Let's go get this over with."

Mike thought he'd get licks again from the paddle, but Father Rich took them into the gymnasium and had all the boys form a circle. He handed both boys boxing gloves.

Father Rich had the two boys face off. He said, "Boys, we've had a policy change. Instead of the board, you two will box your grievances out of each other."

Father Rich never asked what happened, which to Mike seemed unfair, but he said nothing. They went at it. Mike knocked the boy down three times, and the kid balled up in a fetal position, crying, while Mike stood over him. Most of the kids were smaller. They watched, scared to death. Mike's inner demon came out once in a while, and when it did, it scared him, although he hid it from others. Mike was able to move quicker than anyone he'd ever gone up against. He didn't care about being hit, he'd just continue to fight until he'd taken his nemesis down.

Over his two years at the orphanage, he'd watched the younger kids and babies get adopted by nice young couples. In six months, he'd be sent to a different school for older kids, and he'd have to start all over. His grades had improved a little, but his athleticism was off the charts. When prospective couples came to meet with Father Rich, he'd bring the kids out and line them up.

Most of the kids who'd been there when Mike arrived had gone to new families. Mike was big for his age, and most young couples didn't want to take a chance on an older child. Mike played the game. He always tried his best to smile. Though polite, he was passed over for a cute two- or three-year-old, or a baby, every time. His time was running out. This saddened him. He was comfortable in the routine and close to the Fathers.

A few months later a lineup was called. All the kids stood still and quiet, a few shuffling their feet nervously. The older kids introduced themselves to the uniformed man and his pretty wife. Mike observed the man's commanding presence as he shook hands with boys down the row, and a slice of self-respect rose out of the depths of his pain. As the man approached him, Mike stepped forward, looked him steadily in the eyes, and stuck out his hand. "I am Mike, and I'm eleven years old."

This caught the man completely off guard. He said, "Hi-ya, Mike, I'm John O'Shea." He smiled at the boy and shook his hand, then he moved on down the line, like an officer inspecting his troops.

Following behind the man at a slower pace, a beautiful lady introduced herself to each of the children. She walked up to Mike and smiled. Mike, who was trying to put on a strong front, looked into the woman's eyes and saw a softness there that gave him a warm feeling right into his soul, something he desperately wanted at that moment. Nurture and love were things he'd never had before. The woman hadn't moved on. She made eye contact with him one more time, and as she moved on down the gauntlet, she kept looking back at him. Mike tried to cover up his vulnerability, hoping no one could see it. He looked at the ground, his heart hurting as he braced himself for another rejection.

As usual, they weren't going to take him. Father Rich dismissed the children and sent them outside for the rest of the day. After an hour or so Father Rich waved Mike over. "Follow me," he said. "Some folks want to talk to you." Mike's footsteps picked up a little as he followed Father Rich into his office. Maybe there was hope after all. The nice lady and the big man sat on the sofa, and both leaned forward when Mike walked into the room.

"Sit down, Mike," Father Rich said. "This is Major O'Shea and his wife Ann." Both smiled at Mike. "They want to chat with you for a few minutes."

They asked the usual questions—his age, what he liked to do, his favorite color—the things a typical eleven-year-old would respond to. Mike spoke softly, his answers slow and methodical. He wanted to make a good impression. Though he tried not to hope too hard, after an hour, John and Ann asked for a few moments to come to a decision. That day changed Mike's life forever. He would become a full member of a real family with a real name. He belonged to someone now. His new name was Michael O'Shea.

SEALS

January 2000

Had he done the right thing? He wouldn't be human if he didn't ask himself the question.

"O'Shea, get that girly look off your face and get your shit together," his team leader shouted. Mike didn't know if he could get his shit together. Why was he here? He couldn't think straight. Cold water dripped off every part of his body and the fifty-two-degree breeze whipping around him added to his misery as he shook from his hypothermic condition. He'd need dentures before this was over. His mother had once told him that the way she got through the agony of childbirth was to think about how many women before her had done it and survived, and by God, she could too. His father had made it through this as had many other men, and Mike could too.

"It pays to be a winner." He found himself repeating the mantra whenever the temptation to call it quits overcame him. He'd already endured the first two weeks of culling and next week would be Hell Week.

He'd wanted to bond with the other men but knew if he did it would be harder when some of them washed out. By now he had a pretty good feeling who of the remaining fifty percent would make it through Hell Week. He hoped he'd be one who made it, but he had to admit to a sliver of doubt. He'd heard up to half of those who remained at this point wouldn't make it through the next week, as its purpose is to separate the undecided from the committed. The shame of washing out would be worse than anything physical he'd have to endure, and that helped toughen up his mind and his resolve. And the thought of Stacy's silky hair, vibrant green eyes, and soft, shapely curves buoyed him and lit a fire inside. He hoped she'd be proud.

Kent Halbert, Chase Jones, Mark Jamison, and Don Carpenter were all part of his boat crew as things stood now. If these four made it through with him, he'd be recommending them to his father for recruitment into PAL. He had developed high respect for each of these men. They had the fortitude, cool heads, and leadership ability to be a huge asset to the team. Another man on their team, Ahmed El Massier, an Egyptian who fast-tracked through the elite international guard, had already been recruited by PAL, hence his place in the SEAL training program. Knowing this and seeing Ahmed's skills and capabilities through the demanding training had already made them friends and brothers.

After the boat evolution, the next event in the training schedule for this last day before Hell Week would be the fifty-yard underwater swim. Mike was grateful that this would be done in a pool rather than the frigid 57-degree waters off Coronado, California, even though he knew a significant number of men passed out at the end of the swim. He understood, from hearing the leaders talk, that the goal was not to hurt anyone, but rather to push their limits so they knew what they could endure. The two main things the culling process accomplished was to determine their limits and to train them to give great attention to details. His was the only one of the boat teams that listened well enough to catch the leader's omission of the word "boat" when he told them to get themselves to the next evolution. Every team but his hauled their boats unnecessarily.

The swim began. Mike's team lined up behind Don Carpenter, then Major Mark Jamison, their team leader, followed Mike. He watched Don swim the entire length in one breath, which was the requirement for this evolution. He made it to the other side, his tall, lanky frame seeming suited for this kind of challenge, and although he had to be helped out of the water, he still had enough in him to stand and put his arms up in victory. The guy further down hadn't been so fortunate. He had gone limp a mere foot from the side of the pool. The instructor in the water went for him and hauled him to the edge where other hands on the side pulled him out. They slapped his face and yelled at him to come back. After a long ten seconds he coughed and ejected water from his lungs.

Mike's mind had ceased thinking. Pulling on some inner core of strength he didn't realize he had, he defied the inner voices that told him to be afraid of death, and instead, he embraced the challenge. He would only do what was set before him, reaching for that edge, pulling to perform better than his ability. Whether he did it for family, country, or only himself, he didn't know.

Probably all three. This trifecta made a thick, strong, three-stranded cord, a melding of purpose that he could use to propel himself forward in this and everything to come in Hell Week. His mind stopped, and his focus narrowed to the task before him as he took several deep breaths and dove in.

Giving it all he had, he kept reminding himself as he swam that even if he passed out he'd be okay because his oxygen deprivation would be well under the amount of time that would cause brain damage. When they pulled him out at the end, his brain had gone completely blank and he couldn't remember where he was or what he'd been doing, but there was Don leaning over him and yelling, "Hooyah! Mike, you did it!" and pumping his arm around like a fool.

When Mike stood, he pulled air into his lungs and straightened his back. This had been their final evolution before Hell Week. He'd make it through all right, and so would the rest of his team. He watched first Mark Jamison, then Kent, and last but not least, Ahmed, pulling themselves through the water and knew they were all forming a bond right here in Basic Underwater Demolition SEAL training, or BUD/S. The honor he felt at this moment, training and serving with these top heroes, increased his violent shivering, yet strangely warmed his heart so he hardly noticed his body's extreme reaction to the fatigue and pain accumulated over the last two weeks of near-torture. He smiled and clapped his buddies on the back and said, "Hooyah!"

And they all repeated, "Hooyah!" together.

CHAPTER FOURTEEN

Law School
Fall 2001

Stacy Lyons stormed into her apartment and threw her handbag down on the table. The nerve of this guy to try such a thing on a first date, especially when she had fended off his groping hands several times earlier in the evening. Guys shouldn't even try to hold hands with a girl if she doesn't give them any encouraging body language, like flirty eyes or genuine smiles. She'd had to say, "Take me home. I'm ready to go home," not even caring how rude it sounded.

She would never find anyone like Mike O'Shea. Some days the sense of loss and longing threatened to overwhelm her, and at those times she would force herself to get out for a bike ride or spend time with a friend.

After months of phone tag and silence, they'd given up trying to stay in touch. She'd occasionally call and talk to Mike's mother when she grew desperate to hear something about him. To deal with the pain, she poured herself into her studies, and this kept her plenty busy, and the satisfaction she gained from her professors' positive feedback and her good grades only inspired her to double her efforts to be the best she could be. She found that corporate law on an international level held no end of fascination and keeping up with it seemed to be no problem for her. Next step was her semester abroad. She'd chosen to go to England, although her biggest interest, sparked by interactions with General O'Shea, lay in the Middle East. But all in time.

Her phone buzzed, rattling on the table next to her purse. She looked at the screen.

She slid her finger to unlock the screen and shouted, "Mike!"

"Hey, babe, I just wanted to hear your voice," he said. Was he emotional?

"Are you okay, Mike?"

"I miss you, Stace." Mike was clearly choked up. What was bothering him? She put her fingers to her mouth and pressed them against her lips to forestall the quick tears.

"You too, more than you know," she managed.

"We're heading out on our final training mission in the morning, and I just wanted you . . . to know . . ."

"I do know, Mike. You know I pray for you every day, and the only thing between you and me is distance. You have my respect and my total support. You also have my love."

There. She'd said it. Judging from his voice, he needed to hear that someone believed in him and loved him.

"Thank you. It means everything to me to have the support of my girl, my best friend."

"You are going to be just fine, Michael O'Shea. I can't know what kind of danger you are going into, but I do know that you are trained to handle it. You have quick and accurate instincts. Trust yourself and your training, Sailor."

After a little small talk, she said, "It broke my heart to hear that Amy and Don broke up."

"Yeah, I think Amy is just wired to need more hands-on in her relationships. Don couldn't give her what she needed. At least, that's what he told me."

"It's hard, Mike. Some women, especially, are wired to need frequent connection and closeness. Some of us can function without it while we are pursuing other goals, but when you have nothing to distract you, it can become painful, like a great aching void." She was still trying to determine whether she could live a life full of sacrifice with Mike. Maybe she could talk to his mother Ann about it. Not that he'd asked her to marry him yet.

"How are you doing, Stacy? Have you gone out with anyone?"

She grimaced. She didn't want to tell him about Derek. But she had to be honest.

"I went out with someone tonight, but I had a terrible time. He was pretty shallow. He only wanted one thing, so I told him to take me home." She paused, considering. "Look, Mike, I have only been going out a little bit, just to have something to do. I'm not looking for someone. No one can take your place."

"I feel the same."

And that was the honest truth, for both of them. Mike's phone call would have to get her by a little longer. As the days continued to pass in a flurry of studying and tests, she kept her herself laser-focused on her goals, and eventually she developed a warmer feeling of camaraderie with Mike, as she knew he'd be doing the same thing during their time apart. When the phone silence became deafening, she tried to quell her worry and loneliness for him with the thought that they were a team, and all teammates must pull their own weight. She would honor his deep service to the country and not let him down by moping and pining away for him. They'd be together one day.

With Thanksgiving right around the corner and then her semester abroad, Stacy shifted her focus to the upcoming visit from Mom and her younger sister Rebecca. Tomorrow was Friday, her first free Friday in a long time. Mom and Becca lived in Leesburg, Virginia, but Becca was so involved in school activities that Mom didn't have a lot of freedom to find something she enjoyed with which to occupy herself. Her mom had been a homemaker since she married at the age of nineteen. She'd been a wonderful mother, but since her dad and brother, Becca's twin, had passed away two years ago in the car accident, she could see that her mom had been struggling with what to do with herself. Chalk that up to their traditional marriage roles. No offense to Mom, but that kind of back-burner life did not appeal to Stacy. She herself planned to be an insatiable lifelong learner. She loved academia. Girlfriends made fun of her for attending every free lecture and cultural event the college offered, but she didn't care. To her, boredom was the worst feeling of all.

Stacy's feelings about her mother stemmed heavily from the knowledge of her mother's affair. As far as Stacy knew, no one else was aware of the affair, and no one knew that Stacy knew. But what had happened to the man? In the two years since Dad had passed away, Mom had not outwardly dated and didn't seem to have anyone in her life. Was she waiting for Becca to be out of the house? Was she consumed with guilt over it since the accident? Had he known?

Stacy had found out purely by accident. During her second semester at UT, Mom had come to visit her. She must have thought no one would know her, and that she could be openly together with the man, but why she didn't think there was a chance her own daughter would see her, Stacy had no idea. She'd gone to pick Mom up at the Airport Hilton. Instead of waiting outside in the car, Stacy had been early, so she parked and went inside. She glanced into the hotel café and saw her mother at a table across from the man, their faces close together. Then her mother kissed the man, long and lingering, and caressed his cheek before she stood. Stacy backed out of sight and raced out to her car. Though she tried to partition it off until she had time to process it, the entire visit was strained. Stacy could see signs in her mother that were not ordinary—a sudden smile for no reason, careful attention to her appearance, distraction from whatever they were doing.

Stacy had never let on that she knew, to anyone, although she'd considered telling both her mom and her dad. But ultimately it wasn't her business. Now she was glad she'd made that decision and done nothing that would have hurt her father. The effects of the knowledge of the affair upon Stacy could be summed up in a fear that if this could happen in her parents' marriage, which she'd always seen as strong and healthy, it could happen in any marriage. She didn't want to ever be cheated on, nor did she ever want to think she'd be capable of doing so to someone else. As much as she didn't want this fear to enter into her relationship with Mike, how could it not? Not only did she fear what she was capable of, but what if Mike got tired of her? She'd heard the statistics.

But their focus during this visit would be on Becca. Her sister had found it hard to recover from the loss of her father and brother. Mom and Dad had adopted the twins as toddlers. Marcus seemed to have no physical issues, but Becca had been born with spina bifida. Stacy's mother had devoted her life to the children, and although Becca spent her days in a wheelchair, she seemed to have channeled her limitations into greater intellectual ability, and she had a knack for memorization and recall.

As Stacy flew by her first-floor window, she noticed the car pulling into a parking space in front of her dorm room. Her father had insisted they buy the bright yellow Ford Focus several years ago—a flashy color on a plain car—and her introverted mother hated it. Interesting how something so irritating could make an about-face and become a comfort rather than an embarrassment.

Becca wheeled herself in and Mom followed with a few bags of things Stacy had asked her to bring from home. After giving them both big hugs, Stacy set them up at the small table and served drinks and sandwiches for lunch.

"So, have you heard from Mike?" Becca asked.

Stacy took a bite of her turkey and avocado sandwich. "Not much. I guess he's quite busy. He's about to finish his SEAL training."

Becca gave her a sympathetic look. Mom tried to fill the silence. "At least the lack of distraction of a boyfriend allows you to focus on your schoolwork. How is that going? Are you looking forward to your semester in England?"

"I'm doing fine. I'll have to move out of the dorm, you know, so I'll need to come home with everything at the end of the semester and dump most of it with you, if that's okay."

"Cool, Stace, can I use your car? I think we can get it adapted for me without too much cost."

Becca tried so hard to be positive and face her challenges head on that it was always difficult to say no. Stacy would do anything in her power for her sister. Mom had life insurance money from her dad, but she'd have to be careful with it, as they had a lot of challenges ahead with Becca, starting with college. Becca seemed fixated on a history major. In spite of, or maybe because of her handicap, she had more smarts than Stacy did. Someone had called her an SGI once, and when Stacy looked it up she found it meant "supremely gifted individual." Yep, that was Becca. She'd find a way to manage her life independently, but it wouldn't be easy.

"I think that will be up to you and Mom," she finally answered. "I'm willing, if you can make it work." She hugged Becca when she got up to clear the table. "It doesn't bother you to think of driving, even after the accident?" Becca had suffered terribly from survivor's guilt, having had only minor injuries. She and Becca and Mom had to pull together after the huge loss, and they shared openly about their coping mechanisms.

"I'm sure if I'd had my license at the time of the accident, that it would be difficult to get behind the wheel again. But I have made progress dealing with it. You know how I love quotes?"

Stacy nodded. Her sister could quote long passages from memory.

"Well, here's one I like. 'You gain strength, courage and confidence by every experience in which you really stop to look fear in the face. You are able to say to yourself, 'I lived through this horror. I can take then next thing that comes along.' That's a quote from Eleanor Roosevelt."

Stacy squeezed her arm. "That's great, Becca. Thank you for sharing that. So encouraging to help us keep on during the hard times."

Mom said they should go before it got too late and traffic picked up. They'd planned to do a historical walking tour of Brattle Street and the Charles River.

Stacy grabbed her purse and they took off out the door. "I'll meet you at the car," Becca said, taking off down the sidewalk to find the handicapped ramp up to the parking lot.

"She's something, isn't she," Mom said.

"Yes, she is. We never dreamed she'd be such an optimistic encourager with her handicaps. But she inspires me."

"Not all her days are good, but I find myself inspired by her courage too."

They loaded up and spent a pleasant afternoon walking, the light breeze blowing browned leaves around their feet. As they neared the car, Stacy saw Dave, a guy she'd gone out with a couple of times, stringing Christmas lights on the bushes of the college president's house.

"Hey, Dave, how are you?" she called to him. He swiveled, hands full of colored lights, and he nodded, smiling. They'd parted on good terms, and she considered him a friend. If it weren't for Mike, she would've encouraged him, but Dave had realized she wasn't into pursuing a relationship, and he'd eased up.

Thank goodness she hadn't had to fight him off. Becca asked her why she wasn't tempted to continue dating such a nice, good-looking guy.

"It'll be okay, sis. Mike won't leave you alone forever. I remember the first time I saw him, at your graduation. He seemed bigger than life, so strong, and with that Texas charm, the way he treated you, he seemed to a sixteen-year-old girl like the catch of a lifetime."

"Well, he always seemed that way to me too," Stacy admitted. "Which makes it very hard to be apart, especially since we don't talk much now."

Mom chimed in. "Since Mike seems to be going down a similar path as his father, have you thought about talking to his mother about how she deals with that kind of life as a wife? It might help you see how you could make it work."

"John and Ann seem to have loose reins on each other, and if I'm not mistaken, the time apart and the danger of that life have actually created a strong bond, a strong marriage. They put a tremendous value on family and spending as much quality time together as possible. That is encouraging," Stacy said. "The thing is, how to find a way to settle down together. It's too soon to say. I want Mike to be ready for it. I don't want to drag him into marriage if he's not ready. I'm afraid to think what could happen if he's not."

"He may need a little encouragement," Mom said.

"I bet next time he sees you, that's all it will take," Becca the optimist said.

"Thanks, Becca." Stacy pulled Becca's ponytail. Becca grinned and managed the transfer from wheelchair to car smoothly. "Wow, Bec, you're doing great getting yourself around. Your shoulders are really built up now. Sexy shoulders are attractive, you know. You should flaunt it next summer when it gets hot again."

"There's a guy I'm hoping to see again next summer at the camp. We got to be good friends, and we've been sending letters to each other now and then. It will be my last summer at the camp, unless I return to work with the kids during college."

After hanging out a while longer, Becca had worn down and they departed for Leesburg, with Stacy's reassurances that she'd be home for a couple of days over Thanksgiving.

The bittersweet paradox of life's big moments left one continually trying to cope with stormy emotions, Stacy thought. Better to pour oneself into other interests when there was nothing to do about the things one couldn't have.

CHAPTER FIFTEEN

First Mission
Spring 2002

Mike tied his hammock to the two large pecan trees in the side yard of the ranch house. Perfect for his well-deserved siesta. He'd had few breaks over the last two-and-a-half-years, and today was Lazy Day. Just him and the sounds of the birds, the gentle breeze, the smell of lilacs, and the far-off rumble and clacking of the tractor.

The rallying sound of his new PAL ringtone caused him to startle. He fumbled for his phone to end the annoying sound, and in doing so he caused a shift in his position and found himself face down in the dirt. By the time he'd stood and brushed himself off, he had a text summoning him to headquarters.

Time for his first op. What would it be? When he entered the war room in Austin, the project leader and two tenured PAL officers were seated at the round table with an Arab of unknown descent.

Mike walked around the table to the Arab, the only person he didn't already know, and held out his hand. "Mike O'Shea."

The man stood and shook Mike's hand. "Jamal Awan." He grinned, and Mike sensed immediately they would get along great.

Harvey Davis, the project manager, stood. "Mike, we have a mission for you that Jamal will be helping you with. You'll be backup support on this US-based terrorist plot. Rumors have circulated for days that a suicide bomber is going to infiltrate the Republican National Convention. This particular tip came by way of Jamal, our undercover ISIS operative from Afghanistan."

PAL received constant tips of suspected terrorist activities, some credible and some not. Someone had the job of filtering the tips and deciding what was probable. Not a job he'd want.

Davis continued. "After that, you'll be shadowing Jamal for the next two months. You'll get a two-year education on the Middle East in two short months this way." The briefing continued, and plans were made. The convention would take place at the end of the week.

Mike found Jamal to be the perfect teammate, with his fun-loving, optimistic nature in the face of danger. The perpetrators were apprehended, and Mike was off to the Middle East.

Mike gained respect for Jamal every day and appreciated his intensive knowledge and help with the culture. Jamal introduced him to the Bedouins and the wadis, the language and customs. And he took him home to meet his family, where Mike experienced hospitality like he'd never seen it before. He assisted Jamal that day in delivering a calf they named "Bully" due to his prolonged butt-kicking birth. The poor mama cow could do nothing but lie there and moan. Mike had never heard a cow moan before. Thus began a long and illustrious friendship between Mike and Jamal.

When Mike returned, he found that the team had finally gelled. As he'd hoped, all five of his SEAL teammates had accepted positions with PAL. Mike and Don had come on board together, and Don had been instrumental in recruiting the others. Ahmed El Massier was a given, as he had been handpicked by the PAL leadership, but Kent, Chase, and Mark required a little more arm-twisting, and had come on a few months later.

They'd learned to trust each other, and they functioned like predators, all unified and working in sync to bring down the largest of prey. Considering that only one percent of those who enter SEAL training actually finish, Mike had enormous respect for these men. They'd been together for several months now, and at their first opportunity for some R&R, they headed to Sharm el-Sheik, sometimes called the city of peace because it hosted many international peace conferences. Mike's father had recommended this resort town, located at the southern end of the Sinai Peninsula. It boasted great Red Sea diving. Groups of Russian women filled the hotels during the winter months looking for rich Arabs or Western expats with whom they could hook up and leave the stress of Mother Russia behind. This captivating adult playground featured great music, food, and fun, a festive city few Westerners could imagine in an Arab country. The city had been given back to Egypt at the end of the six-day war in 1967. A full day's drive from Cairo, it developed into a metropolis of adult entertainment and outdoor adventure.

Mike sat at the bar with Mark, his superior, who'd led their first mission. The placard in the entryway said, "You name it, we've got it." He was dying for a smooth, creamy Guinness. They wouldn't have it, he guessed, looking forward to calling their bluff.

"You got any Guinness? Extra stout?" he asked the bartender. The muscular, balding man turned his back and got busy out of sight. When he returned, he slid a couple of mugs down the bar their way. Mike looked at Mark, dumbfounded, and Mark raised his eyebrows.

"Look at that thick, creamy head," Mark said.

"You ever notice how this stuff tastes like tiramisu?" Mike said, sniffing.

The bartend scooted down the bar, having caught up with his customers. "Hoppy, with a slight burnt taste and a tantalizing hint of sweetness. Surprised? My sign don't lie, boys!"

Mike stuck out his hand. "Mike O'Shea," he said. "And this is Major Mark Jamison."

"Neil Quar." They shook and Neil wandered off to mix a drink.

Mike said, "Great place. Someday, I'll bring Stacy."

"We'll all bring our girls and get toasted every day for a week. If you live hard, you gotta play hard." Mark winked.

Mike eyed the contingent of British flight attendants huddled together next to the huge saltwater aquarium. He motioned to them with his head, his eyes still on Mark.

"That's a fine thought, pal. Why don't you go get busy finding a girl so you'll have one to bring?"

"You boys need a refill before my shift is over?"

"No, we're good," Mike answered for both of them. But hey, Neil, you know anything about those flight attendants? Mark here is looking to score."

"So am I, boys, so am I. You want to join me in an invitation? We'll have to break them up so we can pick one." He glanced at Mike, who shook his head. "What's wrong with you, man? You got a chick somewhere?"

Mike lowered his eyes, his dejection evident.

"He hasn't seen his girl for several years."

"My God, why not?" Neil said.

"They were college sweethearts, and they haven't seen each other for . . . what is it now, Mike? Three years?"

"Three and a half," he said, his voice low. "Don't ask me why. We're both on paths that haven't crossed. But you guys go ahead. Every dog deserves his day."

The party would continue on for three days, Mike knew, giving Neil and Mark plenty of time to woo their choices. Don was in his element, cutting up, telling jokes, and keeping all the girls in stitches. And true to character, Mike sat back and took it all in.

One of the girls had been stealing glances at Mike. He recorded her interest. Don wandered over and saw the looks.

"She's quite the looker," he said. "Beautiful brown hair, curves in all the right places..." He laughed and winked. The woman approached, and Mike stood and offered her a seat. They talked, drank, and laughed. She made all the right innuendos, but Mike couldn't follow through, although he enjoyed the attention. He blamed jet lag and left Don to his antics, agreeing to catch up with him and Neil in the morning for the first of many dives in the beautiful waters of Naama Bay.

The next night they ran into the girls again, and the one Mike had spoken with for most of the previous night had found another beau. Although a little hurt for a moment, deep down Mike was relieved he didn't have to deal with it anymore.

Shouting and scuffling broke out near the door where Don and Neil's group were hanging out. Linda, Neil's love interest, had come in the door trailed by a Yemeni Arab, who had chosen to pursue her into the bar, and she turned and told him to back off. He'd chosen the wrong girl to hit on. As Neil confronted him, all hell broke loose. Mike couldn't hear the Arab's response, but Neil must have thought it worth fighting over, and he threw the first punch. Not about to let one of their new friends take on five locals, Don and Mike jumped in and the fight was on. The bar broke out into a brawl.

The Yemeni had been visiting with some friends from Dubai,and they joined the fight as well. The locals had no idea who they were up against as Neil, Don, Mike, and two other PAL operatives gave the young arrogant Arabs, in essence, "a good ole-fashioned ass whippin'." Mike slugged the Arab who had accosted Neil and broke his jaw.

"These guys are Dubai plainclothes special police, Mike," Neil said, rubbing his fist and breathing hard from the exertion of the fight. "They've got Yemeni friends crawling all over this place. I've been watching them all evening."

Mike nodded as he watched them carefully. Several were on the floor in various states of pain. The Egyptians didn't pay these Dubai police any heed.

"These guys have no authority here in the Sinai," Neil said.

The white-faced young guests were tourists and untouchable. Sinai revenue came primarily from tourist trade, and the government had a directive to protect tourists, as they were Egypt's biggest moneymaker.

Several of the pummeled men tried to get up, rage in their eyes, but they realized they were outnumbered and did not try to engage further. Someone had immediately contacted the Egyptian police, and in what seemed like mere seconds, they were surrounded by local law enforcement, arrested, and hauled off.

Neil took them back to the bar and fixed them all a drink, and they laughed and talked until Mike excused himself and retired. When Mike entered the lobby the next morning, he found, as luck would have it, that the Dubai group had rooms at the same hotel as the PAL team. He spent the rest of the day trying to avoid them, and finally decided to check out and find a different hotel.

***

Mohammed rubbed his jaw. Not a day went by that he didn't curse the arrogant Americans for his broken jaw, and the one who'd broken it in particular. Eight months had passed since the fight that had required him to spend a day in the local Egyptian hospital getting his mouth wired shut. He'd seen the man, Michael O'Shea, along with his team checking out of the hotel just as he arrived. He'd flashed his badge at the front desk and gotten copies of Mike's passport. The young American would come back through Dubai one day, he'd thought, and he would have his revenge. Mike's passport was now on the Emirates' watch list.

Mohammed had worked his way up in the world of Dubai's secret police. As the newly appointed lieutenant, he'd just arrived at headquarters for a day's work tracking down and putting away criminals. Criminals like himself, he thought, enjoying the thought.

"You got a passport hit, Mohammed. Lit up like an American Christmas tree," his boss said. "What do you want to do about it?"

"Who is it?" Mohammed asked.

"Name's Michael O'Shea. American. You know him?"

Mohammed rubbed his hands, a rare smile breaking up the hard lines of his face.

He looked at Mike's picture on the computer screen, then ordered him followed. He left hastily and joined the tail, elated at Allah's providence. His jaw still ached, and he could not chew anything firm, like nuts, that required him to bite down. He called his two cousins, the ones who he'd gotten jobs for on the force. They'd do whatever he asked. Once they were on the tail, he'd call off the others and he and these two tough guys would handle this.

He would set his trap and make this Michael O'Shea pay.

CHAPTER SIXTEEN
Revenge
Al Ain

Mike's team entered the city of Al Ain, the desert oasis. This old trade route into the great desert that led into Saudi Arabia in the north and the Emirates to the east overflowed with picturesque forts. They'd all decided to stay the night here and catch up with old acquaintances. They drove through the city and marveled at the many duwars, or roundabouts. The magnificent circular intersections held a cornucopia of beautiful displays of artistry and landscaping that filled the center of each, with more sculptures adorning the roadways. Mark said it was like an open-air art museum everywhere. Much attention had been given to detail. The city had obviously invested heavily in road maintenance, and the streets and shopping districts were spotless. After all, this was Sheik Zaed's hometown, and nothing had been spared in detail or cost. Many comments appreciating the beauty around them made their journey go by quickly.

Traffic patterns, however, were a beast. Driving through Al Ain is frequently referred to as "organized chaos." More like a road rally with young Arabs driving as fast as they can, drivers paid no attention whatsoever to the lines drawn in the road. The mantra "every man for himself" seemed quite apropos, and entering the roundabout was not for the faint of heart. Most of these kids, with their $100K SUVs, take on the personas of Indy drivers. It is a marvel that more accidents don't happen. The ones that do usually involve the safer, more conservative drivers.

As Mike drove the Hummer in his self-described NASCAR event, none of them noticed the tail they'd picked up. Most of the vehicles were Range Rovers or Land Cruisers—white, with big tires and blackened windows. Each of the team members believed they had entered the country undetected, and being followed was the last thing on their minds. All eyes were focused on the landscape and at how close each of the cars came to hitting each other.

They pulled up at the Al Ain Hilton and were greeted by their old friend Neil. Although he'd been assistant general manager of the hotel when they met him eight months ago, he'd enjoyed working in the bar. Now married to the flight attendant Linda, they were expecting twins. They ribbed him and clapped him on the back, congratulating him for the quick work.

***

Mohammed was especially happy when he received the report that the Americans were leaving the city of Dubai and heading toward Al Ain. So far, they wouldn't suspect they were being followed. The Americans stopped at the hotel where a big event was taking place. The parking lot was already full. He'd have trouble finding a place to park where they could follow. Inside, he learned that this was a Coca-Cola sponsored concert, and by asking around, he caught the name Neil Quar, the new general manager. He remembered that name. He'd been involved eight months ago.

Mohammed arrived and watched from the back of the ballroom, hardly able to tolerate the classic rock band that was the evening's entertainment. Mike and his group seemed completely unaware and had let their guards down. They were not watching, only having fun. They left the ballroom and moved to the downstairs bar where the afterparty would take place. Mohammed cursed. This would make it harder. He and his cousins followed and jogged down the steps, then eased their way around the packed room, eyes on Mike and the crowd, jostling drinks as they went. Mohammed flashed his badge several times, and an aisle opened for him and his men. When they reached Mike, standing with his back to the wall, Mohammed flipped open his badge once again and said, "Come with me, Michael O'Shea."

"What is this?" Mike said. He braced his legs and stood firm, confronting the Dubai police officer. "Do you have jurisdiction here? Let me see that badge." Mike wasn't going to come along peaceably, Mohammed realized. His eyes fixed on the service elevator not far past where Mike was standing. They'd have to use that. It exited up on the other side of the ballroom.

Well aware of Mike's teammates across the room, Mohammed took note that they and other expats sang and laughed, getting more intoxicated by the moment. The band, due to arrive momentarily, would keep them partying the rest of the night, if he could find a way to get Mike to come along without notice.

But that didn't seem to be possible. Mike held his hand up and yelled across the room. "Hey, Don!" just as a fist slammed upward into his gut.

Thirty minutes later, Mike came to, groggy from alcohol and pain. He sat up partway and said, "What the hell?"

The Arab in the front seat turned and smiled a sadistic, broken-toothed smile and said, "You don't remember me, do you, Michael O'Shea?"

Mike sat up a little further and said, "You must have the wrong Mike O'Shea."

"Oh no," laughed Mohammed, "I have the Mike O'Shea I want." His crooked smirk caused a dark fury to enter Mike's eyes, but he held it in check for the moment.

Mike said, "Okay, humor me. Do I know you?"

The Arab began to lose his patience. "Do you remember Sharm el-Sheik? You were there, no? The bar, the fight—it was none of your business."

Mike thought for a moment until the pieces clicked into place. "Oh yeah, were you one of those chicken shits that jumped my friend? Four-on-one is hardly a fair fight."

With impeccable English he yelled back at Mike. "You will pay for what you did that night!"

It was Mike's turn to smirk. "You mean for kicking you and your little friends' butts in a fair fight, which *you* jumped into to make it unfair?"

"Laugh now, infidel. You won't be laughing when I am through with you."

"So again," Mike smirked, "you're not man enough to go one on one."

Now the Arab laughed. "Why should I? I have nothing to prove, and my cousins here saw how much pain you have caused me. They want revenge as well. See, infidel, blood runs deep here in our country, and yours is going to run into our sands."

"*Allatooh*," Mohammed commanded, telling his driver to go straight, and then, "*Yameen*." They turned right as directed, then headed down an old camel trail with an ancient Bedo adobe hut displayed in the headlights, many outbuildings surrounding the structure.

***

Don had heard Mike yell and turned in time to see his friend being sucker-punched and dragged away. He immediately shifted gears. He yelled to Mark, who was socializing on the other side of the room. After a few well-placed kicks, blood poured from Mike's nose and he was limp as the Arabs dragged him into the elevator.

Don and the team jostled their way through the crowd to the staircase, but the band was on the way down with equipment, making their progress agonizingly slow. Chase had the widest bulk, and as he tried to squeeze past a guitar case, he lost his balance and tried to catch himself with a hand on the guitarist's back, thereby pushing him down into his bandmates. Several lost their footing and ended up cursing the team. "Sorry," Chase shouted, but none of the team stopped. Then they were upstairs and out the door.

Mike had already been zip-tied and shoved into the back seat of a Range Rover on standby. Don ran to the valet, grabbed his keys, and as there were limited roads into the hotel, he took careful note of the direction the Range Rover was headed. They all piled into the

Hummer, Don threw it into four-wheel-drive, and they took off. The Range Rover's taillights were still in sight, and he stayed far enough back to avoid detection. Don saw the Range Rover turn, then the car stopped and the headlights went out. The moonless night was pitch black, with millions of stars dotting the dark dome of the nighttime sky. He turned the Hummer off and crept closer toward the hut, taking his time and scoping out the surroundings. None of them could see anything moving outside. He braked and shut off the Hummer. He and his crew jumped out and moved stealthily toward the building. The door opened and an Arab stepped out, sucking on a cigarette, the red tip bright in the darkness. He leaned against the SUV with his back to them.

Don took his shoes off and crept up silently behind the Arab lookout. As the Arab turned, Don hit him with all his strength, knocking him flat. He struck him across the back of the head, putting his lights out. He quickly searched him while Mark and Chase rifled through the SUV. Mark pulled a Glock .45 out of the glove box. He confiscated it and headed toward the door. As he did, he noticed a broken window on the side that gave enough of a view to see what was taking place. Don joined him and they peered in. The Arabs had hung Mike from the ceiling with his shirt off. A fire had been lit in the center of the room, flames starting to crackle.

Ahmed joined them at the window. "I scouted the perimeter. Nothing else," he whispered. The men watched and listened while the Arabs jabbered in Arabic.

"What's he saying? Can you tell?" Don said.

"He's mumbling. The short one asks about the Warrior. The other says his strength has grown and he won't be able to be still much longer. He says . . . all the years of hiding and growing stronger and planning will pay off. Allah will have the victory. Eyes and ears everywhere . . . many followers . . . much power and great destruction. The other asks when."

The man attending the fire stuck what appeared to be an old-fashioned branding iron into the coals. He turned and spoke to Mike.

"You will tell us what we want to know," Mohammed said.

"You'll get nothing from me," Mike snarled back.

"We will."

What kind of information they were hoping to get out of Mike was unclear, but it was not hard for Don to assess the situation and see what was about to take place. He moved around the outside of the partially cracked door and listened.

"You bloody ragheads are gonna find yourselves wiping up your own blood with those towels," Mike said, and the darkness in his soft voice could not be mistaken for anything other than his deepest rage.

Mohammed, sniggering evilly, said, "You're not going to be such a joker when I get done with you."

Don had heard enough. He could see only two, so if there were a time to react, it was now. He eased the door open just as Mohammed picked up the red-hot branding iron. He held up the glowing tool and turned, raising it above his head where Don could see the brand. The iron had been formed into a misshapen heart, an ugly mimicry, glowing hot and red. The Arab raised it to the level of Mike's chest and snarled.

At that moment, Mike's long-time friend said, "I don't think so!"

The Arab whirled around as his turbaned cousin started toward Don. Don put a shot through the leg of the approaching Arab and stopped him dead in his tracks. Then he raised the Glock toward Mohammed and said, "Put it down now or I'll shoot a little higher than what I did to your little scumbag friend there."

Mohammed's scumbag cousin had rolled over in pain. Full of rage now, Mohammed raised the branding iron to throw it. Don shot him in the shoulder, and he dropped the glowing tool, which bounced and came back at him, landing on his bare feet. He screamed from the double insult to his body. Although wounded, his adrenaline took over and he propelled himself at Don, who looked at him at amazement and backhanded him across the face with the butt of the gun, as though hitting a badminton birdie. The Arab went down.

Don looked over at Mike, still hanging from the rafters, and said with a big smile, "How's it hangin', cuz? What did ya do to piss these boys off?"

Mike returned the smile and laughed. "I gave that boy there a little dental work when we were in the Sinai and I think he wanted to return the favor. Now come on and cut me down and let's get the hell out of here."

Don took the branding iron and burned the ropes off Mike's arms. They left both of the injured Arabs laying on the floor and turned as the rest of the team entered the building.

"Where you boys been? You think it was a good idea for you to leave us alone with these goons?" Don said.

Ahmed spoke up. "One on guard, two scouting. If you'd gotten yourself into trouble, we'd have had your back, brother, and you know it." He slapped Don on the back with one hand and Mike with the other. "Let's search this place before we go."

They pulled out their flashlights and opened the cabinets that lined the wall, finding papers and supplies.

They grabbed the stacks of paper and hauled them to the vehicle. "Headquarters needs something to occupy their time, don't ya think? They'll love this," Chase said.

"What's this over here, Mike?" Don said.

They went outside where Mike saw the Arab on guard duty also laying on the ground. "That your doing also?" he said to Don.

"The boy was smoking in a nonsmoking area, and I had to help him put his cigarette out." They both grinned as Don shot out three tires and took the keys from the ignition.

As they walked off toward Don's vehicle, Don looked over at Mike and said, "Damn son, you just can't seem to keep your butt out of trouble! If'n you keep this up I am going to have to start chargin' you for saving your bacon!"

Mike laughed as they got into their vehicle and headed back to the hotel. When they arrived, Neil was out front and smiled when he saw Don and Mike jump out of the Hummer. Neil said, "What happened? Where's your shirt?"

Mike laughed. "I had to look after my boy Don, and a couple other fellers back there took the shirt off my back!"

Don said, "Yeah, right, you keep snowin' and I'll keep shovelin'! Ha!"

Mike looked at Neil and said, "Well, son, this is mostly your fault. Remember our shindig down in the Sinai?"

"Yeah, what does that have to do with anything?"

Don said, "Well apparently, pards, those boys back there took exception to our helpin' you out."

Mike laughed. "And ole Don here decided that I didn't need to be barbecue!"

"You got that right!" Don said, laughing. "So, we left a couple of them in bad shape back at an old shack about ten clicks down the road. You might send somebody out to get them, as they ain't goin' far."

Mike poked at Don and said, "Speaking of which, we probably ought to get the hell out of here so there are no questions asked. Not sure how they found us, but they must be connected if they got to us so quick."

They left and returned to their room. They grabbed their gear and all left for the field headquarters in Muscat, Oman, where they expected to be given their next assignment to China.

Yelling at Neil standing out front, they said, "See you next time 'round, Neil!"

Don looked over at Mike and said, "Ya know, cuz, we might not ought to come back to this sandbox for a while. Seems we're not too welcome here anymore."

CHAPTER SEVENTEEN

The Kidnapping
Oman

The evening cooled from the sweltering heat as a slight breeze removed the intensity from a stuffiness that could take one's breath away. General John O'Shea had been back in the field for seven years now, and he was still going strong at the age of fifty-one. This was where he felt most comfortable, and while he knew he couldn't keep it up forever, he'd not give it up until he had to. He'd been glad to leave his desk and the burden of out-of-control politics. He asked Ahmed if he knew the address in Shatti al Qurum, a suburb of Muscat on the eastern border of Oman.

"*Taman, Taman*, yes sir, General." They wound through the newly paved streets into what was commonly referred to as the Diplomatic Area, where all the embassies populated the streets. They passed by the buildings, all surrounded by ten-foot-high white walls, one after another. The villa, with its snow-white façade, sat back behind one of the many gates. They arrived fashionably late, as expected, and passed through the gate into a large, well-lit garden, manicured to a level that would rival the Master's golf course. Like a lot of villas in the area, overbuilt and large enough to give it almost a hotel-like image, the gate was manned by two locals, only one armed. The gate closed behind them as they entered, and the general's black armor-plated Suburban fell in behind a line of S550 Mercedes, limousines, and exotic cars.

Sheik Saud had asked the general to attend, then begged his forgiveness, as he had already committed to another event that evening. The sheik asked this favor in order to send a message to the diplomats that his reach to the Americans included senators, ambassadors, and high-ranking military officers, and the relationship was still strong. Sheik Saud wanted the hierarchy that would be attending to see that he still wielded "*wasta*"—in other words, power and influence—with the Americans, and that the local ministers should listen and take notice of his ability to bring US business to the Sultanate. It was a favor that the general could not refuse.

Sheik Saud himself had overseen the seating assignments and had seated the general next to Hamid Bin Sali, one of the Omani secret police, in hopes they would have a few minutes to chat. Hamid was a loyal and high-ranking official in this branch of Oman's intelligence agency, which was the equivalent of the CIA, although Hamid's position was not common knowledge with the guests that evening. His purpose at this event was to let the general know about a security meeting that would take place in two days and which included all the players involved in protecting the Sultanate.

This dinner event was a typical means of communication by the Arabs. Though not a state dinner, those present included many influential locals, along with VIP guests. A perfect setting for a clandestine meeting, it afforded the perfect cover to pass along a clandestine message. The room filled with forty or fifty guests, and as they entered, the occasion became quite colorful, with the local ministers outfitted in official robes, or galabias, the desert kaftans adapted for evening wear. The western guests wore tuxedos, and all of the women dressed elegantly. Visiting military arrived in full formal attire, and the whole atmosphere reeked of wealth and power. Many businessmen and entrepreneurs would have loved to attend such a hot ticket in town.

The minister of oil himself, Sheik Mohd, hosted the event. The general knew him as Sheik Saud's nephew. As John entered the foyer, lavish with massive flower arrangements, he and the other attendees were announced individually, by both who they were and by their respective titles or ranks. This proceeding was a throwback to when the Dutch ruled the Emirates and was still carried out as more of a tradition than anything. The atmosphere was noisy as the general entered, and no attention was paid either to the announcements or to John's presence. He was not offended, as he had some familiarity with the routine traditional ceremony, but he thought it a little silly. An Arabian combo played in the corner, the sounds of the guitar, drums, and flute perfect belly-dancing fare. A variety of juices were offered for the locals, along with alcoholic beverages for the Westerners. Sheik Mohd, the host, immediately came over and greeted the general. As they embraced, the traditional kissing of each cheek took place.

The general said, "Sheik Mohd, so great to see you again and to be in this magnificent home. I am happy and honored to be back in your beautiful Sultanate." He truly meant this—without a doubt, this was one of the general's favorite places to visit. The Sultanate maintained cleaner streets than in the US. Its clean air and geographical location, with rugged black volcanic mountains, white sand beaches, and emerald-blue waters with thirty-meter visibility, were stunningly beautiful. His Highness insisted on the clean streets, as well as that the cars and trucks be washed and modern. Although not the richest of the Arab countries, this was certainly the cleanest and most hospitable spot in the region.

Sheik Mohd, excited to see his old family friend, walked the general around, introducing him to everyone. They approached a young woman with her back to them. She wore a beautiful form-fitting Yves Saint Laurent dress, her wavy hair loose and falling below her shoulders. As she turned around, a surprised smile burst across both faces.

"Stacy! My lord, what are you doing here?" He shook his head with disbelief and said, "What has it been? Three, maybe four years? How are you?"

Sheik Mohd smiled. "Obviously you know each other, so I will take my leave to allow you two time to reacquaint." The general nodded his thanks.

Stacy smiled and hugged the general like a long-lost daughter, which is exactly the way the general thought of her. He stepped back, and intending his words as a compliment he said, "That silly son of mine should have never let you get away." She lowered her head, more demurely than he would have expected back home. "Now, what in the world are you doing in Oman, Stacy?"

She smiled at his bewilderment. "I'm here representing a client in an oil deal. It's quite complicated as it relates to oil rights, payments, and legal ownership. You know, General, the Arabs base their laws on the Koran and Sura law, which is quite different than how we do contracts in the states."

"That's right. If I remember correctly, your law degree was in international business."

"Kind of you to remember, General. I'm here working with the minister and His Highness on a directional drilling contract for a client of ours. I was supposed to be here three days, and that was two weeks ago. As you know, nothing moves fast here. The minister was kind enough to invite me tonight, because I've worked closely with him and his staff. However, I should be finished in a couple of days, then I'll be back to New York."

A look of sadness filled her eyes. "How's Mike?"

The general smiled, understanding her unspoken longing for his son. "Doing great, just busy with various missions. I seldom see him myself. But I know for a fact he has not looked at another since you. Stacy, you put a spell on him, and I would love to see you two kids hook up again." Stacy smiled and nodded without a verbal response.

Hamid appeared again, and the general asked, "Hamid, would it be too much to have Stacy sit next to me tonight? She has always been family to the O'Sheas."

Hamid bowed and said, "*Inshallah*, no problem, Mon General."

A man dressed in Indian attire came through with a bell announcing, "Dinner is served," and the guests started to move into the main ballroom, decorated in richly colored curtains and art from all over the world, done by famous Italian and Dutch painters. The plates and goblets were gold-lined, and the setting was magnificent. Even considering the social class that was there that evening, most were in awe of the decor and setting. The giant curtains covering the windows were pulled back, displaying fountains, and in came Asian artists dancing in ritualistic formation to flutes and drums. The colorfully decked-out dancers attracted all eyes to the entertainment they provided.

Outside, a black Suburban pulled up to the gate. With darkened windows and no license plate, it had been stolen an hour earlier from the Oman Oil Company's parking lot. At this point, the first security mistake was made when the gate to the villa opened before the passengers were checked. Two guards approached each of the Suburban's front windows, and as the windows came down on both sides, both guards were killed instantly with silenced .45s. At the same time, an old beat-up station wagon pulled up behind the Suburban to block the gate entrance, and five heavily armed, masked Arabs got out and rushed to the front of the villa. Four additional assassins jumped out of the stolen Suburban. The second security mistake occurred then, as no one was guarding the front door. The four of them entered stealthily while the other five moved around back. The terrorists methodically moved through the kitchens and back rooms, quietly killing every worker and service person they encountered. This was also the first time an attack had taken place in Muscat, which made the attack a complete surprise.

The five gunmen entered the ballroom. The eyes of the guests all faced the garden, lending a perfect setting for a surprise attack. As one of the Asian artists turned a flip in midair, his chest exploded, and screams erupted from the onlookers. The guests looked toward the garden in shock, and the five that had entered from behind them opened up with AK–47s, deafening and deadly. The general grabbed Stacy and pull her to the floor. He lifted the long tablecloth and they scooted under the table as the carnage raged. He hovered over her as screams and absolute terror gripped the entire room.

Hamid pulled his concealed Ruger and fired at the closest terrorist. The man was dead before he hit the floor. As Hamid turned, two of the perpetrators unloaded full clips into him, killing him instantly. The slaughter proceeded—yelling, screaming, and blood splattering everywhere as some raised their hands in surrender. But it didn't matter. These fanatical killers showed no mercy, murdering everyone who breathed. As the smoke cleared, the general held his hand over Stacy's mouth and looked at her, communicating nonverbally to be still. He held a finger over his mouth, hoping to avoid detection under the table. Stacy's chest heaved with suppressed sobs and John hoped she would not lose it. He tried to maintain a calming arm around her to help her stay in control.

General O'Shea's luck ran out when the leader of the strike force lifted the tablecloth and saw the two looking right back at him. "*Fadual, Fadual*," he said, motioning with his hand for them to come out.

As the general and Stacy stood facing the terrorist, he said to them in a British-educated accent, "Who are you? Why are you here?"

The general looked the Bedo right in the eye and said, "I am General John O'Shea, and this is my daughter-in-law Stacy, an international attorney working on contracts for a major US firm. She is here visiting me, as my guest." If this killer standing in front of him thought she was with him, she might have a chance of survival. Tears rolled down Stacy's face as she took in the bloodbath before them. No one else moved in the entire ballroom. All were dead but them.

The terrorists turned to two other comrades and said something to them that the general couldn't understand. The other masked assailant was walking around the room putting bullets into those who were moaning in pain. It was an execution-style killing. One of the Arabs ripped a cord off the wall-length curtains and grabbed Stacy and the general, then tied their hands behind their backs. He led them to the front door, grabbing two turbans from two expired local guests. When they reached the door, he used the turbans to blindfold them.

John O'Shea knew some Arabic. He kept his eyes shut and listened as the leader spoke to his comrades. "We can ransom these two for money and guns," the man said. "The general has the power to do so and he will not be any trouble while his daughter is with him. *Inshallah*, we will help our cause, and if we are right, we will not bring the Americans down on us until we release Allah's message." John inferred that the cryptic remark "Allah's message" meant the rumored bomb.

They pushed the two into the car, and the general whispered to Stacy, "Whatever you do, do not speak. Do not look them in the eyes and keep your eyes on me only, subservient and humble. Remember, these are fundamentalists with no regard for life, and they look at women as lower class. Do what I say."

These terrorists were congratulating themselves that the whole operation had taken less than fifteen minutes and had been executed just as they'd rehearsed. They'd done what they came to do—send a message to the upper

Sunni faction. Their intention for this attack was a warning for things to come—a message that the locals could not stop Ali Al Sharif and his followers. *Inshallah,* the jihad was coming, and there was no way to know from where. While the attack on Sheik Mohd's dinner took place, a bomb simultaneously went off in the old souk where Sunni traders had done business with the Dutch for a hundred and fifty years. This attack killed everyone in a three-block radius. Just another instance of ruthless killing, with extensive carnage that the Sultanate had never before experienced. The leader knew Ali Al Sharif would be pleased, and they would be rewarded.

One of the terrorists turned and slammed his weapon against the general's forehead, knocking him out.

***

Stacy gasped. Blood trickled down the general's brow. The laughter coming from the front seat terrified her. She had never seen war or killing, and she existed in a hazy state of shock, worried about the general and whether he would come to. She could not see him, so she had no idea how badly he was hurt.

They drove for what seemed like an hour. Blindfolded, Stacy had no idea where they were being taken. All she could hear was the call to prayer by what had to be a nearby mosque. Sultan Qaboos's law indicated that a mosque must be built within walking distance in every city, so they could have been taken anywhere. A garage door squeaked on its metal rails as it raised, and the car slowly pulled in. Again, she heard a door slam. Arabic chatter, then yelling, and chaos erupted. They yanked Stacy's blindfold off and sat the general up. He started to come to, the dried blood that had run down his face cracking as he moved his facial muscles. She remembered what he'd told her. She lowered her head and moved closer to the general. At that point, the leader came over and slapped one of the Arabs, a string of vile words pouring from him. He didn't want to upset the Americans, as he knew he could get money and weapons for these two infidels. Deep inside, he held respect for the foreign warrior, as he could see the ribbons and medals on the general's formal uniform. This he could relate to and would be the reason the general and Stacy were alive, along with their value as hostages. He said something to another Arab standing near, who then left. Shortly he returned with water and clothes, at which point they cut their captives' hands free.

The rough, bearded man told Stacy, in English, "Take care of your father, and no harm will come to you, if you do as I say."

Stacy nodded, lowered her head, and took the makeshift bandages. She whispered, "*Shukran*, thank you." She turned to tend to the general. They got him onto his feet, but he was only semiconscious, and they had to help him, one on each side, to move him into what looked like a warehouse office. The room contained a long table and a couple of chairs, with a couch in the corner. A washroom sat at the back wall, not closed off to the rest of the room. They laid the general down on an old torn couch and when the door closed, Stacy heard them lock it. She hurried to the sink for more water and continued to clean and dress the general's forehead while he remained unconscious.

She had no idea where they were, what would happen next, how bad the general was hurt, or the cause of all the killing. Angry tears ran down her cheeks and she was shaking, hard. All she wanted at that moment was to buck their traditions and lash out at their captors, but after a few minutes she got hold of herself and to the empty room she said quietly, "Okay Stacy, don't give them the satisfaction of letting them know you're angry or scared. Remember what the general said. Someone will come for us. If they wanted us dead, it would have already happened." Then she waited, wondering when— or if—the general's senses would return.

CHAPTER EIGHTEEN

The Threat

PAL Headquarters

Mike and Don had just returned from China on a top-secret mission to deter a steel magnate from sabotaging the world steel industry and were feeling quite good about successfully thwarting the situation. Without their intervention, the situation could have escalated into a full-blown depression for the entire auto industry. They were on a roll. The two entered the PAL office with more than a hint of swagger.

Don headed over to the recap board on terrorist activities, shook his head, and turned to Mike. "Damn, son, we can't catch a break. Just look at that lit-up thing. They have added pert' near twenty new ops! Don't those guys ever take a vacation?"

Mike looked at the board and smiled, eager for a new assignment, then he headed toward his dad's office. As he neared the door, his name came over the loudspeaker asking him to pick up the phone for an urgent call.

"Hello," Mike said. He immediately recognized the voice on the other end. "Jamal, you ole camel thief, where the hell are you? I haven't heard from you since Bully was a calf!"

"*Marhaba*, Mike, listen—I only have a minute, and time is of the essence. I just got word from a reliable source that there will be a message sent to the fort Wadi Ben Khalid next Tuesday night and *Inshallah*, you need to be there and intercept it!" Jamal was so worked up he was nearly yelling at Mike. "It is of most importance to the region. There are rumors that a nuclear trade is going to take place that would change the balance of power in our most Holy Land. Mike, you must get there. We will have only one shot at this, and it is vital to intercept this information."

"Hold on there, big fella, you say this is about nukes and someone is going to buy them and use them? Rumors of these types of deals have been circulating for years, so why is this different? Who's saying this? I'd like to know, before I go traipsing off into the Big Sand Pit. If you recall, Jamal, I am not the most popular guy in the Dhofar these days."

"Mike, please trust me, the information coming in is the real deal. Have I ever spoke to you wrong?"

Mike hesitated a minute. Sure, he'd go and find a way into that fort, but it wasn't going to be easy. That old fort had, at one time, held off the entire Saudi army for ten days, and although it needed a good face lift, it was still difficult to get in unnoticed. With a water well inside, it had been built with only one way in and out.

"Okay, I'll see what I can do, Jamal."

"Praise be to Allah. Get there as soon as you can and intercept that message, as it can unleash the wrath of a holy jihad, killing many, not to mention the political imbalance it could bring."

"Okay, okay, Jamal, I will get over there and have a listen. Be safe."

Mike hung up and walked down the hall to his father's office. As he entered, Sandy looked up and immediately moved to grab him and hug him.

"Wow, Sandy," Mike said, "what gives?" Sandy didn't seem to be in any mood for levity. She released him as suddenly as she'd grabbed him, and he flopped backward into a chair.

"Sit down, I'll be right back," Sandy said. In less than a minute she came back with Captain Bill. Given that Mike was aware of Sandy and Bill's history, for them to be in the same room together told him this must be important. The two sat down directly across from Mike.

Bill, with an almost military cadence, said, "Mike, you know that Sheik Saud and your father have been friends for years, and that Saud trusts the general above all people. What we know is that the general received a call from the sheik and then an hour later another call from His Highness Sultan Qaboos. General O'Shea gave us a story about the sheik requiring his presence at a dinner the next day and he was immediately on a plane to Muscat. We have no idea what exactly he was doing there, but we do believe the general would not have left if it was not of the utmost importance. We have just received word that he has been taken."

"What do you mean, 'taken'?" Mike said, planting his feet, his body tense.

"That's affirmative, Mike. All we know is that the sheik asked him to attend a dinner with some high-ranking government officials, and the facility was attacked. He and some of the others might have been taken. We cannot reach him."

"Was he alone? When did this happen and why?" Bill stepped back, and Mike realized that his rage, close to the surface, made the man uncomfortable.

Bill looked empathetically at Mike and said, "Mike, you know the general better than anybody, and his actions would not have been such as they were if it weren't important. Two longtime allies requested his presence. We have been in contact with Ahmed. He dropped the general off at the door and returned to base. No signs of anything amiss when he was there."

Mike looked over to Sandy and said, "I want on the next plane to the Middle East, either domestic or military, and I want it now."

"Yes sir, Lieutenant," Sandy said, and she hurried out. Mike strode out of the office and as he walked by Don, he gave him a curt nod to come with him, and now. As they drove to the Bachelor Officers Quarters, Mike brought Don up to speed. Two hours later, they were on Emirates Air headed to Dubai. He thought hard about his next steps. There couldn't be a coincidence between his father being taken and the arms deal Jamal had briefed him on, could there? Something definitely stunk, on both fronts.

After reaching Dubai, they'd enter Oman from the outermost checkpoint to the Emirates from the eastern outer border, with no one suspecting. They'd have a five-hour trek to get to Oman, but the travel would be worth it if it meant entering the country unsuspected.

They would pass through Al Ain and pick up their contact, Ahmed El-Massier. Al Ain was Sheik Zayed's hometown, the largest inland city in the UAE. Located on the eastern edge of Abu Dhabi, it was known as

"Garden City of the Gulf" due to its greenery, which was fed by many springs. Here they'd meet up with the other PAL staff that had traveled over with the general.

Mike and Don picked up Ahmed, and he brought the two up to speed on the terrorist activities.

"An awful affair, Mike," Ahmed said. "And I have news you are not going to like."

"I've already had that. What could be worse?" he asked his old training buddy.

Ahmed adjusted his turban and shielded his eyes from the blinding sun. "Not only the general, but a Western woman has been taken. They're being held for ransom. The attackers accomplished what they set out to do in killing the minister and slaughtering the other diplomats and nearly everyone at the dinner, and now they have the added benefit of a beautiful Western woman and a two-star general for ransom. It was too good to pass up, especially knowing that they would need money for weapons with the overthrow of the Oman monarchy in their near future."

Ahmed had grown up on the streets of Cairo and was self-educated. He'd entered Egypt's mandatory army and found his station in life. Placed on the fast track within the elite international guard, they taught him manners, hygiene, and self-defense, then sent him to liaison with the US Navy SEAL training where he'd met a young Mike O'Shea going through the same training. The two became fast friends with similar backgrounds, both learning how to survive, kill, and acquire all the talents and skills necessary to move in an underworld that is unknown to the average soldier, much less to civilians. PAL needed assistance in the Middle East, so it had been a no-brainer to recruit Ahmed El Massier from Mike's

SEAL group. He came over to the US after his family lost everything when Mubarak was overthrown. Ahmed appreciated the freedom and democracy of the US, and gladly signed on to assist PAL. He'd been a valuable asset over the last couple of years.

When they arrived in Oman, Mike sent Don over to headquarters to get everyone up to speed and manage logistics, while Mike went in search of his old friend, Master Sergeant O'Dooley. He checked at his villa and then at the local gym. His next stop was the local Embassy club. It was more like a small-town bar, decorated with hats from oil companies, including all the major players doing business there. An American flag hung over the bar, and money from every country in that part of the world was stapled to the walls and poles, along with college flags from many US universities and a few European schools.

Mike spotted Sergeant O'Dooley hanging onto both the edge of a bar stool and a Jack Daniels bottle that had about three shots left in it. Mike looked down at him and said, "Hello Sergeant, what are we celebrating this fine day?"

With slurred words and bloodshot eyes, O'Dooley said, "It's Monday isn't it?"

Mike said, "Yep."

"Good enough for me."

As Mike reached down and helped him up out of his chair, he reeled from the smell oozing from O'Dooley's pores. "Come on, Sergeant, let's get some coffee in you. I need you to get your head on right."

They left the Embassy Club and went straight to the army café. Mike poured hot black coffee down him. Then he grabbed a bucket of water and dumped it over his head and finished by giving him a few slaps to get his attention. The cold water seemed to work. As soon as he sobered up enough to listen, Mike explained that he had gotten a tip that a message was being sent to the fort at Wadi Ben Khalid, and they'd have to intercept it.

"Climb in, O'Dooley, we have a three-hour drive, and this gives you to time to finish sobering up and be ready."

They picked up two days' worth of supplies at the supply chain tent, a couple extra RMEs, and additional water. Mike glanced over and saw a rocket launcher sitting in a corner, so he reached down and threw that in the back of the jeep. They left out with plenty of time to formulate a plan to get into the communications tower at the fort.

CHAPTER NINETEEN

Interception
Wadi Ben Khalid, Oman

Mike O'Shea lay shivering on the orange desert sands watching night fall quietly over the Arabian Peninsula. The lack of sound lent an eerie stillness to his predicament, and he couldn't shake the thought that it must be the sound of death. The pain hadn't subsided. He had to get pressure on his wound to stop the bleeding if he expected to survive. He reached for his pack, pulled a sponge-like square of medical gauze out of an emergency first-aid package he always carried, and tried to apply pressure over the bleeding gash.

The pain he'd endured during spring football practice at UT was nothing in comparison to this. Today, the bleeding from the wound in his side had turned the golden sand crimson, some of it having already turned to maroon as the blood slowly oxidized. His blood. His eyes fluttered shut and his mind wandered, delirious, two weeks back—or no, even further. Much further. Stacy. She was the one he'd thought about through all of his

training, through the months of physical pain and
endurance, her image always fresh in his mind. More
than three years had gone by. She'd dated other guys,
she'd said, but she hadn't found anyone else. He could
see her now, those flirty green eyes twinkling and her
long, taut legs tormenting him . . ..

The pain still hadn't subsided. How long had he been
unconscious? Stars twinkled in the night sky, but what
he remembered had taken place during late afternoon.

Mike and his partner, Master Sergeant O'Dooley, had
left the old, abandoned fort called Wadi Ben Khalid
hours before after radioing in from the fort's ancient
adobe tower that he'd intercepted the meeting place
where the nuclear warhead buy was to take place. Then
Mike lost contact as he and O'Dooley came under fire
and he didn't get a chance to finish his current intel
report. They grabbed the ropes that had been latched to a
large beam and rappelled down the jagged walls of the
tower. As their pursuers fired shots, they hit the soft sand
hard and rolled. They crouched and ran, then jumped
into the UN jeep. Eager to get to a place where they
could radio in their report, loud shouts erupted behind
them as they retreated.

"*Yella! Yella!*" He heard the Arabs' machine gun
truck start up and pull out with a screech to come after
them.

As they raced from the outskirts of the old fort, three
desert-terrain 4-wheel-drive vehicles started after them,
two with short-range rocket launchers, and one loaded
with a high-powered machine gun.

Their mission had been a success. They'd been able to
sneak close enough to overhear conversations, both by
the individuals in the fort and the communications over
the radio.

They raced into the desert, and O'Dooley took out the first vehicle with a bazooka that they'd hastily thrown on board this tank destroyer, just in case. They rounded the old Bedouin trail when the sergeant caught the next jeep with the machine gun at a bend in the road. As they made for the desert, they knew their jeep was no match for this last vehicle. The sand buggy had bigger wheels and a suspension built for the desert terrain. By the time they got caught, Mike and Master Sergeant O'Dooley were thirty-five miles into the deep desert, with the setting sun glaring into their eyes so they couldn't see their pursuers.

The booming noise of mortars exploded around them as their white NATO jeep flew up and down the dunes of the Wahiba sands. "There's only one, Mike," his partner said, blasting behind them. As O'Dooley fired, he repeated that he thought only one machine gun and rocket launcher were pursuing them. Then their jeep exploded from the back end and that would be the last thing the sergeant would ever say.

Smoke rose now from the burning wreckage of their jeep, fifty kilometers away and out of Mike's sight behind one of the high, arching dunes. Loud voices speaking Arabic and the sound of boots kicking metal sent the fear of death down his spine. He listened and thought he could distinguish five voices. He knew they were searching the wreckage and the surely deceased sergeant. Mike had his Colt .45 with three rounds of ammunition in the chamber, though he'd be no match for the terrorist group if they found him. His teeth began to knock together as his sweat dried. The light was nearly gone. The night would be to his advantage if it caused them to move on without searching behind his dune. He kept his head down, hearing the voices nearing and then retreating from his position. As the voices and flashlights grew more distant, he managed a one-arm crawl to the top of the dune and peered over. The Arabs were dressed in galabia, the long white robes worn by most Arab nationals located in the Khaleej, and the moon lit them up like ghosts floating across the dunes.

He rolled over and tried to take stock of his situation. In the floorboard of the jeep would be a radio he could use, if it hadn't been found. Would it have the necessary range to allow the satellite to pick up his distress call? He got his feet under him and painfully straightened his body to a standing position. The bandage seemed to have slowed the bleeding, but he was lightheaded and would need medical attention soon if he were to survive. He climbed over the ridge that had kept him out of sight, stumbled at the crest, and rolled down the cool sand toward the smoldering jeep. He dragged himself up and lifted the hidden door to the bottom of the vehicle. Mike flipped on the shortwave radio, and with a harshness of breath that was barely a whisper he said, "Mayday, mayday, this is foxtrot-one-niner, do you read? Over." He waited for a response. Nothing. He tried one more time. Nothing but static. Not wanting to run the batteries down, he had to get to higher ground if there was a chance to be heard. PAL's base camp would be searching for him.

Mike looked over at the stripped-down body of Sergeant O'Dooley with a heavy heart and great remorse. He'd make sure the sergeant's death was not in vain. He conducted a quick search for water and other supplies, but the Arabs had cleaned everything out. Water in the desert was of great value, and he hadn't expected to find anything, but he was desperate.

Death from dehydration was his biggest threat now, and Mike knew he had to move while it was dark. The sun and desert heat would not bear down on him for the next twelve hours. He'd been in the region enough to understand that the Arabian desert is blistering by day and bone chilling by night. He scanned his location. He'd need to make it to the top of the mountain just north of his position to find shelter before daybreak. It was imperative that he get his costly information to PAL headquarters. Mike was a realist, and his training had taught him that he had one, maybe two days max that he could survive with his wound and no water. With all of his strength, rage, and anger, he started up the silky sand pyramid toward his mountaintop refuge. The pain was excruciating, but he ignored it, summoning up his inner dark side and another gear that allowed him to keep moving forward. The summit appeared to be miles away, but he kept at it—crawling, falling, lurching—and he continued moving as the sun began to lift its head over the dry, barren terrain.

***

Mike's swollen eyelids opened to slits and revealed his predicament in all its futility. Sheets of glass with a reddish haze was all he could see. He must have passed out. Next would come the hallucinations. He tried to move his body, but he lacked any volition whatsoever. Across the sea of smooth glass something seemed to be moving. He might as well give one final effort to move. Either the desert would kill him, or the enemy. Mike couldn't remember sending out another message, but he knew there was a GPS transmitter on the radio. Had he engaged it? Would there be enough signal to bring help?

He couldn't be sure—he was hurting, and his tongue traced the blisters lining his mouth. Parched and barely conscious, he suddenly felt a lightness, as though he was rising off the sand. It finally registered that he was being lifted into the back of a truck.

"Boy, if you want a suntan, let's do Cabo next time," a voice said. It seemed familiar. Mike tried to smile, but his eyes would not open. "Drink, now," the voice instructed, and he tried to swallow, coughing a few times before the cool trickle ran down his throat. When he'd swallowed as much as he could take, he passed out.

***

Don and Ahmed drove Mike through the side streets of Muscat into a high-rise neighborhood. The field hospital had been built on a sleepy side of town. The discreet three-story adobe building with a half-painted garage door sat on the rear side street, blocking any street view of what went on beyond its walls. In passing, the front blended with the other buildings, giving it the appearance of just another rental flat.

Ahmed drove at a snail's pace, Don thought, and although he knew the reduced speed was necessary, it took control to execute. Mike was unconscious but stable. Don filled Ahmed in on the neighborhood and the hospital, as Ahmed had never been there before. Most of the locals living around the building thought it was a communication center for the Omani secret police, so they asked no questions, and no one dared try to break in. Like most small communities, speculation and rumors flourished, but no one really knew. The building had been updated recently. Infrastructure had been put into place, such as new reliable electric power, a water treatment tower, lateral lines for waste disposal, and street repairs. The locals welcomed whatever had moved into their neighborhood, as it also provided them with the use of these upgrades.

Don had radioed ahead, so as they approached, the doors opened and they pulled in. Mike was still unconscious. Don and Ahmed carried him into a large open area that held three SUVs. This area had been set up as a façade, made to look like a parking garage or warehouse. As they opened the side door into the back of the warehouse, a sterile hallway beamed white lights out through the door. They struggled through with their unwieldy cargo and placed Mike on an old gurney that had been in use thirty years earlier when the British controlled most of this part of the world. Then they rolled him into a private room. The gurney was the only piece of equipment that had been on backorder when the US had set up shop. Otherwise, the facility was conveniently modernized and staffed with doctors who spent most of their time at the Royal Hospital, a hospital built in conjunction with UNICEF.

Royal Hospital employed prominent doctors from all over the world. They also provided free health care to Oman's citizens. The American doctors on contract had been specially selected through PAL's organization and were ex-military, with expertise in combat field care and diseases such as malaria, dysentery, and yellow fever— not the normal run-of-the-mill family physician's daily diagnostic challenges. Donations to the hospital from the US in the form of money and technical expertise had enabled them to secure permission from the Omani government to set up shop. The caveat, of course, being that it could be used by Oman's high-ranking government officials, if necessary. Thus, PAL was enabled to provide extra equipment that could be placed strategically in the Middle East for just such occasions, with no questions asked. The doctors had plenty of free time to help teach and provide assistance to the local medical staff. And some of the best medical care in the world was provided to the locals, free of charge.

They transferred Mike onto a new state-of-the-art medical bed, then the doctor started an IV, as Mike had suffered extreme dehydration from heat exposure. His lips were parched, and he had lost over ten pounds of water weight. On the verge of delirium, his weathered appearance and sunburn would rival any European beachgoer early in the season.

Doc Edwards, the tall, brawny young doctor taking care of Mike, had just finished medical school and his required service to the army, and he wanted to give back to the entity that had provided the funding for his education. He took vitals and bandaged the wound. The shrapnel had penetrated clear through Mike's side, luckily not hitting any vital organs. After removing this and finding no bullet or other metal lodged inside, the wound was considered clean. Because Mike had applied the makeshift bandage and had kept dirt and sand out of it, the young doc felt Mike would recover quickly with a tetanus shot and some rest.

Don waved a hand at Ahmed, who was headed back to field headquarters, then he sat intently outside Mike's door, getting up every few minutes to pace, like a caged lion. The mountain where Don had finally found Mike was like a high desert sand dune, volcanic rock inlaid with golden sand. Seeing Mike lying motionless on the hot sand, he'd had serious doubts about his condition.

When Dr. Brad Edwards came walking through the door, Don jumped up and damn near tackled him.

"Hold on, big fella," he said, looking down from a few more inches of height than Don's 6'2". He held up his hands. "Your partner has had quite the shock to his system, but with a couple days of TLC, he'll be okay."

Don's expressive face morphed from a scrunched-up frown to a grin that stretched from ear to ear. "Can I go in and see him, Doc?"

"Yeah but be quiet and let him rest." He moved on and Don did not waste time with any more small talk.

Dr. Edwards' voice carried from the next room. He addressed the nurse and said, "A little rest, hydration, and burn-care ointment and the boy will be fine. He's built like a rock."

Don sat in the lone chair in the corner, remembering another time he'd been here. The makeshift hospital had seven rooms and a dentist's office. Unknown to all but a few highly classified military and embassy personnel stationed in the region, the state-of-the-art equipment was the best in the world for mobile hospital care. The doctors had everything from instant x-ray machines to specialty equipment for the operating room, as well as a full pharmacy at their disposal. They had the capability to do heart transplants along with satellite connections to the Mayo Clinic and had access to the best military triage hospitals around the world. They could handle anything thrown at them. With US-trained doctors, the health care was as good as any on the planet.

***

Mike woke up disoriented, and discovered he had no clothes on. The smell of fresh sheets enveloped him, and his gaze shifted over to rest on a familiar face. Don, his old friend and cohort, slept in the chair. Mike threw a paper cup at him and said, "I'm all in for Cabo!" Don's eyes opened wide and he jumped from his chair, making appropriate exclamations of relief.

Mike's senses were slowly creeping back. He threw his legs off the bed and tried to stand. Don caught him on the way down. "Whoa, big fella, you lost a ton of blood and were more dried up than a dehydrated prune!"

"How long have I been out?" Mike asked.

"Since yesterday morning when we found you laid out in that giant sandbox. It's a good thing you turned that GPS on, or I would have never found you."

The nurse came in for her routine checks, congratulating Mike on his recovery and telling him to give it an hour or two before trying to ambulate on his own.

After she left, Don asked, "What about Dooley?"

Mike looked down and shook his head. "He didn't make it. He gave it hell. He's the sole reason I'm alive." Saying it out loud brought on a pain as intense as the pain in his side.

Mike suddenly sat up straight. What day did you say it was? I've got to get my report in!" he shouted.

Don looked down at his Rolex Submariner and said, "Wednesday, why?"

Mike tried to yell, his voice barely getting past his traumatized vocal cords. "The buy is going to take place Friday, near the old fort at Nizwa! We have to make plans to intercept those warheads or we can kiss this region goodbye. Their target is Al Bustan next Tuesday in Muscat at the Sunni Summit. Sheik Zayed from the UAE, His Highness Sheik Hamid from Bahrain, and Sultan Qaboos from Oman will all be attending. This could wipe out a majority of the Sunni leadership with ties to the US and could put the entire region in a holy war waged against the western allies."

The Al Bustan Palace was the site of the first Arab League summit for peace in the region. If they didn't stop this, not only would it wipe out most of the prominent Arab leadership, it would set the peace process back a hundred years with an all-out war. This war could erupt not only the Arab peninsula, but bring Russia, Egypt, Turkey, Iran, and Iraq into a world war. By attacking here, it would strengthen the symbolism of what they were trying to portray. This had to be stopped, and PAL needed to act now.

***

Ali Al Sharif and his cohorts had heard about the happenings at the old fort at Wadi Ben Khalid, but thought nothing of it, as the three Arabs that had chased Mike and O'Dooley into the desert assured Ali that they had killed all the infidels. It was decided that the treasure stashed in the black caves overlooking the Arabian Sea would be taken to Nizwa and traded for the instrument of their revenge. The warhead would give them the ability to make a difference that the Arab world had not seen since the dividing of the Arab tribes into countries. It was their chance at glory and to finally bring notice of the unfairness of the Sunni rulers. It was Allah's call to arms. They would arrive Thursday at sunset, break their fasting with some of their most trusted followers, and make the exchange Friday at the Muslim religious festival of Eid. Afterward, Ali would celebrate with his men. After he made his plans, he uttered, "Praise be to

Allah, all honor to his name," a benediction that lent him
the justification he needed for his vile actions.

Ali made his way to the outskirts of western Yemen
to Aden to meet with two of his most trusted men who
had returned from Saudi Arabia. He'd scnt them to meet
with the fanatical Taliban side of the Shiite regime. What
news had they brought?

He greeted his band of warriors by name and custom,
kissing each on both cheeks, alternating three kisses,
then he spoke to the team's leader.

"Did you make progress on finding a location for the
operation?" he asked Yasin, the young man whose long,
curly black hair blew in the hot wind.

"We found an ideal spot, Sheik Sharif. As we talked
before, due to its central Oman location and its continual
use for Bedo arms trading, the cover is good for the
exchange of the warheads."

Ali said, "This is good news. I'm aware of the small
arms repeating rifles being smuggled into Yemen and
Saudi in this location."

The men with Yasin nodded their heads, and one said,
"They've been carrying on successfully with these trades
for as long as I can remember."

"*Inshallah*, Yasin," Ali said. "Friday next is a perfect
day, a day of celebration at the end of Ramadan. Plan to
carry out the deal at Eid al-Fitr. This will be seen as
nothing more than another small arms deal." He clapped
first Yasin and then his comrades on the shoulders, and
said, "Good work, men! May Allah be praised. The
infidels will not know of the danger occurring right
under their noses."

CHAPTER TWENTY

The Plan

The nurse gave Mike another dose of painkillers and made sure his IV had plenty of glucose to rehydrate him at a steady pace. When he woke again Wednesday evening, Don entered the room with a burger and fries from Hardees, located just down the street. Mike was famished. He sat down, started to eat, and Mike asked, "What gives, didn't you bring me anything?"

"Why no," Don said, "they have you on a strict hospital diet of fowl and tortillas. You know, with those brown mashed-up fava beans." As he took a big bite out of a giant cheeseburger and opened a bottle of Sukar Gold beer, Mike grabbed his pillow and threw it at Don. His pal laughed and pulled fries and another burger out of the Hardees bag, then he handed them and a cold beer to Mike.

"I thought so," Mike said. "I knew you wouldn't let your old college roomie starve to death!"

"If I had," Don said, grinning, "I'd never hear the end of it!" As they chowed down, Mike began to feel whole again. His side had a bit of an ache to it, and he was told he had a decorative row of staples—twelve, to be precise—after they removed a piece of the wheel well that came from the exploding UN jeep. He was feeling much better with that foreign body removed. After a couple more beers, it was time to get down to business.

While Don was out, he'd called Ahmed as well as Major Mark Jamison, who was in charge of the region. Don asked them to come by the hospital for a briefing. He told them Mike was up and around and had vital news from his mission, and that Mike was anxious to hear news about his father. Major Jamison was followed into the room by Captain Kent Halbert.

Kent had gained weight since BUD/S training, but it was all hard muscle bulk. His receding hairline was a little more prominent, and his gray eyes still held the intensity that had stood out during training. As Kent peered down at his classmate, Mike distinctly felt the assurance those gray eyes afforded. Kent was in charge of all ground operations, and any incursion would come under his watch, as he would lead the mission. Any mission Kent led had a better chance of succeeding than most. Chase Jones stood next to Kent. He'd been busy since training, working as an operative on a successful mission out of China, and although his hair was thinner, he'd bulked up, and now looked like a large piece of gristle. He was a solid soldier and a great asset to any op they would run. Mike was also aware of Chase's Olympic bronze medal in shooting. These two, along with Ahmed and Don, made a great team that could take on anything. After Mike's briefing, they thought it best to go back to their headquarters where they could move satellite imagery and review all the data they had on Nizwa. It was agreed. Mike would join them in the morning for ops planning of the mission at hand.

As they started toward the door, Mike asked, "Any word on the general or the woman that was taken?"

Don looked over at the rest of the team and said, "I'll bring him up to speed on what we know." Mike easily read their expressions. There was something here they didn't want to tell him. As the others left, Mike's total attention shifted to focus on his lifelong friend.

Don related what had happened that night, how the minister and his entourage were the targets, and that the general and the lawyer were collateral as an opportunity to trade for money or arms.

Mike asked, "So have we heard from them?"

Don said, "Early this morning a messenger brought word that they would trade the pair for either one million dollars, or ten rocket launchers and twenty-one grenade launchers. They are prepared to make the trade early tomorrow morning if their terms are met. If not, they'll kill the general and sell the woman."

Mike, unable to process the information, tried to think through their options. PAL would never negotiate with these radicals.

Don looked at him and then down at his feet and said, "There is one other thing you need to know, Mike. The woman lawyer they have taken with the general is . . . is Stacy." A sudden shot of pain-laced adrenaline coursed through Mike's body, from his scalp to his toes.

"What? How can that be?"

Don told him of Stacy's chance meeting with the general, as she was the legal counsel negotiating with the OOCC and Exxon/Mobile for new drilling sites. "It was a fluke," Don said. "A chance meeting at the wrong place at the wrong time."

A rage boiled up inside him like never before. Two of the most important people in his entire life were in harm's way, and he wanted answers now on what was being done. He ripped out his IV, tubes dangling and dripping, and jerked on his clothes that Don had brought over for him, heedless of his injury. As he strode to the door, Mike looked over his shoulder and said, "You coming?"

Don jumped to his feet and followed Mike out in a mad dash through the hospital's front door. He said, "Our ride is over there. Where do you want to go?"

"Headquarters."

Don peeled out as fast as the Hummer would go.

No one had informed Mike that Stacy was with the general. He'd last seen her when she graduated with honors from Harvard Law School. She had been on her way to a bright career in international law. His stomach churned. He needed to punch something.

They reached the field office headquarters, and Mike walked straight into the situation war room. Major Jamison and Captain Halbert's heads snapped up.

"I guess Don briefed you on the situation with your dad and Ms. Lyons?" Kent said.

Mike nodded, not trusting himself to speak, his mouth a thin, straight line in his battle-scarred face.

"Mike, I know how you feel, but we are spread thin here, and our primary mission right now is to take out Al Sharif and retrieve those nuclear warheads. Then we can deal with the kidnapping," Major Jamison said.

With all the composure he could muster, Mike said, "Admit it, Mark. That will be too late. We have to act now and get ahead of this."

Kent spoke up. "We just don't have the manpower or the firepower to pull off a complicated mission at this point along with securing the nuclear weapons."

Mike focused on him for a few seconds, acknowledging Mark's skill and expertise, yet not willing or able to accept the verdict. He scanned everyone in the room, who all looked back at him with sympathy but doubt and said, "Then I'll do it."

All of them but Don shook their heads. Mark said, "All we know is they expect firepower or money tomorrow morning at 0900. We do not have the resources, nor do we have the ability to make, that kind of trade."

To Don and Ahmed, Mike said, "Then we will run the bait-and-switch with a bluff and kill them all before they know they have been had." Mike mustered up all the self-control he could, looked at Kent, and said, "Saying we can't do it is not good enough, Kent. We don't have time to wait. They will kill the general, and Stacy will end up as a sex slave to some Bedouin sheik, or else sold to Russia. We have to make a play in the morning."

Kent started to say something, and Mike held his hand up. "Hear me out. Let's pull the bait-and-switch op. We can get them to think they are getting what they asked for, but right before the trade goes down, we kill them all before they know what hits them. This has been done many times with other hostage situations. It will work, provided we control the place and timing."

Kent cleared his throat and looked at the others. Mike watched the faces of his team, gauging the thoughts of each. No one spoke for several minutes.

"I know this place, and it's perfect for this," Mike continued. "We have two world-class snipers in this room. We know the enemy will have at least one of their own. We'll go scout the area and identify the most likely places they would secure an elevated gunman. We then place two of our own, well ahead of time, and when the play starts, our guys take out their gunmen. We bring in empty gun boxes from a tugboat, giving the appearance that they came from our carrier. We'll have a SEAL team hidden around the building, which also has an oil-change pit that is perfectly secure. They'll be so arrogant in their thinking and excited about getting money and guns that they will agree to the place, and that's when we will strike. Guys, I'm telling you, this will work. After we get our own back, we'll go to work on the nuke trade."

Passionately, almost pleading, Mike said, "We have done it before, and this is our only chance! We have to recover our man. And woman," he added quietly.

Kent sucked in a long breath. After watching Mike keenly and considering his plan, he said, "It might work, but it would be a long shot. We have limited intel on the location where the trade will take place."

Wanting to seal the deal on his proposed mission, Mike said, "Then we change the place for our best chance at an immediate strike, with no room for error. We tell them we've had a tough time meeting their exact demands, but that we have fifteen rocket launchers and two hundred fifty thousand US dollars and six thousand UAE dinars. We'll say the rocket launchers are being delivered to the port of Muscat from one of our US freighters offshore. We tell them that they will arrive at 0900 exactly, and we will meet them at the port. The trade will take place at pier number five, as it has cover all around, and we can easily secure our two snipers and give them crossfire ability. We have two world-class marksmen in Chase and Ahmed, right here.

"They will exchange if we dangle this carrot at them. We'll require them to have both of our kidnapped victims at the trade, or no deal. They want the money and arms worse than two collateral people picked up at a party, even if one is a two-star general. As they bring the captives forward, we'll have one shot, one chance, to kill them all. If the general is not secure, he knows how to handle himself. They'll certainly have a sniper of their own, and we'll have to find him before the trade and take him out." All still listened, intent on his plan.

"Don, that's where you come in. Scout the layout, then think as they would. They have to come in from the south, so this helps our chances of finding the sniper ahead of time and preventing him from getting a shot off."

Mike finished by saying, "Then we go get the warheads."

Major Jamison said, "You know, it might very well work." The others in the room nodded. "I will make a call, secure the dock, and arrange for the façade of crates of rocket launchers to come into the port—that is, after I contact our kidnappers and get them to buy off on this." With eyes full of sympathy for Mike's position, Mark Jamison made eye contact with him and said, "Mike, understand that this is our one-and-only chance. If we can't get them to come to us, we will have to try and delay, scrap the mission, and hope for more time."

Ahmed then spoke up for the first time. "I know this type of people. They are thinking of nothing but guns and money. Because of this, it will blur their judgment. They will come."

Kent said, "I hope you're right, my Arab friend."

The men left the room, each having a task to complete. Mike and Don stayed, studying the overhead surveillance, which showed a break in the roof of the warehouse where the meet was to take place. Mike and Don located two points where the enemy could place a sniper. Close by was large crane for hauling containers off ships. The crane sat on higher ground and offered good cover, and though the distance was further than they would have liked, it was doable with the talent they had. They'd put Ahmed, their best marksman, in this location on the crane. Across the backside of the open storage building was a decrepit-looking water tower, typical of all structures in that part of the world, and Chase would be adjacent to this, behind an old water cooler on top of the building next door. This would create a crossfire within the opening in the ceiling of the port storage room. Mike would have to arrange to fill the covered areas, forcing the trade to take place, all the while providing shelter. This is where his pal Don would come into to play. Don had connections with some of the local merchants who had daily freight brought into the Sultanate. They'd build a facade of goods in the enclosed area. Behind that, a platoon of trained SEALs would be concealed, ready to move at a moment's notice when the first shots were fired.

At 1600 hours, they reconvened to brief the frontal assault team on their progress. Ahmed had been right, the Arabs had agreed to move the meet, but it took convincing, and they'd encountered another snag. The enemy wanted only one person at the trade. They also wanted to move the trade to 1000 hours. Both concessions were given, and now the task became angle of gunfire, how much firepower would be used, and how to not kill the two victims. Mike knew, as they all did, that the rescue would be tricky.

Kent was late in joining the meeting and when he came in, everyone listened intently as he filled them in on the location the meet would take place. While he was scouting it out, the whole takedown was nearly blown when a truck carrying four Arabs arrived with their own scouts. Fortunately, by the time the Arabs showed up, the container facade was already in place. Kent and crew hid behind the containers in a pit that was apparently used for oil changes. The Arabs never looked down. Kent pointed out that this pit would be a good place to station two or three men out of sight—men with the ability to engage quickly and perform well in a crossfire behind where the vehicles were most likely to enter. With positions on both sides of the room and the advantage of concealment, the pit would provide great cover while securing a tactical advantage.

The trick would be getting the victims out and away from whatever vehicle they arrived in. Mike had given some thought to this. They'd stage the money and the fake crates of weapons at two separate locations and put a vehicle in between, thus requiring the Arabs to get out on foot to examine the goods. This would be the tricky part, as Mike knew the Arabs wouldn't like this. But it was his team's best chance to get clean shots. Ahmed, on the crane, would have to take out their sniper first before anything else could take place—timing was everything for a successful hostage exchange. With that said, the team felt that they had covered most of the bases and hoped no surprises would occur during the trade.

It was agreed that Saeed Al Gama would be the translator for the exchange. This was going to cause some irritation, as this would make two people at the exchange instead of the one they requested. The team would explain that Saeed was there as interpreter only.

Saeed was ex-Egyptian Special Forces and the best with a knife that anyone on the team had ever seen. He had several specialized throwing knives secured within the multicolored wrap around his waist. He could move and hit a target from fifteen to twenty yards, faster than any gunslinger seen in western movies. He struck fear into the most hardened fighters, once they saw him demonstrate his prowess. The team was thrilled to have him with them, as he was a huge asset when it came to surprise. Saeed was a Sunni whose family had been killed during a small raid in his village by a fundamentalist Shiite band terrorizing the Sinai. Ahmed had recruited him. Mike had quickly noticed the man's quiet soul, but when he spoke, his voice demanded that you listen and pay attention, as he only spoke when it was truly important or when a situation could have negative consequences. Though quiet, he could also be a charmer, perfect for his role in this operation. His unassuming, sheepish presence and nonthreatening temperament belied a deadly killer, and even those who knew him best feared him.

The only thing to do now was wait, Mike thought, as all attention centered on this first op. As soon as the hostage trade had been managed successfully, the focus would turn to the warheads. A small team had been dispatched to Nizwa to validate where the nuclear warhead trade was most likely to take place and who was going to be involved. Intel would also come in from a state-of-the-art satellite that would be moving over the area later that day. Though he was already sweating like a sinner in church, Mike nodded his head, satisfied that he'd done everything he could to save the ones he loved.

CHAPTER TWENTY-ONE

The Rescue

Morning sun broke out over the city and the mosques began their morning songs of prayer—leisurely, sustained, vibrato-infused tones, beautiful and peaceful, if one embraced the intent of such a call to prayer. Loudspeakers with similar calls could be heard blaring throughout the land.

Mike took stock of was about to happen. He knew that the plan had been vetted and rehearsed, all angles checked, but he also knew only one slip, one small mistake, could cost the lives of the two people he held most dear. As his anger swelled within him, his focus on the task at hand intensified. He knew much of the success of this operation lay squarely on his shoulders, and his ability to move and kill with deadly force would be the only way his loved ones would survive.

He watched the plan unfold over and over in his head, thinking and imagining every move that needed to take place, as well as foreseeing any possible complications and marking them off as he found ways to counteract them. He could see it play out, much like it would on the big screen, before it occurred. He put on his Cavalier vest with his .45 Glock stuck in his back waistband as he had done a thousand times before. He practiced with the speed of a cobra strike, removing the gun and focusing it on the person staring back at him in the full-length mirror. As he'd learned to do many times before in the field, he engaged in some positive self-talk after he'd done all he could to prepare. This time, he told himself emphatically that he was ready, he knew what to do, and he would be successful saving those he loved.

Ahmed and Chase had already left and would move into place long before the Shiite's sniper made his way to the exchange site. They were counting on the sun and port activity to help conceal their activity. The rest of the operational PAL team were in place, hidden in the oil pit behind the fake wall they'd built. They had jammed the door of the entrance to the cargo bay so there would be no room to maneuver in case someone had a change of heart or something went south. Mike and Saeed would be inside waiting to carry out the exchange, knowing that the enemy sniper would have his sights drawn directly on Mike. He was counting on his hidden teammates giving him cover, as his whole focus would be on what was before him as the exchange played out.

Mike and Saeed arrived ten minutes early. They wanted to allow the enemy sniper time to radio in and give the go-ahead, even though two people were in sight rather than the one they'd demanded. Mike and Saeed drove up in the 1960s hippie van that Kent had arranged for, with red and green paint and different-colored fenders, black smoke bellowing from the exhaust. In contrast to Kent's no-nonsense get-it-done focus for a job in hand, the man could let loose with a good sense of humor at times. When Kent and Don got going, there was no stopping them.

Everyone was tense. The hippie van was a good way to keep everyone a little off balance, Mike thought as they approached. The kidnappers pulled up to the opening, and a masked, armed gunman got out of their van. He tried to open the door of the building wider. Like a barn door on rollers, the heavy door required the strength of two men, so he waved their van through the narrower opening anyway, while scouring the area looking for a trap. The van pulled through and came to a stop. Another masked man in loose black clothing got out while the driver remained in the van, staring straight ahead. The first man immediately began yelling at the two PAL agents. Saeed spoke loudly and explained he was only there to interpret for the "infidel slime" standing next to him. At this, the masked terrorist visibly relaxed his arms, allowing his weapon to drop a few inches. Saeed then told him in a Bedouin dialect that before things went any further, the "white face" wanted to see what he was buying. The Arab turned to his comrade and motioned for him to open the door. As he did, out stepped the two people who were most precious to Mike in this world. He gave the emotion a brief second before his training kicked in and he walled off his feelings, forcing his mind back to focus on accomplishing the mission.

Their heads had been covered with dirty pillowcases and their hands bound with what look like old leather straps. Mike indicated that the hoods be removed. When the light hit their faces, both the general and Stacy covered their eyes. Both appeared exhausted and dirty, but apart from the gash on his father's forehead, they did not appear injured. Mike counted three terrorists—the driver, the gunman, and the Arab making the exchange. The sniper on the roof made four. What he didn't know was whether any others were in the van.

Mike raised his hand slowly and wiped the sweat from his brow, his signal to take out the sniper. Ahmed put a bullet through the right temple of the Arab perched in the rafters high above the exchange. His kill was silent to the actors in the drama below, and as hoped, the sniper's body did not fall. Saeed translated the negotiator's demand to see the money and weapons. His team struck with a speed that stretched out in the moment, like an action scene that has been deliberately slowed. The ability of Mike's brain to slow time gave him the edge he needed to follow the events and to act at the precise instant necessary. In a burst of shattered glass that sounded like a bomb, Kent sent a bullet into the driver. Saeed wheeled around with the speed of a ninja and buried his knife three inches into the chest of the negotiator. The man stood still for a moment, looking down in horror at the handle protruding from his chest cavity before crumpling to the hard dirt floor. Mike held the sights of the Glock on the other gunman and fired three times before the man could raise his snub-nosed Uzi.

While this took place, the team hidden in the oil-change pit emerged and charged the open door of the van. Blasts of gunfire entered and blew through the walls of the vehicle. This was Don's first opportunity, and he rushed forward and rammed into the general and Stacy at the same time, knocking them both to the ground and covering them with his body in case another sniper or more terrorists appeared than they had counted on.

A bullet exploded into Mike's chest from another hidden Arab who had emerged from behind a pallet of feed bags. The shot lifted him and knocked him back three feet. With a large thud, he hit the ground. Only faintly aware of what happened next, from his position on the ground he could see the end of a barrel sticking through the fan blades of a large, ancient overhead fan. He tried to get sound past his lips, but he got nothing. He did manage to raise his arm and point, though. A female voice sounded. Stacy must have seen him, and she yelled at Don, who was standing near enough to hear.

"Look up at the fan!" she shouted, loud enough that even Mike could hear. Immediately all eyes and weapons were trained on the spot and the entire PAL team fired. The shots flew upward toward the fan, puncturing the metal in a sound of fury. The last sniper fell twenty feet to the ground, dead on impact.

For what seemed like an eternity, Mike lay on the dirt floor, ears ringing, with a pounding chest and fuzzy head, but the bulletproof vest had done its job. They were all extremely fortunate that these terrorists were not too sophisticated and did not have armor-piercing rounds. He'd be sore and have a large bruise on the right side of his chest, but he was alive. His eyes were open and unfocused, but he soon grew aware that his father's fear-filled, strikingly dark eyes were looking down at him. He didn't know if he'd ever seen fear in his father before this moment, and he knew it came out of the seasoned general's concern for him. He smiled, and his eyes closed.

Don helped Stacy to her feet, holding her tight in the tense moment. His adrenaline-fueled shout included the entire team when he said, "He'll be all right—he's got his vest on!"

Stacy burst into tears and buried her head in Don's chest as the general knelt down over his son. With a tight smile on his face he said, "Thought I taught you better than this, son. Weren't you supposed to duck?"

Mike's tight smile became a good-humored smirk, eyes closed now. His chest hurt like hell, as though it had been hit with a railroad hammer. He trembled hard with the pain and the adrenaline response. The rest of the PAL team remained focused on scouting the area, then the all-clear was given. Time to move. The kidnappers' radio squawked loudly in Arabic, asking about the money and guns they'd never see. The enemy's friends would not be far behind, so as soon as they got Mike to his feet and mobile, they cleared out in a hurry.

CHAPTER TWENTY-TWO

Eid

Nizwa

When Mike came to, his brain engaged, and he realized where he was. The pain in his chest was the first sign he was still alive. Then soft sheets and the antiseptic smell of a hospital seeped into his awareness, and realization dawned that he was in the same bed as the last time he'd been in the field hospital. As he turned his head to the side, he saw Stacy and his father asleep in reclining chairs pulled close to the bed. He hit the call button for the nurse. As she opened the door, the general awoke, his worn face lighting up with a huge smile. He reached over and said to a groggy Stacy, "Our boy's awake."

Mike mustered a bit of a smile and asked, "How long have I been out?"

The general said, "About three hours. I'm starving— we've been waiting for you to wake up to get some chow."

As the nurse checked his vitals and charted, Mike locked eyes with his girl, who smiled sweetly at him. That was the best sight in the world. Stacy's hair looked wet, but boy, did she look good. They must have both showered and changed clothes before taking up their vigil. Mike reached for her hand and looked deep into her eyes, their gaze saying much without words. The same co-ed he'd been crazy about so many years ago looked back at him with trembling lips. He could see the toll that her kidnapping and his injury had taken. Her eyes were a mix of relief and sadness, but this only enhanced her beauty, he thought. The nurse finished and took off to get him something to eat and drink.

When the cobwebs cleared, he groaned and sat up in the bed. SEAL training had conditioned him to suppress pain and get back up to continue a mission to its end, whatever that end might be.

"I have to get out of here, now," he said, trying to move. "The warhead trade takes place tomorrow, and I told Kent that I would be there, come hell or high water. This is neither."

The general uncrossed his leg and leaned forward. "I expected you would say that, but the team is on it. They have already left for Nizwa and are trying to locate the place where the trade will take place. They've been equipped with the latest in nuclear detection units and have local checkpoints set up. They're disguised as Omani police looking for an escaped convict. We've placed this escaped convict smokescreen on the front page of the morning's paper and on the radio as well." The general went on to say that this was nothing new to the area, as this sort of thing happened frequently and wouldn't arouse any suspicions. An outdated prison sat ten miles outside Nizwa's city center, further diluting any cause for suspicion, alarm, or concern for the participants of the weapons buy.

Mike picked at the tape holding the bandage that covered his chest. He needed to see how much damage his body had sustained. Stacy rose from her chair and stood by his side. She leaned over and helped him peel it off, surprising him with her attempt to join him in his personal assessment. She lifted the bandage, eyes narrowing at the obvious trauma, but not passing out or having to sit down. Good, he thought. She's not too squeamish. If they were to be together, she'd have to be strong. And God, he still wanted her.

They all looked at the damage. The bruising had spread into double grapefruit-sized circles on the upper right quadrant of his chest, and a burn mark could be seen in one spot. "Looks like you took a little Uzi fire, son," his dad said. "You'll be fine after the contusion heals."

Mike sat up, ready to move out, still connected to his IV line. "Get that nurse in here to dismiss me. I'm ready to go," he said to no one in particular. Reluctantly, Stacy went out into the hall to find her.

Mike and the general walked into the field command office on the outskirts of Nizwa and found that a flurry of activity had been taking place as the Omani military, the secret police, and PAL set up a base camp at what was affectionately known as "The Camel Dump," an outpost with line sheds that had stood for centuries. This area was located about four miles outside of Nizwa where the camels, used for long-distance desert trips, were outfitted. Here they fed them and gave them massive quantities of water before heading into the desert. As automobiles and SUVs replaced the camels, very little activity occurred at the mostly abandoned adobe hut. It was perfect for what the teams needed, as it was off the main road. If the location were not known, one would drive right past and not see it. There was no real need for anyone to visit because its location was so close to Nizwa.

Mike and his father entered the small structure, its clay walls keeping the interior cooler than one would expect. Rustic, but usable. Wouldn't be too comfortable for sleeping, but they'd have to do that at some point. Mike and the general nodded at the Omani police officer, the only other person in the hut besides Kent. Mike asked to be brought up to speed on how the op would go down.

"We've detected the warhead, set up surveillance, and secured the site," Kent said. "Apparently, our road checks were too late. We can block all roads in and out in a matter of seconds, so we'll wait until the buyers show up and then move in."

"Any word on the location of the warhead?" Mike asked.

"Not yet," Kent said. "Eid will be starting soon. The team is out with the box. Hopefully we'll get a hit soon. Our goal is to intercept the target inside the location where this 'Warrior' is holed up so we can minimize the ruckus. There's no parking in the pedestrian area of the souk, which is an advantage. We've got the local police at our disposal. We've asked them to be ready to move all vehicles in the area. Besides that, as a safeguard, all roads in and out of the city are primed and ready to be blocked."

"So now we sit and wait," John said. "Got anything to eat? We're starving."

Mike and the others sat on boxes and heated MREs on the portable stove. Jokes were traded and Mike found a use for some of Don's best. It was great to have this time in the field with his father. The camaraderie they shared seemed to him like they were equals rather than father and son. He let the moment sink in and settle in his soul. The knowledge that one of them could be killed at any time always sat like a rock in his chest, but he realized that if it did, this moment would live on. He couldn't have asked for more.

They leaned back and shut their eyes, listening to the chatter from the radio as the Omani team strolled the streets.

***

The city came alive on the first night of Eid at sundown. The team members hoped the nuclear detectors would be able to pick up radiation activity through the mud plaster walls common throughout the city. They had been informed that this construction would not hinder the detectors.

The eight Omani operatives struck off down the street on foot. The radiation detector they carried had the appearance of an old-time ghetto blaster. They walked through the streets with the pretense of celebrating the festival, stopping at booths and indulging in special foods. This was the meat Eid, and they enjoyed lamb and fish and other delicious foods. They had split the city into sectors, and all chatted and sang as they walked. These Omani secret police were Arabs from Muscat and knew the dialect. Starting out from the newly laid ring road around the outskirts of the city, they walked most of the night. Headquarters believed that the terrorists would not place the warheads close to the inner city for fear of being seen.

By 0400 the Eid crowds had died down to a few young misfits on the streets. They walked the perimeter of the city most of the night and then made their way closer to the center. Team Three entered the souk and picked up a hit of radiation. It didn't take long for the team to isolate where it was coming from.

Now that the nukes had been located, field command went into action devising a plan. As they pored over local maps and satellite photos, they agreed that they should place their most sophisticated surveillance equipment in a three-block perimeter around the location. The local police, posing as merchants, could and would block a road in seconds.

Ten PAL agents and another twenty-five undercover Omani special ops agents, posing as buyers and traders, had been placed nearby. These were the elite Omani Special Forces that had been trained by British and US military. Last, the rotating satellite had been stopped and stationed where it projected images so clear that you could see sweat on the brows of the undercover agents. Every precaution that could be thought of by the experienced team had been put into play, and each person was ready to act. All they could do now was wait.

***

Sheik Ali Al Sharif, holed up in the local home of a true believer of his cause, had surrounded himself with his own operatives. They'd gathered in a circle while he infused them with instructions and courage. Almost giddy in his anticipation of imminent success, he stood and walked around the group, laying his hands on every head and calling on Allah to bless their efforts. The house was located three blocks from the old fort in a row of tenant buildings that looked like dilapidated huts from the outside. Most of the traders lived here, behind a long brown façade with doors spaced every fifteen to twenty meters apart. Across the street were the shopkeepers' places of business. All kinds of wares and goods were sold here, from tourist trinkets to fruits and vegetables. The street stretched on for a long distance, the narrow side streets wrapping around on the ends, where more dwellings and shops could be found. This souk, or marketplace, was small, although it had the flair of the great bazaar at the port of Oman or the Grand Bazaar of Istanbul.

As Ali Al Sharif had grown in power, so had his arrogance. He was convinced no one knew he was in Nizwa—or if they did, they wouldn't know why he was there. Only this inner circle knew he carried a stash of gold and coins for trade to feed his destructive jihad wrath. Word in the underworld regarding gun running and trade was not trustworthy, and one could easily find himself shot and robbed. But Ali was too smart for petty criminals. He was sure they'd arrived undetected. What he had neglected to take into account were the nuclear signals his prized warhead was sending out. He'd never given it a thought.

CHAPTER TWENTY-THREE

The Op
Nizwa

This op would be difficult and perhaps nearly impossible, Mike thought, considering the sheer number of traders and buyers who arrived every day to visit the souk, not to mention this being the open market where locals could come and barter goods or buy at cost with discounted prices for their family's survival. On a typical day, one- to two-thousand Bedos, tourists, and traders frequented this souk.

Since the Eid had kept most everyone up breaking the fast, mornings were typically for sleeping after a late night of bingeing. A few older men moved about before daylight, eating before the day's fasting was to begin. However, nothing at all was spotted moving into or out of the target adobe. So for now, they had a waiting game, with a rotation of military personnel watching for any movement.

About an hour before sunset the second night, Eid dinners filled the souk with smells of fish, lamb, and spices once again. People visited the small stores, buying fresh vegetables and fruits for the upcoming feast. The surveillance monitors came alive when movement was detected at the door of Ali's hideout. They would hit the house full force, front and back, exactly ten minutes from the moment the team was in place.

Mike and the general made their way to the site and crouched behind a row of vehicles three blocks from the target. They were ready to move in at a moment's notice to back up the Omani Special Forces. Ali Al Sharif, with four of his most trusted followers, all heavily armed, made their way to the door being watched by the team.

At this moment, three teams moved in on the house, two from Oman and one of PAL's, making a total of fifteen. All were armed heavily and were elite fighting forces. They carried battering rams to use on the front and back doors. Eid partyers began scattering upon seeing the armed, uniformed men running and crouching. All roads within a square block area had been shut down with barriers. Everyone on the teams knew what was at stake. The first priority was to secure the warheads and then take as many prisoners alive as they could. The consequences of letting the warhead get away would be earth-shattering.

Four of the Omani military team moved stealthily to the door where the terrorists had entered. Two carried a battering ram and the other two carried their automatic weapons, ready for the assault. All four grabbed hold and slammed the ram into the crack in the middle of the double doors. Both doors ruptured inward at the same time. The startled group of men sitting at a long table jumped up and grabbed machine guns and pistols and fired into the special forces. Three of the Omani military were killed instantly, and as more team members poured into the house, most all of the inhabitants were shot and died instantly. The hope of taking a big group of prisoners was now out of the question. Although ordered to try and take as many prisoners as possible, a crazy hysteria had commenced, with the Omani police killing everyone in the room as revenge for the blood of their fallen comrades. The two large suitcases they'd witnessed being carried in were on the table, splattered with blood. Every terrorist in the room was dead.

The team blasted the second door open and made their way into the back room. Empty. However, a tunnel opening was visible on the back wall of the room, and the team immediately radioed in this intel. It looked like an old smuggler's tunnel, built years earlier, and it was dimly lit by a string of old lights hanging down on wires, one light every fifteen meters. As they descended the steps into the tunnel, they could hear movement far ahead. After the equivalent of about a half block, they entered a large room where the warhead crates had been stored. All looked to be intact except one, and it had obviously contained a warhead that was now missing. Three other Arabs lay dead near the crate. A sense of urgency rushed through the eight Omanis in the room as they radioed in what they had found. With great speed they hurried through the tunnel, hoping their prey would be slowed down by the warheads they were carrying.

***

Just as Ali Al Sharif entered the tunnel room that held the five nuclear warheads, he heard the explosion of the doors upstairs and the sound of massive gunfire. He immediately turned around and opened fired at the men with whom he was bargaining, killing all three. He'd been set up and betrayed. He broke open one of the crates and to his surprise, the warheads were there and intact. The technology gains that had taken place had produced a lethal weapon half the size of what a typical nuclear device would have been ten years earlier. Ali ordered his two young followers, who were speechless and scared, to hoist the warhead onto the shoulder of one of the largest muscle-built men in the Middle East. He was six foot four and could bench press a VW. Ali knew he would have no problem keeping up as they made their escape.

He hollered, *"Yella, yella,"* encouraging them to hurry as they took off through the opening into the next section of tunnel. They passed several wooden ladders going up to other adobe homes. They continued on with cat-like stealth, passing three more ladders, and Ali had one of his men climb the ladder and open the door to a house. Lucky for them, no one was home, but his hope was that the followers would have to follow up each outlet, thus buying the Yemenis more time to escape. He'd blow the tunnel behind them with the two sticks of dynamite he carried and hope for a cave-in, thus allowing them to slip away. His pursuers would have created a perimeter, but what Ali did not know was how wide their perimeter was. He'd have to trust Allah for guidance.

They continued to move swiftly through the now-darkened tunnel. Ali and his two young followers, along with the large man carrying the warhead, had put a good distance between themselves and the pursuers. One pulled out a flashlight, turning it on so they could all see. Ali held up his hand for them to stop, and from his backpack he pulled out a thin, wired claymore mine. As Ali set the mine behind a stud and ran the wire across the tunnel, he smiled, knowing this would be a devastating blow. It would kill anyone within a half kilometer and would certainly slow the rest of the pursuers. They continued on down the tunnel, gaining more distance.

***

The explosion rocked the inside of the narrow-walled tunnel, whose ceiling was held up with rotten planks. Two of the Omanis were badly injured, and one was killed. One of the soldiers had a piece of old splintered wood penetrating his side, and it had ripped him almost in two. The other soldier's head had been split open but he was still alive. Another soldier had been standing directly beneath the spot where the explosion had taken place. He was killed instantly.

The Omani Special Forces were wearing body cameras, their activities being transmitted to all involved with the op. An eerily dusty haze where the hole in the ceiling had been became the only light in the tunnel apart from scattered holes in the ceiling before and behind them where light filtered through the floorboards. Cameras projected all of this back to field headquarters. The remaining three men on the team had been split, with no way through the obstruction.

***

Ali, his three followers, and the ballistic warhead continued to move as fast as possible through the tunnel. They were sure there would be a perimeter set up but weren't sure how wide the net would be or the location of the last exit up to the street. As they moved, they whispered that this was probably a smuggler's tunnel, built to move guns or hide escaping political prisoners from the nearby prison. A small amount of noise was coming from just ahead, as Eid was now in full swing, with families having dinner and celebrating with music. Otherwise, the tunnel was quiet, and they weren't sure, but they thought they heard movement behind them.

Ali had one of his men climb the next ladder and look to see if it was safe to move up into the city. As the tunnel wound around, they were unclear where they were in relation to their truck. This was a chance they would have to take. The opening would place them in an alley somewhere in the city. Once up on the streets, they would not have any problems getting their bearings, as all streets and passages were centered around the ancient fort. As the Yemenis peered out from underneath the wooden door into the alley, in the corner Ali spotted a large pile of trash next to a wagon wheel and broken storage boxes. They climbed out into fresh air and set down their prized warhead, swiftly dragging everything they could over the door they had just come through. They were only able to salvage one warhead, since the Omanis had taken them by surprise. The two Yemeni followers, along with Ali, took turns carrying the thirty-four-kilo bomb and hoping they had successfully tricked or thrown the pursuers off that it was not a passable doorway. What Ali and his team did not know was that the nuclear detection units his enemies had with them were true tracking devices. Ali was relying on deception and was clearly unaware of the newest technology that would pinpoint his location. He and his men hoisted the bomb back onto the giant's shoulder, picked up their rifles, and moved toward the end of the alley so they could get a better understanding of where they were.

***

A five-man group remained of the Omani Special Forces on Ali's side of the cave-in. These men had continued to pursue the Yemenis. They tried each door as they passed it, but all were locked. When they came to the door that Ali and his team had blockaded, they couldn't open it, so they continued on down the darkened tunnel. Ali's deception had worked. But his was a short-lived victory, as the Omani Special Forces didn't have far to go. Only a hundred meters ahead, the tunnel ended abruptly. The men turned back, once again, to the doorway next to the one Ali and his team had blocked. They broke through and moved upward, startling a family when they came up through the floor boards into their living space. The family had just sat down for dinner. The startled bunch screamed while the five-man team begged forgiveness. They left the dilapidated home and entered the street, not far from where the three Yemenis had come out of the hole, but they saw nothing.

CHAPTER TWENTY-FOUR

The Bomb

Ali kept his little group moving slowly through the streets. Night fell, and the evening shone with millions of sparkling stars. At every other pole in the souk hung what looked like colored Christmas lights, with strands running down the streets like garlands, adding to the festive atmosphere. As Ali and company came to each street and alley crossing, they peered cautiously around each corner, hoping to get a glimpse of the old fort tower so they could maintain a sense of direction. After moving three streets over, they saw what they were looking for. Their biggest problem now was that the tunnels had taken them to the opposite side of the fort, away from their van. Ali's next move was going to be tricky. He could seek shelter in one of the homes and hide until all was clear, but this was not really an option. All three were covered in dust, and they would not be welcome in just anyone's home.

After a frank discussion, it was agreed that their best chance would be to continue to move and try and make it to the van, then they'd exit the city on the old camel trail they believed would not have security, again thinking they could make it to safety with deception and cunning versus technology. Ali and his men weren't far from their van now, the path to freedom in reach, the jihad almost within their grasp. Sweat poured down their dust-covered faces, leaving light streaks and giving the appearance of zebra masks. Almost there, Ali thought, almost there.

***

As Mike and the general watched everything unfold, they took off to where they thought Ali was headed. When they rounded the corner, they spotted the five Omani Special Forces entering the street. They approached and combined forces with the Omani team while the beeping increased in volume and speed. The lighted green screen on the detector showed the movement of the nuclear warhead. Bingo! They were very close.

Mike's team and the Omani forces fanned out on both sides of the signal's location and tried to surround the terrorists. The rest of the search team moved in from the opposite side, boxing the prey in completely. The overhead satellite picked up three images moving toward the north side of the fort. Their target was two streets over, moving slowly. Satellite surveillance enabled them to radio to Mike and the general. The images were only bodies moving. As the satellite was tracking what was going on, Mike and the general could move concurrently along with Ali. When they received it, the plan was to capture the three, although Mike and the general knew there would be little or no chance of that.

As they closed in, Mike caught a glimpse of what looked like the Incredible Hulk's brother, presumably carrying the warhead. The sheer strength of this giant to carry a thirty-five-kilo bomb on his shoulder amazed Mike. What's more, the goliath moved like a leopard on soft feet. They rounded the corner at the edge of the fort's tower. The structure looked over the entire city, a picture of strength from days long ago.

Music filled the air, and dancing, celebration, and laughter echoed off the walls as the whole city celebrated the meat Eid. This is the second, and holier, of the two solemn festivals, honoring Abraham for the sacrifice of his son Isaac as an act of obedience to God's command. An animal sacrifice is made, and the meat is divided in three parts. One for the poor, one for relatives, friends, and neighbors, and the last third for the family. And not one person realized that running through the streets of their city was a weapon of mass destruction that could destroy the entire Middle East and possibly cause a global war.

At this moment, twenty Omani Special Forces surrounded the area where Ali's van sat. They had infiltrated and had four men inside the vehicle. The noose tightened on the three-block perimeter. Mike and the general were coming from behind their prey, and they caught another glimpse of the terrorists looking over at their van parked on Main Street, where automobiles were still allowed to move. Most of the inner city was now blocked to traffic. What Ali and his team could not see was the sniper posted in the tower above, or the other Special Forces hidden behind donkey carts, cars, and corners. The terrorist group moved slowly toward the van.

Mike turned to his father and said, "I have my suspicions that one of these is the Warrior Sheik himself."

The general whispered back, "All hell is going to break loose since Ali killed one of the Secret Police and injured two others, and they won't have any restraint. If we move in right now, maybe we can capture and question one of the three."

Mike nodded and began to move. He didn't hesitate as he rounded the corner and yelled at the top of his lungs for Ali to stop. "*Minfadlic, minfadlic!*"

As he closed in, Ali turned, and Mike paused involuntarily. The man's eyes appeared blood-red, and streaks ran down his scarred face. His visage was a mask of horror. What made the gruesome scarring worse was the expression in his eyes, which were narrowed with hate. His two comrades stopped dead in their tracks. As one raised his Uzi in Mike's direction, a bullet exploded through his chest and his remains splattered all over the weightlifter. The giant stood tall, with his Herculean appearance, the bomb balanced on his shoulder. As he slowly swung around, he raised his free hand and pointed what looked to be a Mafia-style tommy gun at Mike. All at once, several dozen spots of blood appeared in his chest. The bomb dropped and every breath stopped while both it and the giant fell toward the ground. The big man landed on his knees, the bomb right between them. Even those who knew it would not explode couldn't help but cringe.

Two more rounds hit him, and the back of his head exploded. He was dead instantly. The general had been right, all hell had broken loose. Mike watched as the

Omani Special Forces filled the street seeking vengeance. Ali jumped behind a car that was parked next to him, cursing as his plans evaporated before his eyes.

CHAPTER TWENTY-FIVE

On the Run

When the first shots were fired and the giant went down, total chaos erupted. Doors opened and men with guns poured into the square. All hell was about to break loose as screaming women wailed and armed Bedouin men took in all that was happening. Yelling—screams— it was a nightmare.

The old jeep behind which Ali crouched had been given no restoration and had not run in twenty years or more. The vehicle was more rust than paint. A metal-on-metal noise behind him made him whirl around. A door swung out from the front of the shack and standing in the opening was a girl not much older than seven years. Hard to tell, with such a quick look. He backed toward her, and she stood still, paralyzed. When he turned, she saw his grotesque face and screamed. He swooped her up with one arm, and when a man appeared at the door, Ali shot him dead. The girl wailed and kicked.

"*Ya baba, ya baba*," she screamed. He'd killed the girl's father right in front of her. Ali yelled at her to stop screaming, but she wouldn't, or couldn't. He pointed the Glock at the girl's head. Everyone froze.

Ali couldn't have cared less. He would use the infidels' weaknesses to his advantage, knowing that what was left of the Omani forces would not fire for fear they'd hit the girl. He moved along the dusty street with his back to the adobe facade, using it as protection from behind, and the girl as an angel for a shield. They moved in a slow-motion waltz. A waltz of tragedy, Ali thought.

The young girl continued to wail, and Ali rasped out in Arabic, "Stand back! Don't follow, or the girl will meet Allah!"

The Omanis froze in place at this atrocity. They had not been taught to deal with civilians in harm's way, especially with a little girl's life at stake. If they approached, this madman would kill the girl, and with her father already dead, tensions had skyrocketed.

Ali moved along the wall, holding the girl up and protecting his torso, the gun pointed at her temple. He approached the van. Ali's followers had placed the van there earlier in the day, and the van's placement had been caught on-screen by the PAL satellite. Ali approached the back of the van and threw open the back door, fumbling a bit as he held the girl and the pistol. When it opened, Ali turned, holding the girl in front of him and facing the van. The three Omani Special Forces came face to face with the petite young girl. They held their fire, and it cost them their lives. Ali fired on all three, and they were dead before they knew what hit them.

He jumped into the back of the van, flinging the girl toward the front. With a quiet laugh he muttered, "You never know, I may need the child again." He kicked two of the dead bodies out the back and they thudded onto the street. Then he slammed the rear door, climbed into the driver's seat, and started the engine.

The Omani team, as well as the PAL operatives, followed him slowly up the street, staying back about a half block, as they did not want to risk firing and hitting the girl. This Yemeni would not hesitate to kill either the girl or any of them. This outcome would be tragic as well as costly.

The Omani team leader had watched this unfold and he began posturing and withdrawing. The remaining team members gathered around the Omanis and heated words broke out. Ahmed translated when the communication flagged. Apparently, they were not willing to risk any more deaths for this madman. Three more of their men were dead. They had secured the warhead, and if they stopped now, they would not be blamed if the girl did not survive. Much bigger ramifications could be levied on them if the girl was killed while they tried to save her. None of them showed much grief, even after three more of their comrades had died at the hands of Ali. Jamil had taught Mike the hard fact that life has a different value here than what is perceived in Western society, and these men said they could live with the truth that they'd helped stop a nuclear attack. The team leader would be rewarded and given medals for what they had already accomplished, so why should he risk any more soldiers?

The Omani leader said, "Allah has allowed us success. We will live to fight another day. He will set the girl free, so it shall be."

Mike, the general, and the three other PAL operatives could see what was unfolding. The Omanis would not pursue any further, giving Mike's team no further support from their allies. They were on their own. The Omanis, wanting no more of the pursuit, understandably wanted to avoid any political implications. Mike grimaced. This pulling out ate into his craw, even his very soul. None of the PAL team could fathom allowing Ali to escape, and Mike could not fathom letting him have the girl.

General O'Shea drew in a harsh breath. "Nope! Not happening. Not on our watch!" He made eye contact with the team, who all nodded in agreement. They took off on foot at a dead trot, knowing their chances of catching the van were probably nil.

As they rounded a corner, they were nearly broadsided by a jacked-up jeep with desert tires and KC lights. Almost as if it were scripted, Don raised an arm from the driver's seat, and with a jovial look on his face, he hollered, "What's wrong, girls? The bad guys are getting away! Get your butts on board!"

All five jumped into the open jeep as Mike looked over at Don with surprise. Don said, "Been followin' what you boys have been up to the past hour or so from the eye in the sky." He smirked. "I can't leave you fellars alone to finish anything!"

Mike smiled and said, "Shut up and drive. They got a kid, and that Arab is nuts."

Don looked over at the general and said meekly, "Just kiddin' about the 'girls' comment, General!"

John O'Shea leveled a look at Don, then Mike, and then back to Don and said, "Shut up and drive, Sailor!"

"Yes sir, General." Don kicked it in gear and slammed on the accelerator.

The general looked across at his team and said, "He isn't going to come in alive, boys, so pull up your bootstraps and let's take this bad guy out once and for all."

Almost in unison the passengers yelled, "Roger that, General." He smiled and said, "Let's go get that SOB."

***

Ali had the advantage. He'd traded many times at the fort and knew the streets. He'd rehearsed this escape route with his team. He wound around the narrow streets, turning tight corners at different intersections in case he was being followed. He took a quick look in his rearview mirror. "Nothing," he said to himself. He began to relax, thinking he'd made a good escape.

His mind wandered to what his next move would be, giving not a care in the world as to what had just happened, those he'd personally killed, or the loud whimpers from the child behind him. He just did not care. This was a jihad, and to him the dead were casualties of war. Just like the girl's father. The girl might be sent to her death also, but she might be one he could make his personal slave. He smiled at this. Just a year or two more—he liked the young ones. A sick smile scrolled across his face.

The girl continued to wail. Ali yelled at her in Arabic. "Shut up or I will kill you!" He meant to scare her with his wicked look and his staunch command. Even at her young age, she knew her hysteria had to be controlled, so she whimpered quietly. Good, he thought. Her training would start now.

Now that he had some silence, Ali focused on the road, constantly checking the rearview mirror in case he was being followed. If he could get to the outskirts of town and on the camel trail that only the old locals used, he'd be home free.

A wave of rage suddenly washed over him. How had it come to this? The opportunity to grab the nukes was wasted, but he had to focus on his next move and ensure that he didn't lose everything. If he could escape this ordeal, he would live to fight another day. He replayed the night's activities, and his rage built. He sped toward the outskirts of the city. Ten more kilometers and he'd be home free. Then, in his gruffest voice, he grumbled out loud. "They will pay. They will all pay."

CHAPTER TWENTY-SIX

Confrontation

Mike, Don, the general, and the rest of the PAL team chattered on the radio with the makeshift local headquarters. A helicopter had been dispatched as the team at the PAL center watched the progress of this chase. Unbeknownst to Ali, he, as well as the PAL team on the ground, were being tracked by satellite. The Omanis he had killed earlier in the van had placed a tracking device on the inner floorboard, out of sight. The PAL team received directions from HQ through the transmitter, and Ali's every movement was radioed in to the jeep. The jeep paralleled the van from two blocks over, keeping pace with him at every turn, just out of sight. They watched his path and soon realized they had a very good idea where he was headed.

The local sheik, who was a longtime resident of Nizwa as well as the Omani governor of the region, were both in the PAL headquarters tent, watching the op on-screen. He informed them of the location of the camel trail and thought that would be Ali's most logical route. The sheik had been summoned by the local authorities to help. It had been more of an order than a request.

They had guessed right about Ali's route. It was agreed that they would take Ali in the desert, outside the city, in case this whole incident got any uglier. They'd called for air support. Now word had come in that a band of Omani special forces was coming in from the north. If that were true, they'd be able to cut off Ali's only escape route, and there'd be no turning back once he entered the wadi. He'd be trapped. What they didn't know was how to get to him to stop the van without carrying out a suicide run, head-on into any car they might plant to block his path. The bigger issue was how they'd get him out of the van and into the open once his van had been blockaded. Most important was how to do this without getting the girl killed.

The emotion and hysteria this situation had created with the locals in the city was escalating and would only get worse. If they could not get the girl back alive, the local sheik had implied that the entire Omani special forces unit, as well as the police, would lose all credibility, and more chaos would take place. Not to mention that the local sheik would be blamed and would most likely not see morning sunrise. He would be hunted down by the townspeople and held accountable, for he was seen as the national government.

Almost pleading, the sheik said, "This could set our law and order back a hundred years." As these were desert people, they operated under Tribal Law—Sharia Law—the law of the Koran, and it had taken a long time to get the locals to trust the Omani Centralized Government to enforce laws fairly and with justice according to a different set of principles. They would first blame him for everything, then they'd blame the government. This could be comparable to the 1940s in the United States' Bible Belt, were everyone carried a gun and no one from the federal government was trusted.

***

As Ali turned into a wadi, he caught his first glimpse of headlights coming toward him. This was no coincidence—they had found him. His breathing quickened, his eyes glazed over, and as he knew well, he was trapped in this canyon. He had to calm himself, get control of his emotions, and think. What could he do? They were here to kill him. He heard the girl whimper, and then again that grotesque, eerie smile came across his face. He slammed on the brakes and turned the wheel hard to the right, which caused the van to skid sideways into the ditch running along the makeshift trail. He grabbed the girl by her hair and dragged her out behind the van.

She screamed, an ear-piercing sound borne of terror and pain. He knew he was hurting her, but her repulsion of his looks, as though he were a monster, added fuel to his generalized anger. He would wait until they caught up with him, then he would again use the girl as a shield. He'd trade her for the last vehicle in the infidel's convoy and make his escape. They would give in. They were weak, and he was Ali the Warrior Sheik. He did not fear the lesser Omanis and certainly not the weakling Americans. With little or no light, he figured he had the advantage. His overriding arrogance and disrespect for those pursuing him at this point overshadowed his ability to think rationally. As he sat behind the van with the young girl on his lap, he laughed, petting the girl's hair like she was one of the Siberian Huskies he kept in the mountains. She continued to whimper and sob in spite of his petting, but he only smiled malevolently and laughed his sickening laugh.

***

The tracker on the van showed the team that Ali had stopped, about six clicks out from the city and two kilometers ahead of the pursuing PAL jeep. On screen, the eye in the sky reported that the van was stopped on the side of the road at the next turn.

Mike yelled, "Stop right here, kemosabe. I want out."

Don slammed on the brakes and Mike jumped out. Don and the general watched, puzzled. Mike spoke to the guys sitting in the back of the jeep on top of a storage unit. "Sergeant, get into that locker and hand me that sniper rifle. Get the night scope in the case next to it."

Mike looked at his dad, then over at Don, who was still in the driver's seat. He said, "Listen, pards, I want you to ease up on the van. I mean, slow—so slow—like you're driving that high school homecoming float. You remember, don't ya?"

Don nodded.

"When you round the bend, throw on all the lights we have on this bad boy. I want him blinded and focused on the jeep. He has no idea how many of us there are. We will use this to our advantage."

"He won't think there was enough time for a sniper, or anyone, to get a jump on him," Don said.

Mike grinned at his pal. "Slowly, my Texas comrade, go slowly. I've got a hell of a hike to make, if this is going to work. This should give me enough time to climb that hill and get in place for a clean shot." He moved around the jeep to the general and said, "Maybe I can get this trophy hanger on our wall, Dad."

General O'Shea clapped his son on the back, and with pride, he smiled his approval. "Go get 'em, Mike."

Then Mike addressed the other marines who had blank looks and said, "That's what we call a Texas wall hanger. A trophy buck, only this is not one to be proud of, this is just one that needs killin', and I have had enough."

The general said, "Wind and elevation son, wind and elevation." Mike knew exactly what he was implying. *Make it a perfect shot.*

Mike turned to Don. "Now pards, don't go out and try to play the Alamo. We got this one. Just buy me some time to get this bastard in my sights. You read me, Sailor? You're gonna make me awfully upset if you go and get yourself shot. Ya hear me, now?"

"Roger that, cuz." Don grinned at his longtime friend who had taken off at a trot, and the jeep began to creep along at a snail's pace.

The general turned and shouted at Mike. "That goes for you too, son!"

***

Mike gave a quick two-fingered salute and headed straight up the volcanic rock mountain. After a few minutes, all they could see was a black shadow moving slowly up the mountainside.

The general gazed out, straight ahead, and to no one in particular he said, "I estimate it will take him about ten minutes to get to the top and another five or so to get a good bead on our bad guy. Just to be on the safe side, let's try and buy him twenty-five minutes or so."

Don hesitated while he absorbed the general's words, and with an audible lump in his throat for his buddy, he said, "Roger that, sir. He's got this."

To everyone's relief, the Omanis had succumbed to common sense and had decided not to abandon the Americans after all. The team communicated with the Omanis coming from the north, instructing them to slow their pace to the showdown. It wasn't quite the same as the long-simmering feud at the O.K. Corral, but this had all the drama of that infamous 1881 gunfight, and if this evening's events were ever recorded, they would closely mimic the legend that took place in Tombstone, Arizona Territory. But no one would ever know this particular event had taken place—that PAL had intercepted a nuclear weapon that would have changed the world, and not for the better. Nor would they know that death had occurred to people in this desert far from American soil, or that American soldiers died today, sacrificing their lives to save many more. Their families would be told that they'd been killed in a training accident. Only a handful of people would know the truth. The general reminded himself that the right people would know, and that would have to be enough. They'd taken out the bad guys, saved lives, and kept order in the region and possibly in all of Western Europe. His next thoughts turned to the terrified girl and his son, who scoured the mountainside in search of a place from which to take aim at a monster.

As the groups converged on Ali from both the north and the south, the general turned to the marines in the back and said, "Either of you two boys speak Arabic?" It surprised the general when the younger one, who couldn't be much older than the required eighteen, said, "Roger, General, fluently."

When he saw the general's puzzled look he said, "General, I grew up in Saudi. My pa was an old wildcatter working for Aramco, and his pa, my granddad, did also. I grew up with Saudi nannies and lived most of my life in Riyadh. Most of the kids I played with and went to school with were Arabs." He smiled and said, "Hell, General, I can speak better lingo than most of the locals."

Taken aback, the general said, "The Saudi Oil Company? What's your name, son?"

"Colton, sir, Corporal Colton Karpent."

"Well, Colton, you're my guy!" The general smiled. "You've just been promoted to translator on this cluster. You up for that, son?"

"Roger that, sir!"

"Okay, I want you to stall that bastard as long as you can. I don't care what you tell him, just get him talking and stall him. We need to give Mike time to get into position. You might also offer him a chance to surrender, give himself up, tell him we if he lets the girl go, we will be easy on him."

Colton listened intently to the general's suggestions and frowned. The general could see the marine's unhappiness and said, "Okay soldier, what's the problem?"

Colton gulped and look down, then back up, meeting the general's eyes. "General, I don't think that is our best approach."

John looked at the young marine and said, "Why's that, son?"

Colton was obviously nervous speaking up to a general, especially General O'Shea. He was scared as hell and certainly intimidated in the presence of this legend, especially to disagree with him in the middle of an op at a critical time, but he went on, full steam ahead.

"Look, General, 1 know these people, especially these radicals. I have seen and dealt with these guys for years, starting when they were young punks, watching their behavior all the way through, until they turned into dirt bags like our guy out there."

"Go on. What is it you think we should do?" The general was listening and looking intently at his young corporal.

"Well, General, I think we should call him out, question his manhood, his religion, and his bravery. In other words, piss him off and get him talking. I have found that when you challenge scum buckets like this, they tend to talk, then to lose control and become blowhards or braggarts. They want you to know they are not afraid. But deep down, they are. Most, I say most, General, will tell you all about their bravery and how big a stud they think they are. It is emotional to them. Usually they will repeat themselves over and over. The more they say it out loud to themselves, the more they believe it."

"Okay," the general said, "how are we going to get him to stand and talk to us?"

The marine swallowed and said, "That's where you come in, General. He will most certainly talk to you. Although he has no regard for Americans, none whatsoever, and in this guy's case, apparently no regard for anyone, he will talk to you."

"And why do you think he will talk to me, son?" the general said, still skeptical.

"General, you're 'big *wasta*' to him!"

The General looked back. "*Wasta*?"

"That's right, General, *wasta*! Powerful, important. Think of it this way. As our Native Americans of old would say, 'big medicine.' General, he will talk to you, 'cause you're big medicine in his eyes. That boy up there has probably never spoken to such a high-ranking military man as you. He will want to measure himself against you. Most of these punks want to prove they have big *wasta* also. No better way than to have him come face to face with you. He will jump at the opportunity."

The general paused, head in his hands, thinking about the young marine's words. When he raised his head, his mind was made up, but he had another question.

"And how, son, do you propose we let this dirt bag know that I am big medicine—big *wasta*?"

Colton smiled. "I will lie to him, sir! Well, not completely, sir." Colton was a little embarrassed, turning a light shade of red, but he went on. "What I mean, General, sir, I mean, after all, you are two-star general John O'Shea, sir, and in the circles I run in, that is big medicine. I will just embellish a little more, and I mean no disrespect. I mean, you are important, with big *wasta*." He had begun to stammer.

The general smiled and said, "Relax. I get it. I don't care if you tell him I date dogs or even howl at the moon, just get him talking to me or to you, I don't give a damn. I need to buy some time, sailor, you got me?"

"Roger that, sir," Colton chimed in.

Don smiled, easing the jeep forward around the bend. The general looked over at him and said, "Wipe that smile off your face, soldier."

Don couldn't do it and just said, "Aye, aye, sir," and kept grinning as they moved closer to the van.

The Omanis were approaching from the north in the same fashion, with KC off-road lights on, the new powerful LED lights coming from both sides of the trail. They lit up the entire van as well as the hillside behind it, giving it an eerie glow. The clarity of illumination was astonishing.

***

Ali was sweating, although with the sun down, it was cold. The desert fried you by day and froze you at night. The girl next to him shivered violently and continued to whimper. He couldn't care less about her. He'd deal with her later, and she would learn and know he was master. Caught off guard, the sudden illumination from the jeep's lights made him slam his eyes shut. With gun in hand, he raised his arm to shield the light, cracking his eyes. He had been about to yell out his demands when the speaker crackled from the jeep that had followed him in.

"Sheik Ali, I have with me Big American General O'Shea. He wants to talk to you. If you're not afraid," the voice said, in perfect Saudi dialect.

Ali paused, needing to think. Afraid? He was not afraid of any man, especially an American general. This insulted him, so he waited.

The speaker came on again with a slight echo. "I told the general you would be too fearful to talk to him. He thinks you are a coward. He wanted to look into the eyes of a true warrior, a worthy adversary, but he didn't think the son of a camel farmer would be such a man."

To Ali, this was an insult, and his blood boiled. He would look this general in the eyes before he killed him. He would let him know that Ali Al Sharif was not a small man, but a great man, a true warrior. Not like those American officers who sit behind their desks and don't know honor and true jihad. He would tell him, and then kill him.

Ali yelled back at the jeep in Arabic. "Tell this general I will speak with him. I want to see the fear in his cowardly eyes. He is a pig. He is not worthy of my words, but I will speak with him before he dies."

CHAPTER TWENTY-SEVEN

The Shot

The general whispered to Colton. "Now what. How do we move forward?"

Colton said, "I will go out and meet with him first. I'll go unarmed with my shirt off and my hands held high. I will try and get him to meet me halfway, with my arms on my head, no threat to him. He will probably be holding the girl as a shield, as he will not trust us, once he moves toward me. I will tell him that you are coming to meet him."

The general nodded and continued to listen.

"Look General, he is going to be all worked up and pissed, as you have questioned his manhood as well as having insulted his family. He won't know a word of what you are saying, so just leave this to me and pretend you're telling me to say things to him. Let me handle it. We will let him talk and he will probably start yelling. Look him straight in the eyes and show no emotion whatsoever. And whatever you do, do not lose eye contact. If you do, he will see this one of two ways—as either a weakness or a trap. General, if we play our cards right, this should take no longer than five or ten minutes, depending how worked up he is and whether I can get him cooled down. My guess is that he is pretty worked up, so let's be sure we keep this thing going as long as we can and get him to tell us what he wants to do. If we're successful getting him to talk, it may take a bit longer."

"You're a godsend, Colton," the general said, his voice still low, matching the young man's tone.

"I'm hopin' the lieutenant got to the top of that mountain and is able to get a clean shot. Arabs like to talk with their hands, so I am also hoping that this guy gets worked up enough to lower the girl and give us a clean shot. You okay with all that, General?"

"Roger that, Corporal!"

Colton pulled his shirt off, and as he did, the general said, "Listen, son, if that bastard out there lifts a gun toward you, I want you to move as fast as you can and get behind me. I have a cavalier tactical vest on that is able to take a handgun hit. We know he carries a Glock, and my vest can handle that caliber. You hear me, son?"

Colton smiled grimly. "Roger that, sir."

***

Mike was on the move. It was slow going, the sharp, protruding lava rocks making it difficult to proceed quickly without injuring an ankle, and he knew he could not afford to let that happen. It was cold out, but Mike had worked up a sweat, climbing as fast and as carefully as he could. When he'd made it about halfway up, he saw the jeep round the corner, and he got a glimpse of the van pulled off to the side. They were getting close. Mike knew he'd have to take a chance and get moving faster. Drawing on all of his speed and ability, he pushed on up the mountain. If he didn't make it, their efforts would all be for nothing.

He pulled hard, hand over hand on the steep terrain, then pushed forward more quickly on the flatter surface—like running wind sprints in college. When he finally reached the top, muscles burning and fingers cramping, he knew he had to be careful. He couldn't dislodge any rocks or make any sound whatsoever. Complete stealth was needed to get into position so he could take a shot at this monster.

He found a bit of clearing and quietly moved some sharp lava rocks around enough to give him a surface where he could lie down. He assembled his rifle in record time as he had done hundreds of times during his training. As he was attaching his scope, he heard someone using the loudspeaker. He was too far up to understand what was being said, but from the bits he got it wouldn't have mattered, because the voice spoke in Arabic.

He attached his scope, put his tripod down, lowered his sniper rifle, and looked through the night scope. He could see clearly now. The scope gave off a light green haze, but the clarity of the new Bushnell Equinox Z scope was amazing, and Mike could see everything quite well.

As he looked way down below at what was going on, he said to himself, "What the hell?"

The young marine who had been in the back of the jeep had his shirt off, walking with his hands on his head toward the van. Mike shifted the scope to the van and caught glimpses of the girl and the Arab.

Mike couldn't find out what exactly was going on. He tried to speak into his mic but got nothing. Had it broken? Must have been damaged when he slipped and fell on the lava rocks early in his climb. He quickly adjusted his sights and made the calculations on distance, wind, and speed, to ensure a clean shot. He waited, then he saw the Arab move toward the front of the van with his back against it, holding the girl in front of him. Mike had, at best, a head shot, but with the kid in the way, the odds were not good for missing the kid. He knew he could kill Ali, but the girl was too big a risk at this point. He would sit, be patient, and hope the Arab would make a mistake.

As he watched, he saw movement coming from the jeep. He continued to sweep the kill zone, then he froze, wiping his eyes as the sweat poured off of him. His father—not the general, but his dad—was out of the jeep and walking forward behind the young shirtless marine. What was he doing? This was crazy. This Arab had taken out and killed, without any hesitation, more than six people, tonight alone. For the first time, fear came over Mike—not for himself, but for the man that meant everything to him. Mike knew that his dad trusted that he'd made it to the top and would deliver the shot. What if he missed? What if he didn't have a clear shot and had to make a choice, the girl or his dad? What if he wasn't fast enough? Mike was near panic, as he hadn't counted on this. His breathing became rapid and he fought it, continuing to sweat, again wiping his burning eyes.

A cool wisp of air came across, and its effect was like being slapped in the face. Mike had to calm down, breathe slow, and use the confidence that he'd made this shot a hundred times at this range. He'd also made this shot every year for the past eight, hunting with his dad.

With a wicked smile, he said to himself, "Mike O'Shea, you got this!"

Funny, he thought, that sounded like Stacy and was just the extra boost he needed. He focused on only the Arab. Moving steadily, adjusting ever so slightly, he tried to produce a clean shot. He knew it would take only one. All he needed was a split second.

CHAPTER TWENTY-EIGHT
The Outcome

The general looked over at Don and said, "Listen, son, if I raise my left arm, I want you to have that helicopter throw a spotlight on that bastard. I am hoping when he looks up, he will drop the girl enough to let our boy up there have a clean shot. You wait for my signal, but if this thing starts to go bad, do it anyway and kill the SOB, you got me?"

"Roger that, sir, left arm up or no other choice." The smile had finally left Don's face.

John zeroed in on Colton, walking slowly out toward the van. He held his hands high and moved carefully, with no quick or deliberate motions. John could see him shaking, but he was trying his best to not let anyone see his fear. As he approached, John whispered to himself for Colton's benefit as well as his own, "You got this, you got this!"

Colton stopped ten meters from the front of the van. He and John both had a clear view of the girl and could see the terror in her eyes as tears rolled down her cheeks. She was held up in Ali's arms, and peeking around her straggled hair, John could see the eyes of Ali burning out of his scarred face.

Ali al Sharif moved his eyes back and forth. When that wasn't enough, he turned his head, looking from the jeep back to the Omani Hummer and then back again. When he did this, John and Colton got a much better look at the horror the little girl had become familiar with. His visage was something out of a Bela Lugosi silent horror film, except this was not makeup, this was real. Colton had a hard time disguising his reaction, and Ali took notice.

"What's the matter, American, you afraid to look at The Great One?"

In order to get started and set the tone, Colton smirked. He looked him directly in the eye and said, "Show me The Great One!"

Ali's smile morphed into a stern mask, as this pissed him off. In his most commanding voice he said, "I will not speak to a fly of a camel's ass. Send this cowardice general to me."

Colton slowly turned and whistled to the general, who stood in partial shadow fifty meters back. "You're on, sir, come on out. He's plenty pissed off, so go slow, General. We don't know what this dirt bag is going to do."

Right on cue, the general moved out from behind the jeep and stood tall and strong, an imposing figure in anyone's book. He had a .45 pistol stuck in the back waistband of his pants, hidden partially by his vest. He was hoping that if he was asked to turn around, it would be concealed enough so the Arab would not see it. That was a chance he would take, so he'd be armed. He figured even if the Arab saw it, being armed would show he didn't trust him, either.

The general moved forward at a slow walk. He wasn't sure if Mike had made it and was watching this, but again, it was another chance he'd have to take. As he walked, he considered what to have Colton tell this coward. When he reached the bare-chested marine, he nodded at him, not even looking at Ali. He was sending a message, and this offended Ali immediately. He yelled in Arabic at the two marines in front of him. "What, this Big American General with all of his *wasta* is afraid to look at The Great One?"

The general slowly turned his head and looked Ali in the eyes and smirked. This enraged the man even more.

"Why does this general laugh at The Great One, the man who is going to kill him and all Americans?" Colton translated.

The general, still smirking, looked him dead in the eyes and laughed. "I don't know, but I thought this so-called Great One would be taller and not such a coward to hide behind the skirts of little girls. All the Great Warriors I know don't cower to such levels but stand tall in front of the men they are afraid of."

Colton said to the general in English, "He's pretty riled up, sir. I seen this before. You sure you want me to say that to him?"

The general did not lower or take his eyes off Ali. He continued to stare and smirk. "Every damn word, exactly like I told you."

This was a dangerous game, testing who was the biggest, baddest dog on the playground, and the general had been in this position before. He wasn't about to let this lunatic rattle him. Colton translated every word, and that's when the general saw the doubt in Ali's eyes. But his message really got the terrorist going. As if on cue, just as Colton had said, Ali began to yell in Arabic, waving his gun hand, and his yell turned to a strange scream.

Colton leaned over to the general and said, "Hell, General, that didn't take long to get him riled up. He's plenty mad, no telling what he's gonna do now."

The general continued to stare, not moving a muscle, the smirk still on his face. He could see it in the Arab's eyes, the look he'd seen a million times in men he'd led into battle. This Yemeni was terrified.

Ali, almost hysterical at the blatant disrespect, had begun to lose control. His yelling became more intense, and as they stood, it gave John the impression that they were no more than schoolyard bullies, standing toe to toe. The general stared him down and the Yemeni yelled with rage. John O'Shea was trying to buy as much time as he could. As their standoff continued for what seemed like an eternity, everything slipped once more into slow motion. The girl gave a violent jerk and as she slipped, Ali's arm tightened around her neck. She screamed and Ali lost hold, dropping her to the ground. When the general saw this, he raised his left arm.

Trying to keep the girl as a shield and his gun hand free, Ali struggled to grab her, but the girl slipped away and tried to run. He caught her by her hair and pull her back to his waist. He'd seen the general move and it startled him. He raised his gun and pointed his weapon directly at the chest of the general, not more than ten meters away.

Colton yelled in Arabic. "*La-ah, la-ah*, no, no." At the same time, a spotlight hit the entire group from above. The helicopter's bright LED lights lit up the area like a circus ring. Ali shot multiple times, hitting the general in the chest. The vest had done its job, but the 9mm bullets caused him to move backward and slightly sideways, and the general felt a hot searing sensation go through his side, just under the edge of the vest. At this moment blood spattered and then flowed from Ali's neck as the sound of the sniper rifle fire came a half-second later, the bullet having traveled faster than the speed of sound.

The bullet had entered the back of Ali's neck. His face contorted in pain and reflected his knowledge at that split second that he was going to die. The next bullet went straight through his midsection.

Ali looked down as he observed the blood dripping down his dish-dash and making a puddle around the front of his robe. As he fell to the ground, all he could think to say in that split second was "Allah Akbar," as he fell face-first to the ground, dead.

Colton yelled to the jeep for help. The little girl wailed in shock. Mike jumped up and traversed down the mountain with no rope, trying to keep his balance to get to his father. Colton bent over and applied pressure on both the front and back sides of the general with both hands. The Glock's bullet had gone straight through.

Mike reached him in record time. Don had the field kit out, pulling out bandages and gauze and trying to stop the bleeding. Don and Colton unzipped the general's vest and ripped his shirt open, exposing his wound. Colton valiantly tried to stop the bleeding with his bare hands. Don moved Colton's front hand away and told the courageous young man to keep pressure on the rear bullet hole. Don, who'd had some specialty training as a field medic, went to work with focused hands. He flushed the wound. As Mike ran up, he saw Don shoot something into the wound to flush it out the back hole as Colton reversed his hands to the front bullet hole. Don now used a syringe and shot coagulant into the wound. Then he applied the gauze and the general fell back.

Mike arrived in time to grab the back of his father's head to keep it from hitting the ground. Completely focused on saving the general, Don employed a cool, authoritative voice and in complete control he said to his two assistants, "Sit him up. I need to tighten his bandage to stop the bleeding."

Don went to work. When he looked up, he made note of the fear in his best friend's eyes. He and Mike had been in a lot of hairy situations before this one, and Don had never seen Mike afraid. But this was not only their general, it was his father, and they both knew it. Mike looked down at his dad and then over to Don with pain in his eyes, not knowing how bad the wounds were.

Don reached out and touched his brother's arm and said, "He's gonna make it, Mike. The bullet went straight through and I didn't see any black coming out of the wound, so I don't think it hit any internal organs. It's just that being at such a close range, it was quite an impact." With all the assurance he could muster in his voice, Don said again, "He's gonna make it, pards, by God. He's the general and a tuff SOB, and on top of all that, he's an O'Shea."

The general groaned as he started to come to. Don reached into the medical kit and pulled out a syringe of morphine. The general looked up into the eyes of his dearest and only son, and with a hoarseness of breath he asked, "Did you bag that buck?"

Mike smiled into the general's eye and said, "Yeah, Dad, I got 'im. I was waitin' for you to help me haul him out." The general smiled and then his head dropped back, and he passed out.

The Omanis had been standing back, but now they came forward. They looked down at the blood everywhere and one grabbed Ali by the hair and raised his head, just to be sure. The man was appalled at the grotesque, frightening sight. The Arab turned to Colton and said, "All done. He has gone to the skies. Allah is merciful and will take him, but I wish this not to happen. He is dead."

The girl was still wailing as one of the Omani soldiers picked her up. He held her softly, calming her down. She looked down at Ali and then started crying again, burying her head into the Arab's shoulder as he whispered softly, "*My-lash, my-lash*, it's okay, it's okay, it's all over now. We will take you back to your mamma now." He walked away and got her some assistance from his comrades, who placed her in their Range Rover.

A portable stretcher was brought out and they lifted the general onto it and moved toward the jeep. The other marine was on the radio talking to the helicopter pilot who was still hovering over the scene. He yelled into the radio. "Go find the closest place to land, we have a man down who needs to be evac'd to the hospital in Muscat." The lights dimmed as the helicopter left to look for a landing spot. They loaded the general into the jeep.

Mike looked back and forth at both Don and his father. He'd heard what Don had said, but he was still worried. Don noticed his worry, and with a small, forgiving sort of smile, he said firmly, "He's gonna be okay, cuz."

Mike shook his head and looked down at the ground. "This is my fault. I should have been faster." For the first time in all the years he'd known Mike, he saw tears in his eyes.

Don looked up at him and said, "This is what we do, Mike. This is the life we have all chosen. All we can do is our best, and what we were trained to do. You got him, cuz. Your dad is going to be fine, and we got the bad guys. We saved the entire Middle East." With a bit of a smile he looked into Mike's still-pained eyes and said, "Damn, son, don't ya think you're just bein' a little hard on yourself? There are only a few people in this world who could have made that climb and made that shot from where you were. We'll be drinkin' Lone Star longnecks, or in the general's case, Buds, by the end of the week."

Mike looked up and said to his longtime friend, relaxing a little. "What are ya doin'? Tryin' to cheer me up again, or what?" as he hit the bill of his best friend's Longhorn baseball cap.

CHAPTER TWENTY-NINE

Al Bustan Palace
Muscat

The general took three full days to get a jump on recovering from his injuries, two of those days devoted to wrap up and debrief with the US State Department and the Royal Families from Saudi, Oman, and the UAE. Ali Al Sharif had been officially identified, and the Yemeni police were to pick up his body along with the other deceased terrorists in Salalah, where they were sent to be returned to Yemen, but this was not as smooth or cordial as expected. The Omanis were upset and wanted payment, or "*bacshish*," for their losses, to be paid to the families of the soldiers that were killed or wounded. Additionally, the Omanis wanted tribute from Yemen to pay for the entire operation. Of course, the Yemeni government denied all knowledge of the failed attack, once again, unsettling the lower portion of the Arabian Peninsula and the Shiite–Sunni relationship. Mike and the general let the two respective countries deal with that as they continued to try to identify where the warheads

had initially come from. Not much luck there, as the
participants of the trade were on the lower end of the
Shiite Brotherhood. The general and Mike realized that
there was no sense in pushing it any further, as none of
the captives had any valuable information. They were
only following orders and were not decision makers or
leaders.

***

Mike had arrived in Muscat early that morning and
was immediately transported to the Al Bustan Palace, the
Ritz-Carlton hotel where the upcoming peace conference
would be held. The luxury hotel lay between the Al
Hajar mountain range and the Sea of Oman, the crescent-
shaped beach rimmed with blue ocean and backed by the
mountain's darker tones. He checked in and deposited
his bags next to the bed in the luxurious suite. When the
thirty-year-old palace was remodeled, every detail was
artistically amplified, with great attention given to form,
lighting, color, function, and enjoyment. Not only was
the palace entrance spectacular, with its huge domed
lobby and mix of traditional and modern style, but Mike
stood still in the center of the suite, taking in the
fragrance of Bakhoor, the sound of the Ud—a traditional
stringed instrument—and the Arabian white onyx. He
didn't want to mar the beauty by leaving his things out,
so he changed quickly into his beachwear and stuffed his
scuffed bag into the large, mirrored walk-in closet.

He headed out to walk on the warm sandy beach. The
soft grains of golden sand between his toes, created from
eons of buffeting, lent a comfort of sorts to his own
battered soul. He'd hardly had time to breathe since
college, let alone figure out what his future life might

look like. Years of grueling training, several years of intense and dangerous missions, and a few rounds of physical trauma, injury, and recovery had worn him down. A longing for connection with a life partner stabbed through him as the cool surf washed over his feet, the bubbles tickling his skin. His injuries were healing, but his heart had been sorely neglected, and he could feel it.

Stacy's departure for law school over six years ago had affected Mike more than he'd realized at the time. He'd never before had such a feeling of obsession for something he wanted. He had learned to deal with letting go at a young age as his family moved from one assignment to the next. He'd dated other women off and on, but the four years with Stacy at UT had been different. A vivid memory of kissing her goodbye at her empty apartment that last day, the kiss sweet and bitter at once, played in his mind like a mournful violin. He'd felt a huge loss. No, not a loss, a gut-wrenching hurt. As he watched her walk to her Ford Taurus, the feeling of regret and loss had swept over him like a wildfire. He hadn't wanted to let her go, but neither of them could prevent the separation. Their love emulated the first unconditional love one feels in life, and the deep hurt in its absence.

Stacy was special. Their lovemaking had been tender and innocent at first yet expressing a passion unlike any he had ever felt. As they grew together and explored each other, the unreserved passion escalated to an intensity one only dreams of. They both knew this was right for them, and as they looked into each other's eyes they shared a pure sense of knowing they were giving everything to the other—no holding back, no intimidation or regret. Their coming together had been pure, loving, and special.

As Mike thought of Stacy over the last six years, he tried to tell himself it was a college affair and that it just hadn't lasted. This was his attempt to try to ease his pain. Maybe it was a first love—a puppy love—the kind you read or hear about when you're young. Yet he'd dreamed about her repeatedly, and for the first time in his life he was actually scared, as he couldn't control his emotions and longing for her. Because these feelings were out of control, he could not bring himself to contact her. He knew if he did, he ran a better-than-average chance that he would throw caution to the wind, leave his post, be AWOL, and risk his career—or worse, that she'd reject him. But the thing that ate at him the most was that he would not and could not bear to let the general down by leaving his job at PAL.

He'd thrown himself into his career, scoring higher than any SEAL had ever scored on the physical training test. His classroom grades were decent, but his physical abilities were off the charts, and he'd been put in charge of PAL's missions that carried the highest risk, hence the handful of injuries he'd sustained, any of which could have proved fatal. But when one is tormented from the inside, a natural response is to live on the edge, taking risks one would normally avoid. Mike understood this, and although he well knew his abilities, he did not have either a feel for—or a fear of—his own mortality.

The other women he'd dated since his SEAL training had all been short, menial encounters, ones Mike could take or leave. He'd date these women, but his thoughts would inevitably return to Stacy—her smile, her warmth, and her passion for him. He tried not to compare, but it became clear to him that none of these relationships came close to what he'd had with Stacy, even though the physical characteristics of the beautiful women he'd dated had been enviable to his guy friends. The way Stacy walked and handled herself and her carefree attitude seemed a custom fit for him. Beauty aside, the one thing she did was make him laugh, and he felt at peace with her.

***

When Mike didn't call and she'd waited for what seemed like an eternity, Stacy cried, felt used, and did exactly what Mike had done. She'd thrown herself at her studies, finished second in her class, become head of the law review, and then moved on to Brown and Root as a lead litigator and negotiator for the oil company of which her dad had sat on the board. She worked for them for two years, then joined the international law firm of Page, Becker, and Bennett, making partner in record time, and was given the highest worldwide profile assignments the firm had to offer. She didn't disappoint, which explained why she was in Muscat today. She often thought of Mike and hadn't been able to get him out of her system, but honestly, she'd not tried to rid herself of every thought of him, knowing it would have been impossible to do so. She'd dated from time to time but had nearly always sent the young men on their way after a single date.

Would he be here at the palace for the peace conference? It was possible. She'd keep her eyes open for him. What would it be like to see him again? Trying not to get her hopes up too high lest they be disappointed, she decided she'd leave the exquisite immersion in the beauty of the hotel and go for a little nature instead. The beach was compelling, with its beach pavilion restaurant and tables and chairs set up against the clear blue waters of the Gulf of Oman. The entire place oozed sensuality and romance. What a setting to enjoy with Mike. Hoping against hope that he'd be here, she threw on her suit and flip flops, then donned a below-the-knee, light but modest cover-up for the occasion. As she skirted the lobby, she rounded a table, gaze fixated for a moment at the monstrous chandeliers hanging from the domed lobby ceiling, and her right side bumped a human figure so hard that she stumbled. A hand reached out to steady her, and her head snapped back to see who it was so she could offer her apologies.

"Well, I'll be," a thick Texan accent drawled out. "If it ain't my old friend Stacy. I haven't seen you since college!"

"Don!" Stacy said, going slightly weak at seeing such a familiar, friendly face. She grabbed both of his arms, aware that her nails were digging in, but not caring. If Don were here, wouldn't Mike be here as well? She looked away and scanned the area. An intense feeling of pain swept through her.

"He's here, darlin', and he knows you are here. You'll find each other."

"Do you know where he is?" she asked breathlessly.

"I think you're headin' in the right direction. The beach."

Stacy couldn't wait another second. "Catch up with you later," she hollered to Don over her shoulder.

Attempting to walk through the hotel in a dignified manner, she gave that up when her feet hit the sand. The flip-flops were only slowing her down, so she took them off and carried them, looking for lone figures in the bright morning heat. Where was that son-of-a-gun, anyway? He could have tried to find out if she were there, but he hadn't. Maybe his feelings had changed. Nervous now and a little less eager, she kept going, shielding her eyes from the glare on the sand. Finally, she saw a lone male figure. Was it him? When she was sure, she took off at a run, unable to contain herself in spite of her qualms.

***

She was here at the palace, and he knew he'd see her eventually. He didn't know how to make that happen, let alone what he'd say to her when he did see her. Did she know he was here? Would she welcome him? He reached the end of the walkable beach and turned, heading back. The palace, with its creamy white façade against the dark mountains took his breath away. As he continued on, a slim figure with curves came into sight. The woman's head turned, her golden locks still there, but shorter now, as a professional woman would look. She was stunning and had not lost any of the model's figure that Mike had dreamed about continually. He could tell, even from a distance, the moment she recognized him. Her steps faltered for an instant, then she smiled, waved, and started running. If she was running eagerly toward him, that must mean she wanted him. He picked up his own pace and as they ran into each other's arms they embraced, and the bodily contact felt like heaven, as though nothing had changed. They were still one. The rush and thrill came back immediately, just as he'd experienced it so many years ago when they'd been inseparable. An intense, indescribable wave of heat attacked his whole being and he lifted her and swung her around and around on the golden sands, her arms around his neck and her flip-flops lost to the fresh breeze. They collapsed onto the sandy beach and as Mike held her and brought his face in close for a kiss, only one thought came to mind—uncontainable passion for this beautiful woman he still loved so deeply.

Some hours later, the couple came up for a refreshing breather and they pushed their masks and snorkels up on their heads. Stacy and Mike marveled at the natural coral reef off the beach shore of the Al Bustan Palace. The water was an emerald blue. Visibility was five meters, and full of colorful coral, pink, blue, and red, and so beautiful. Lion fish and brightly colored moray eels were also a delight to see.

As they enjoyed the day in the beautiful Arabian Gulf, the wait and anticipation of being alone again was almost more than either of them could stand. As always, Mike's faithful friend and cohort Don stirred the pot and kept their drinks filled, being silly and making them both laugh as if they were at New Braunfels on the Guadalupe River. Most all the kids that went to UT at one time or another would load up with coolers of beer and take an all-day float down the river. It was fun, and all enjoyed great memories of relaxing summer and fall days that had taken place, along with bonfires and long-term bonding that cemented their friendships. His faithful pal Don had no idea of the pressure he felt as he and Stacy waited to return to their rooms.

As the day went on, Don hooked up with a young marine officer stationed at the US Embassy. Kelly was fun, carefree, spoke five languages, and was a complete intellectual. Maybe that's why she and Don were attracted to each other. They laughed and joked without a care in the world, basking under the hot blue skies on the white Arabian sands, swimming and embracing without a care in the world. It was growing late in the afternoon, and as with most Arab functions, the banquet would start late, around ten p.m. They picked up their ice chest, towels, and beach chairs, then headed back to one of the most beautiful hotels in the world, the spectacular Al Bustan Palace. All the lights came on at once at the hotel, with the soft white light glowing past the repetitive arches as the breathtaking sunset dimmed and night fell. The four were suddenly not in a hurry, and they sat on the sand and watched what appeared to be a beach setup for an open-air wedding dinner. Crossed torches and large lighted globes provided a romantic atmosphere around the scattering of round tables, luxuriously dressed out and decorated in reds and whites. The hotel had been built with no budget and was meant to be a showplace for peace. Mike believed this destination was one of the most romantic getaways in the world, and he was here with the girl of his dreams.

CHAPTER THIRTY

The Gala
Muscat

They would have several more hours together before they'd be expected at the event. As Mike walked up to the hotel, his stomach did back flips. Mike was nervous—okay, scared—and excited all at once. This was what he'd dreamed about, the one that got away. His first true love. The object of his desire was holding his hand, taking him back to his youth. Afraid to look over at her for fear she was still just a conjured image of his mind, he felt like he was dreaming. She held his hand, her walk almost a sidewalk-skipping pace, giving away her lighthearted feelings. Good, he thought. This is going well.

His room was two doors down and across the hall. As they approached her room, she opened her door and stepped inside, closing it quickly until only a body's width was left open. Her face leaned through. She looked at him then, only inches apart, and while holding the door with her leg, she took his face in both of her hands and kissed him with a quick smooch, then pulled away quickly.

"Michael O'Shea. You, young man, are not coming in here, and it serves you right for never, ever calling me in three-and-a-half years! You have not earned the privilege of visiting my bedroom after your lackluster courting skills. Not a phone call, a card, or a 'how do you do' in all this time, and you, cowboy, think you're gonna have me jump right back in the sack with you? As we say down home, ain't happenin', big boy."

As he'd walked her to her room, he'd been as giddy as a schoolboy with high hopes of rekindling their long-lost passion. Mike stood in front of the now-closed door. His expectations and hopes while sitting on the beach, and what he'd dreamed about for the past three-plus years, were lost. Completely deflated, he stood there like a lost puppy. It was obvious now that his failure to contact her had been a poor strategy. He said out loud to no one in particular, "But I just risked my life for you. I took a bullet in the chest! What's a guy got to do?"

After several minutes he realized she wasn't coming back. With his head hung low, he walked the few doors to his room and poured himself a vodka on ice.

***

Stacy stood with her back against the door, a little smirk on her face. That will teach him, she thought. But her insides were completely knotted up. When she'd held his hand walking back to the room, electricity had shot though her whole body, leaving her weak and defenseless. She wanted him so badly. With the exception of a few more scars on his back, he had not changed one bit. He was still the hunk she used to squeeze her pillow and dream about. He was truly beautiful, and she was smart enough to see and know that there was still something between them, something strong.

She smiled, cocked her head, and said, "Better to make him wait." So, simultaneously, in two different rooms, thousands of miles from where they'd started, both stood under cold showers.

***

At nine p.m. Mike walked down to Stacy's room and knocked lightly. She opened the door, and in her black low-cut dress and Hong Kong pearls, she looked amazing. She didn't have much make up on, but she'd never needed it. Her face wore a serious expression, and even with that, Mike openly admired the girl who had turned into a young woman. *Don't screw this up, O'Shea, or you will never have another chance.* He offered his arm, complimented her on her dress, and they turned to walk to the function, feeling every bit like long-lost lovers, though neither openly acknowledged that fact.

Mike, Don, and the general, with their dates, were attending a black-tie dinner with the heads of state they had so gallantly saved. Along with the other PAL leadership, they were to be the guests of honor, with the general himself giving the Americans' keynote address. This was truly an honor, as it is usually the US Ambassador who opens such galas and events.

Ambassador Ken Minogue visiting from Dubai was more than happy to let two-star General John O'Shea give the keynote address this time. And the general certainly didn't disappoint.

Dignitaries and guests entered the ballroom, their elegant dress as beautiful as the setting. The eight hundred people invited to this gala would be guaranteed to show, as this was the hottest ticket in town for several weeks. Many different VIP guests and renowned World and Arab leaders were given access to the party. Though unusual to see alcohol served at these events, Eid had ended. Fifty percent of the invitations to this event were extended to British and US expatriates and government and Embassy high-ranking officials and the other half to Arabs, so drinks were served. When Stacy and Mike entered and were announced, all eyes turned their way. Stacy could still cause a stir in any room she walked into, and she certainly did this evening.

The greeting line had grown considerably, and lucky for them, Mike and Stacy held VIP passes and were ushered through a different line with no waiting time. As they moved through, they shook hands and bumped noses in greeting as per custom in the Dubai Emirates. [Is this the right way to say this? ...in the Dubai Emirates?]They moved through, shook hands, and bumped noses. Standing with the honored US military and the British contingency in the greeting line, Mike shook hands and saluted while Stacy provided air kisses on both cheeks of the greeter.

After they finished running the welcome gauntlet, Mike and Stacy headed straight to the ice sculpture surrounded by a beautiful setting. Dom Perignon streamed into a spectacular river leading to a dispenser that collected the nectar into a champagne flute rimmed with solid gold. Stacy ordered one from a server who was fully attired in the traditional Indian Kurta, a silk pajama-looking outfit. Many of the servers and waitstaff at the event were expatriates.

Mike collected Stacy, headed for the fully stocked open bar, and ordered a new botanical vodka, a Ketel One and soda. When he turned around, he was looking straight into his dad's ribbon-filled chest and was startled to see his mother standing next to him in a Chanel silk dress. Even at her age, she could turn heads. He didn't say a word to his father, just embraced his mom with a bear hug, a huge smile on his face. His voice betrayed the degree of his emotion, and he choked up when he said, "Dad didn't tell me you were coming, Mom. What a great surprise!"

Smiling, she said, "After the success of your latest mission with your father, whatever it was, Sheik Hamid sent his private plane for me so I could be at the conference with your father."

As Ann moved over to give Stacy a hug, it seemed like old times, with the family all together. Mike watched Stacy with his mom. They chatted warmly, their faces close together like a mom and daughter would do. While he was lost in thought, his arms were grabbed from behind by two women. He knew who it was before turning, as neither Kim nor Sharon could keep from giggling and giving it away. Surprised, Mike turned and gave them each an Arab greeting by touching noses. Mike glanced at his father and saw him grinning from ear-to-ear, watching them. The last time they had all been together was when he and Stacy had graduated from UT.

After General O'Shea gave his opening comments thanking Sultan Qaboos and all the other diplomats in the room for their generous hospitality, the party began. His opening line was, "I will be brief, as it is I who is standing in the way of you enjoying a Châine five-star dinner." As Mike waited for the laughter to die down, Mike thought about the general's speeches he'd heard and seen many times before. This one proved different— his authoritative demeanor was electric as his speech spoke of bold new alliances and the embracing of all religions, as well as all Arabs, both Sunni and Shiite. It was a call to arms for peace in the region, with the US military safeguarding that peace. The trade pact had been signed earlier in the day by the rulers of each of the three Arab countries represented at the banquet, along with the US Ambassador. General O'Shea called it a new path forward and concluded his twenty-minute address by thanking all on behalf of the President of the United States.

The dinner lived up to its buildup. The meal was served to every person at the gala at the same time, with the five chefs flown in from across Europe standing at the back of the room, arms crossed proudly. Dressed in their traditional white smocks, they watched as the food entering the gala brought pleasure to the guests, who oohed and aahed as each course was served. As they finished their meal, all the chefs were formally recognized for the world-class meal and their superb cooking skills. The presentation of the food had a distinctive sculptural flair.

The time had come for the Arab rulers to say a few words, and they presented the general with a silver whalebone Khanjar, a traditional curved knife made of silver, mounted in a shadowbox with engravings of thanks to the general and his PAL associates. The general accepted this graciously, bowing and shaking hands.

General O'Shea walked back to his seat where he leaned over and whispered into Mike's ear. "This belongs to you. Without your tenacity, the outcome tonight would have been much different. I am proud of you, son."

CHAPTER THIRTY-ONE

Shortest Kidnap in History

After the gala, the family decided they would change and go to the Embassy marine bar. The marines who had been stationed here over the years had made the expat hangout into their country club. The dive resembled a local neighborhood bar and grill, more or less. Hats hung from the ceiling from past visitors from all over the world and from all different kinds of companies. A party was in full swing, with one of the young marines acting as a DJ, playing '70s and early '80s rock. As they ordered from the bar, Hootie and the Blowfish blasted out of four large speakers surrounding a makeshift dance floor.

By the time the O'Sheas arrived, the place had attracted about sixty people. They were celebrating Master Sergeant Joey Higgins's departure, as he had been with the US Embassy in Oman for the past two years on a single-status contract. He was headed back stateside to reenter his family's lives. Toasts and speeches were given and gag gifts were opened while his old unit roasted him good-naturedly. Not knowing anyone, Mike and Stacy sat and watched the festivities, catching up on each other's lives with some intimate conversation. Mike got up and pulled his chair around to sit closer. Holding Stacy's hand, he watched his sisters with concern. The young single marines were paying them a lot of attention, and they were thrilled. They each danced with every marine there at least once. He kept one eye on them, not as relaxed as he'd like to be. Stacy picked up on it.

"You know, your sisters are really big girls now. They can hold their own."

"You are probably right. Old habits die hard."

"After all, aren't all marines gentlemen when it comes to ladies?"

Suddenly it seemed very important to him that Stacy believe him to be a gentleman, a man of honor. If he couldn't feel that from her, he wondered if he'd be able to love her enough.

"I don't know if all marines are gentlemen. I doubt every one of them is." Mike looked down at his glass.

"But you think some are? Are you basing that on your experience with your buddies? I'd wager to say that every one of your team are as good as they get."

He nodded in agreement. Maybe that's as close as he can expect to get tonight. But it would be nice to have the assurance that his girl thought of him as a gentleman. Respect, that's what he needed from her. His father had it from his mother. It was written across her face.

He figured he was wired to protect and defend as much as a person could be. And honestly, it felt good. After everything he'd been through growing up, this was what he needed. Self-respect. He recognized it and it was enough. He sat back and drank in the party atmosphere, the life and vitality of everyone there who had a job to do and who all faithfully performed their jobs with dedication and skill. After the carrying on had died down and the dance music slowed, Mike stood and held out his hand to Stacy. She met his eyes, gave a sweet smile, and held her hand out to meet his. He pulled her up and brought her close to him.

"Dance with me?" he whispered into her soft hair. It smelled like honeysuckle. He felt drunk on the moment, even though he'd only had a couple of drinks all evening. Stacy nodded, and he led her out on the makeshift floor with several other couples. They danced a couple of slow dances, holding each other close. Mike could hardly pull his head back from Stacy's, and she pressed into him. He began to hope for the best rather than the worst.

His mom and dad sat several tables away and reminisced with some long-lost friends about the good ole days when they were young, recounting some of the pranks they pulled on each other. At one point his mother got to laughing so hard that she had to pull out her tissues. It was great to see them having such a good time together. He glanced at Stacy and saw that she was watching too.

"Your parents have made it work somehow, haven't they?"

"Yeah. I'm not sure how, but they have always been such strong people. Not only physically, but they're tough. Mentally tough. Yet they didn't lose the spark between them, even after all the danger and times apart. You can still see it between them. They knew they needed to be strong, and being strong during the tough times has made the good times that much sweeter. They are something to emulate."

"Not many children think so highly of their parents," Stacy said. She had a strange expression on her face. He watched as her face began to scrunch up like she was going to cry, but suddenly it changed again, and she brightened visibly, her eyes suddenly full of hope. And what? Anticipation?

"You okay, Stace?"

"I just figured something out, Michael O'Shea. It is life-changing. Treat me right and I'll tell you about it," she winked.

He smiled at her. *Soon*, he said with his eyes. She got the message and blushed slightly. His smile grew, and he reached over and took her hand, tenderly, rubbing his thumb across the back.

The O'Shea party began winding down when one of them realized it was two a.m. The general and Ann gathered their troops and walked out the door.

Over a dozen young marines sat outside in the cool desert air, relaxing. As the general held the door for his family, Ann walked ahead to the Hummer, as she was the designated driver for the evening. As she stepped up to the street, she turned. A van swerved, skidding, and moved at high speed right toward her. She stood frozen in place, seeming to not know whether to run or which way to go if she could. It came to a screeching halt right in front of her. The middle door flew open and a young Arab grabbed her and pulled her inside. In seconds, the door slid shut and the rear wheels spun on the drive, kicking up loose gravel. The general had seen the abduction and as Mike watched him run toward the van, he too sprang into action. The general reached down and pulled his .45 Glock out of his ankle holster, as did Mike.

John O'Shea aimed and opened fire, hitting both back tires, which caused the van to slide sideways out of control. The careening vehicle smacked into two parked cars in front of them. The whole incident lasted less than a minute, and as John and Mike rushed the van, nine or ten Embassy soldiers were right behind them with guns drawn, all pointing at the driver and passenger of the van. Mike arrived just before his father. He yanked open the door and stepped back and Ann leaped out into her husband's arms. Mike's gun was aimed at the head of a young Arab. None of the three potential kidnappers could have been older than their late teens or early twenties. Why they chose such a venue to try to capture an American, Mike hadn't a clue. Must have something to do with the recklessness and invincibility of youth who wanted to prove themselves.

All dropped their guns and raised their hands at the overwhelming firepower in front of them. The Omani police were called, and when they arrived, the three young men seemed to have a lot to say. They gesticulated and spoke quickly, pointing and apparently trying to explain themselves. The police hauled the young men off and everyone breathed a sigh of relief. Apparently, according to the translation, they were looking for an expat to hold hostage for ransom money. As everything settled down and no real harm was done, the O'Sheas laughed at the fact that this was the shortest kidnapping in history.

CHAPTER THIRTY-TWO

Together at Last

As Mike watched Stacy through the evening, he'd decided his best move would be to assume nothing. The woman of his dreams deserved his respect and honor, and after being rebuffed—somewhat unfairly, he thought—the next move would be hers.

Their footsteps on the sound-absorbing carpet of the hallway slowed as they neared Stacy's room.

"Good night, Stace," Mike said. "Sleep well. I enjoyed every moment of our day." They reached her door and stopped. "I will see you in—"

Stacy reached up and her soft, slender arms circled his neck and she kissed him, long and slow. Then she whispered in his ear, "Five minutes, your room," and she slipped her room key in and was gone.

Eight hours earlier he'd stood in the hall talking to himself after the door shut in his face. Stacy must still love him. True to her word, five minutes later a soft tap sounded on his door.

Stacy's eyes crinkled and she tried to speak but the words wouldn't come. Tears sprang forth and she became incapable of taking the next step. Finally, she got the words out.

"I don't think I could do this if I didn't respect you highly, with everything in me," she said to him. I love you, Michael O'Shea."

Mike reached out and enveloped her in his strong arms, gentle at first, then tightening as the warmth and strength of his feelings took over. Denied for so long, their mutual longing erupted and burst from both of them as passion took over. They made love until nearly dawn, neither able to get enough of the other. At one point, Mike rose and turned the thermostat down to its coldest position, as both were sweating and out of breath. When all passion had calmed and they'd snuggled under the plush bedding, Mike knew without a doubt there'd never be another girl for him. Overwhelmed with his emotions, he took Stacy's face in his hands and lifted it so he could see her mesmerizing green eyes. Peace and a deep happiness shone from them.

He couldn't hold it back or wait for a "proper" setup. "Stacy Lyons, I have loved you since the first time I laid eyes on you at the Chi O party. I can't live without you any longer. Will you..." his voice trailed off when her expression turned from love to irritation.

"I don't know, Mike, don't you think it's a little late to be asking that?"

"Are you going to say no?" His voice squeaked and she laughed. He lowered his face to hers again and kissed her, long and passionately.

After the longest kiss Mike could ever remember having, Stacy rested her head on his shoulder and fell asleep. Her breathing caused her chest to rise and fall ever so slightly against him. Mike had forgotten how stunning Stacy really was, and at this moment in time she was the most beautiful thing he had ever laid eyes on, an exquisite masterpiece of feminine allure and deep emotional connection. They were meant to be together. This reunion had restored the bond they had shared so long ago, during a simpler time. She hadn't spoken her answer to him, but he'd seen it in her eyes. Now he felt sure they would have each other's support for a lifetime, and nothing on the planet would sever their bond.

He'd take her away for a couple of weeks to plan for the future. Spain, Greece, Thailand—didn't matter where, as long as they were together. Nothing could beat having a home. And a home was worth every sacrifice.

ABOUT THE AUTHOR

Larry McGill's successful career in management in the food services industry has taken him around the world, with operations in Egypt, Oman, China, and New Zealand, to name a few, and most of his career was spent as an expat in the Middle East with the Coca Cola and Golden State Foods companies. An accomplished businessman, Larry is currently CEO of a thriving international company and has been honored with many awards for his leadership abilities. The time he spent living and working in management in the Middle East has contributed significantly to his understanding of the culture and struggles of the region. An Azle, Texas native, Larry earned a BS degree in History from Texas A&M Commerce and an MBA from Century University in Albuquerque, NM. He currently resides in Atlanta, Georgia, and enjoys spending time with his son Richard and daughter Tanya, often at the lake. In his free time, he enjoys skiing, hunting, and fishing, and is an avid golfer.

COMING SOON...BOOK TWO

Spanish Luck
A Mike O'Shea Adventure

Muscat, Oman

Mike O'Shea winked at Stacy. "Listen to this," he said, wiping the gulf waters out of his eyes and picking up his phone off the beach towel.

Stacy wrung water from her shoulder-length brown hair and sat on her own towel, drying off her snorkeling equipment before slipping it into the netted bag. She tilted her head in his direction.

"Hey," he began when the call connected, his tone friendly and confident. A loud voice emanated from the phone, and Stacy frowned.

Mike responded to the heated response with determination. "Listen, pal, neither Stacy nor I have had any R&R for months. She's free, and I'm taking two weeks. This is non-negotiable."

More heated words ensued, but Mike deflected each argument with his characteristic rock-solid determination. They should know better than to bother him, especially now.

The Arabian moon glowed bright and full, thousands of diamonds twinkling in the night sky while palm trees gently swayed, their silhouettes visible against the dark volcanic rock mountains behind the Al Bustan Hotel. Mike ended the call, putting up a hand for a high-five from his girl. He and Stacy had been apart now for four-and-a-half years, and he couldn't bear to leave her side. She held his hand as they walked in to get cleaned up. Dinner awaited.

"What is that dish, Mike?" Stacy asked after they ordered.

"You mean your grilled lobster over a bed of Roz ma mucasarat with a rich Arabian sauce? That's steamed rice and nuts, my lady. Sound good?" She nodded, a smile perfusing her features as she looked into his eyes. Their meal, which included an appetizer of taboulleh and a bottle of hearty Spanish wine, had proved to be as delicious as their accommodations and the beauty seated before him. They toasted their upcoming trip to Barcelona, and headed, a little tipsy, to their suite. They had an early morning flight, with a first stop in Dubai for a few hours where Stacy planned to make the most of world-class duty-free shopping.

The next morning, as they walked through the large airport souk, they were wrapped up in each other, laughing and talking, absorbed in their own world.

"Hang on, Mike. I want to get something else." Stacy darted back into the store, bumping into a swarthy-looking man who looked as startled as she was, and maybe a little nervous. "I'm sorry, sir," she said. He glanced at her bag slung over her neck and across her chest. Weirdo, she thought, noticing the dark tattoo of a knife on his forearm, the ink having bled, making the edges soft. She shuddered.

Mike, not noticing, had reverted back to being a teenager. He'd not felt these deep emotions in years, except in his fantasies. Last night had been spectacular—passionate, nostalgic, and loving—and the luxury of Dubai gave a magical feel to the trip, even a giddiness as they passed magnificent works of art and displays of history. They couldn't wait to reach Barcelona. Two entire weeks of fun, beach, and sight-seeing awaited them. They would chill, eat paella, and drink Spanish wine while they explored the city.

An uneventful flight brought them to the Hotel Ranblas on the famous tourist street of the same name. The city was alive with street vendors, artisans, great boutique restaurants, and shopping. They'd soak up all the Mediterranean had to offer. As they unpacked, Mike's phone rang. He'd ignored his calls over the last few days, but when he saw it was Don, his best friend and cohort, he picked up.

"Hello amigo, what gives? You know I'm out of the loop for a couple of weeks, soakin' up some sun at the beach. Where you calling from, pards?"

After a slight hesitation, Don said, "Malaga."

"So, you and that little filly decided on a Spanish vacation also? Good for you, pards! Why don't you two grab a car and join us for a day or two? Old times and all, you know!"

"Whoa, this isn't a social call. We have an issue." Don's voice was serious. Sincere. Taken aback, Mike knew Don well enough to decipher the tone in the prankster's voice, but he couldn't tell for sure which Don he had. He decided on the prankster.

"Okay, what's up? If it has to do with another mission, those boys back home are just gonna have to wait or send someone else! I am officially on R&R with Stace."

"Listen, Mike—"

"I don't want to hear it! I don't, and that's final. I owe it to us. Just me and her. Tell 'em to take a hike!"

"Hold on, Mike. It's Stacy's folks."

"What? Are they pissed that Stacy is back with me, or what?

"No, that isn't it." Don sounded exhausted.

"Look Don, I will suck up to them when they catch up with us here in Barcelona our last few days. Now get your butt over here where we can show 'em some Texas-sized partying. It'll be fun, pards!"

"Mike! Please stop and listen," Don shouted.

"No, you listen, every time you get somethin' like this in your head and I listen to you, I end up on some wild goose chase or some kind of crazy op! I'm tellin' ya, I am here with Stacy and I'll smooth it out with her folks when they get here. Get your butt here and let's show em' a little Austin, Texas!"

"Mike, please, you're not gonna smooth a damn thing out. Stacy's parents have been taken."

"What did you say?" Mike said, dropping his hat on the bed.

"They've been taken." Mike moved out to the balcony so he was out of earshot of Stacy, who was in the bathroom freshening up.

"Taken?" Mike said. "What the hell are you talking about, Don?"

"Well hell, son, if you'd pick up your messages or your phone, you'd know!"

"I told them at HQ I'd be out of commission the next two weeks."

"No shit, Mike. Why do you think I'm on the phone with you? They got ahold of me and told me to track your butt down. You ready to listen now?"

Mike paused a moment and said, "Okay, okay, are they alive? Who's in charge? How long do we have?" Mike had begun to shift into work mode, his wheels turning, and his operational paralysis taking over.

"Right now I don't know, but what I do know is that back at home base they wanted to ensure you and Stacy are safe and secure. Mike, who knows where you are now?"

"No one. I booked this hotel as an afterthought. Why, and what's going on? Is Stacy in some kind of danger too? Why would someone want to grab her folks?"

Mike could hear Stacy coming out of the bathroom. He slid out of sight so she wouldn't see him immediately through the sliding glass doors.

"Here's what we do know, cuz. Stacy's folks were on a private yacht with three other couples who were longtime friends. They weighed anchor off the coast of Bordrum on the Turkish coastline for some sightseeing. The group was working their way over to Barcelona to hook up with you guys. The day before yesterday, their yacht was boarded by four highly armed masked assailants with Uzis. They shot Dr. Glaess in the leg and threatened the rest of the party. He's fine and going to make it. Then, they grabbed Stacy's folks and left a note, written in broken English. It said, 'We'll be in touch. Meanwhile, get two million American dollars in small bills by Saturday, *Inshallah!*'"

Mike, listening intensely, was still trying to shift gears and process what his buddy was telling him.

Don continued to weigh his words carefully, Mike could tell. "We're not sure if this is a one-off kidnapping by local Turkish Islamic pirates, or if there is more to it. This is all we know now."

"How are they going to contact us, Don?"

"They grabbed Dr. Brad Sullivan and dragged him down the steps to their speed boat and told him to have someone at the base near Sagrada Failia Church at the phone booth on the corner of Carrer de Naplos and Carrer de Mallorca in Barcelona. A call is supposed to come tomorrow at six p.m. They threw the doctor into the water next to their boat and took off with Stacy's folks. And that's all we know now, pards. I wish we had more, but we are dealing with civilians, and you know how that goes."

"Okay, I will be there at six p.m.," Mike said.

"Cool your jets, big fella. PAL has the ball here. We are to stand down, as the boys back at the big playground at Langley think this is too close to home for you. We're to secure Stacy, just in case there is a bigger play than what we know about."

"Come on, Don, what the hell are you talkin' about? I can't sit here and do nothing! What am I supposed to tell Stacy? If she finds out I didn't level with her, she'll never forgive me! I have to do something!"

"Look Mike, I'll be with you in about three hours, and we'll tell Stacy together and figure out a game plan. See you in a bit." Mike hung up and stood looking out across the city, wondering how to deal with his girl over this terrible news. She'd be frantic. Why did it seem they were always out of the frying pan and into the fire?

Made in United States
Orlando, FL
02 October 2022

22910685R00183